# KATE RELEASED

## The Steak and Bourbon Series
### Book 2

## LAURA PRESLAN

Published by Advoture, Inc.

Published by Advoture, Inc.
Cover design by Miladinka Milic of Mila Book Covers



ISBN: 979-8-9915747-2-3

Books by Laura Preslan

**STEAK AND BOURBON SERIES**

Julia Unleashed

Kate Released

Alex Unchained (March 2025)

*To Eric and the brunch divas.*

*Everyone should have a board of directors like you.*

---

## Chapter 1

---

*It's so fulfilling to have a competent boss* Kate thought as she approached Julia's office at LampLight for their one on one. Her bright green skirt swirled around her legs as she walked quickly. She was petite but made up for it with bold wardrobe choices so she wouldn't be overlooked.

In the past, she dreaded manager meetings, but when Julia burst into her life as her manager in 2012, everything changed. The last four years had been pure manager bliss. 2016 was shaping up to be a great year.

Being on Julia's team under the protection and guidance of her strong leadership was key to Kate's long-term success, career advancement, and the financial stability she craved.

They just needed to stick together.

"What's on your list for our one on one today?" Julia finished typing the last sentence of an email before looking up at Kate. "Love what you've done with your hair!"

"Not too short?" Kate ran her hand down the back of

her head where long brown hair had been replaced by a short blond pixie cut.

"You're asking the wrong person. I chopped off my curls and found freedom. I adore your new style. It makes your blue eyes really pop, and you took ten years off your face – not that you looked old."

Kate blushed at the praise. "I'll take looking thirty-five." Kate's forty-sixth birthday was around the corner. "Now we can get back to business."

"What's the agenda today?" Julia asked.

Kate counted topics off on her fingers. "World domination, solving global hunger, proving that short women are fierce, saving baby seals. You know, the usual, J-Money." Kate used Julia's well-earned nickname from leading the advertising monetization team.

"You've already proven that you're fierce… in a good way. Let's start with world domination, or at least office domination." Julia laughed her musical laugh. "There's just one thing first. I have some good news and some bad news."

Kate didn't like that tone. "I want the bad news first."

Julia seemed hesitant which was very out of character. She tapped her finger to her lips. "I've accepted another job."

"Wow. Congratulations." A flash of excitement crackled through Kate. This wasn't bad news at all. She was first in line on Julia's succession plan, and Julia was next in line for her boss' job. They were movin' on up! "That's sooner than we thought we'd move, though. Where's Florence going?" Kate referred to Julia's very French and very effective boss.

"It's a different job." Julia shook her head. "I'm not taking Florence's role."

*Wait. That wasn't the plan*, Kate thought. She waited for Julia to continue.

"It's super hush hush, but Kevin is retiring."

"Kevin?" Kate's eyebrows could not go up any higher. "As in Kevin Donnelly, the head of pricing for all of Lamp-Light?" Julia nodded. "I thought they'd have to pry his corporate badge out of his cold, dead hand."

"Yeah, me too," Julia agreed. "But he told me last week and I jumped at the chance to be considered for the position. The best part was that he was telling me because he'd already narrowed the field down to his top pick." Julia pointed to herself with a flourish. "Me."

"Great news for you and bad news for our team." Kate was genuinely happy for her boss, but part of Kate's brain started working through the implications. "Are you taking me with you?" The plan was to stick together.

"No. But this vacates my role." Julia turned serious.

Kate tasted the adrenaline in her mouth, a sharp metallic tinge. *Here it comes*, she thought. Julia would do the same thing for her as Kevin had done for Julia. That's how these roles worked. You had to be placed into them by an advocate. You didn't just get them for being good at your job.

Kate barreled ahead. "My head is spinning. This is sooner than we thought it would happen. I'm ready to jump in. What's the next step? Does Florence know about your succession plan and my position at the top of it?"

Kate was ten steps ahead thinking through the great conversation she would have with Florence. Kate was the highest rated person in her peer set. She was in the talent development program for fast-track advancement. She had just won the Outstanding Contributor award complete with a trip to Monaco. She had been rocking her role for four years. She had paid her dues.

Julia interrupted her energy. "Yes, and I agree wholeheartedly you'd do a great job." Kate's cheeks pinked at the praise. Julia sighed and her shoulders dropped. "But here's the bad news."

A crackle of dread snaked down Kate's spine and landed in her stomach. "That wasn't the bad news?"

"Afraid not. Randall is only considering external candidates as my backfill. Florence and I tried to change his mind."

*Boom.* Randall was Florence's boss. The energy drained from Kate, leaving a shell of disappointment. The sting of unshed tears pricked her eyes. She never cried at work and was good at pushing them away. "That wasn't the plan, Julia. We were working toward this together. It's the next step in my career plan, as we've discussed." Kate was rambling but didn't care and continued anyway. "Do you know why Randall made that decision and didn't at least give me a chance?"

Julia leveled her gaze at Kate. "We all agree you're doing a great job, Kate. Randall has other plans for you."

The way Julia said it sounded ominous. Kate didn't like it. "What plans? Has Randall shared them with you?"

"Yes, but I'm not sure how you're going to feel about it, honestly." Julia paused, her discomfort visible across the office desk.

"C'mon J-Money. Talk to me."

"He wants you to be his Chief of Staff."

"Crap."

"Exactly." Julia flumped back in her seat, seeming to share Kate's opinion of the role.

"There must be a silver lining in there somewhere." Kate wanted to be optimistic.

They looked at each other trying to think of a good thing.

"I've got it!" Julia extended her index finger. "Since you won't be working for me anymore, I can invite you to my board of directors meeting."

"The Professional Pricing Society?"

"No. I mean my personal board of directors. Steak and Bourbon."

"Whoa." This was really big.

Steak and Bourbon was legendary. Their mutual friends Melanie and Lesley talked about Julia's monthly brunches with deference.

Kate couldn't ever go because she worked for Julia and Julia was a stickler for fairness. "I could be one of your brunch ladies? It just might be worth the trade-off."

## Chapter 2

"I hated being a Chief of Staff," Kate lamented to her partner James that evening over dinner. "You do all that background work and stay in the shadows. I like the spotlight." Kate shoveled another mouthful of garlic bread into her face. "And now I'm carb-loading in my anger. Bad, bad news."

James leaned forward and took her hand. "You might be overreacting just a bit." It was a typically optimistic James statement.

She took a moment to look into his beautiful hazel eyes. She was lucky to be with such an amazing and supportive partner. Five years in, things couldn't be better between them.

Except that he was pressuring her to get married.

"I hear you, James, but I worked hard as Darren's Chief of Staff a couple of jobs ago and then the dude quit on me since he didn't get promoted. It was a tough few weeks before I landed my next gig."

"Yeah, but then you got another job, and then you got

the job that introduced you to Julia. Look how that's worked out."

"I'm pretty sure that whole ordeal shortened my life from the stress. But I've certainly had fun on my current team."

"Don't forget success." James let go of her hand to add jazz hands to his next comment.

"Winning that huge award had to be satisfying. And the stock. And the bonus. I know I enjoyed the free trip to Monaco last October."

Eve, their favorite server, approached the table. "Can I refill your drinks?"

Kate had a chance to reflect on her year as James chatted with Eve. She kept one ear on the conversation about dessert specials.

James was right, as usual. It had been a great year. Three great years, actually. She loved her boss, learned a lot, implemented a whole new monetization and pricing strategy that had increased revenue and profitability, and helped sellers be more successful.

She had built a vision, defended her ideas, incorporated feedback from her peers, and worked through strong resistance to change. She could write a book about her success. She *wanted* to write a book about it. She had to keep making money for the next several years so she could support her real dream and actually write that book.

"What was so bad about being a Chief of Staff?" James turned his attention back to Kate when Eve left the table. He continued to sop up the pasta sauce with a piece of bread. He was happiest while eating. Except when he was having sex. His happy place would definitely be eating in bed.

"Other than everything?" Kate's laugh showed her dismissal of the role. "I mean, you get access to very senior people and get to be in the room when major decisions are being made, but there's so much wasted effort."

"Wasted how?"

"Like, let's have a meeting to prepare for the meeting about the big meeting. By the time we get to the big meeting, we've had so many prep meetings everyone just nods and we didn't need the big meeting."

James looked perplexed. "You lost me."

"You'd know exactly what I meant if you'd done the job. It's all background work and behind the scenes shit to make sure your boss always looks smart and prepared – never surprised or caught off guard. It's exhausting and thankless."

"That sounds really bad. But you like access to important people. And you could use your influence in these meetings, or at least in the meetings about the meetings." James laughed at his joke.

Kate sighed as she sipped her Sangiovese. James was on a roll. "And Randall isn't Darren. Just because Darren had a hissy fit and left doesn't mean Randall will. Maybe you'd get the next promotion from Randall, and you could continue on the fast promotion path. You'd like that. How long would you have to be a Chief of Staff?"

He was right. That appealed to Kate. She wanted to be on the fast track – what LampLight called having "high promotion velocity" – so she could make the money necessary for phase two of her career. She wanted a promotion.

She wanted to have high impact. And she wanted to get paid accordingly. Julia had certainly helped with that, getting her a two-level promotion and commensurate increase in salary. She wanted to stay on that trajectory. "They're typically two-year stints."

"Two years? Please, you can handle anything for two years. I mean, we've been together way longer than that, and it whipped by. And you want to get promoted quickly. This kind of exposure would be great for you."

"Yeah, it'll be good money."

He wagged a finger at her. "Money isn't everything."

It was to her. "Julia helped me get on the fast path to retirement and I want to stay there. I have to maximize my earning potential, James, and this is a great way to do it."

"Katiebug, sweetie. That's just not true." James had started calling her Katydid shortly after they got together. She didn't love being likened to an insect and pointed that out. He had, of course, asked if that "bugged" her and she had been Katiebug ever since. "You actually have plenty of money. You could do whatever you want. Don't take this job if you don't want it. Don't put yourself in a box."

"Not true? It's abso-fucking-lutely true. You don't get it. I have to be in this box. Someday, I'll break out, but for now, I need to stay in this box where I keep my head down and work."

There was no way to know what was ahead. She could be in an accident. She could get fired. Her ability to make money could be stopped somehow. She had to buckle down and make as much money as possible to protect herself for the future. Money was scarce. Obviously.

"Kate, you're in the top five percent of wage earners in the entire world."

"No I'm not, I'm way behind where I should be. Julia helped fix a lot of it, but now I'm losing her."

"Kate, I looked it up. In 2015, you had to make $335,000 to be in the top five percent worldwide. You're a top five percenter. Why do you persist in this scarcity mindset when you have so much?"

"Because it's not enough." He didn't understand. "You never know what's going to happen."

Kate flashed back to when she was six years old. Every night, her father came home from work, exhausted. He went right to her parent's bedroom, hung up his suit, and lay on the bed with his arm over his face until dinner.

One night, he came in and told her mother, whom she called Moaning Marilyn because of her persistent negativity about, well, everything, he just couldn't do it anymore. He had decided to get his MBA and change careers.

Kate remembered how beaten down he looked.

Her mother had yelled at him. Even as a six-year-old, Kate knew that wasn't the right move. Her mother screamed that he had to pay off the house before he was allowed to leave his job because he had responsibilities, and she wasn't going to lose her house because he wouldn't pull his weight.

Kate basically hadn't seen him for the next year as he worked hard to make enough money to meet her demand and pay off the house. He did it. And then he got his MBA. He got a new job as Director of Finance for a social services agency in Chicago.

Things were better for a bit.

When she was nine and he had been at his new job for a few months, he started coming home, hanging up his suit, and laying on his bed with his arm over his face until dinner.

Following your dreams didn't pay off. Switching jobs or careers didn't pay off. They just got you yelled at by the people who were supposed to support you. And even when you persevered, it was just the same shit different pile.

That was a core lesson of her childhood. It wouldn't be any better if she went to another company because people were people and politics were politics.

It was fine for James to follow his dreams, but someone had to be responsible and keep going, even when they hated it. Otherwise, she would never have enough money to quit corporate life and become an author. To be her own boss. To choose how she spent her time.

Their dessert arrived, giving Kate a chance to think while James, again, chatted with Eve. Maybe being a Chief of Staff again could be a good thing. Maybe she had just done it for the wrong leader. She would learn new parts of the business because Randall had software sales, marketing, and the customer care organization in addition to the advertising business. His team was over five thousand people. This was the big leagues.

She didn't want to share the other reason she didn't want this role. She shouldn't have to hide things from James, and it probably wasn't a surprise to him, but it embarrassed her.

Kate was a perennial people pleaser. She had been labeled "the nice one" when being compared to her younger sister Nina when they were growing up. A huge part of her identity was wrapped up in everyone liking her.

Having people mad at her all of the time as a Chief of Staff was really difficult. She was always saying no to something and even had to lie, or at least fib, to keep things moving in the role. Could she learn to curb that?

She'd been relieved when Darren quit because she wasn't the right personality type to excel as a Chief of Staff. Could she put herself into a role like that again and deal with the stress of not making everyone happy?

Of course she could. She was nice, but she was no pushover. She could get along with everyone, she always had.

How bad could it be?

Others were successful Chiefs of Staff. She wouldn't crash and burn again. Her gig for Darren was just a blip.

James pulled her attention back to the table by taking her hand. "Your birthday's coming up. What would you like to do?"

"Oh jeez, I haven't even thought about it much." Kate went along with the subject change. "It's a Tuesday this year. It's not like we can make a whole thing out of it. Let's just have dinner. We can celebrate it for real in Hawaii in two weeks. Glad that's scheduled before I get sucked into the Chief of Staff grind of skipping vacations and changing plans." *Did she just make a decision?*

"Okay. Leave it with me." James nodded. "I'll make birthday dinner plans and come up with some options to continue our celebration in Maui."

· · ·

KATE COULDN'T SLEEP. Her brain was working overtime trying to process her options. If she stayed in her current role, she would have a new boss and be angry she hadn't had a shot at the job. It would be another two years, at least, until she'd get another chance at the role. And the embarrassment of being passed over! Everyone knew she was next in line – Julia hadn't exactly made it a secret. People would talk.

If she took the role as Randall's Chief of Staff, she wouldn't enjoy the actual work, but she'd get a ton of benefit out of the exposure and the placement into her next role.

The divine goddess of career management clearly thought she had more dues to pay. She could explain the situation to Randall and get his assurance it wouldn't be like her last Chief of Staff gig.

She didn't want to get him coffee or hold his laptop while he went to the bathroom. She didn't want to be responsible for delivering him to his hotel room door and then standing there for ten minutes to make sure he didn't head back out to the casino during sales events in Las Vegas.

No way. Not again. Not another Darren. Maybe Randall was different. He had to be.

Her tossing and turning disturbed James. "You okay over there?"

"Yeah, I just can't stop thinking about my job situation."

He scooted over to spoon her and began stroking her thigh. "Now that I'm awake, how about I take your mind off that?"

"It'll be a tough job, sure you're up for it?" she asked.

James pressed against her, and she got her answer.


THREE ORGASMS LATER, they were snuggled up enjoying the afterglow.

"How'd I do? Did I take your mind off whatever was bothering you?" He tucked her into the crook of his arm.

"Yeah, you're good at banishing all negative thoughts when you touch me. I always feel safe and loved when we're naked cuddling."

"Hmm." James sounded thoughtful. "Safe is not the first word a guy wants to hear after great sex, well, great for me. Maybe it was just safe for you."

"Oh don't be like that. Safe is good. Safe is great. I love it. It means I trust you and can be my full self one-on-one with you. You spend a lot of time with other people, but I know you only get naked with me. It makes me feel safe and connected. It's a great thing. Don't knock it."

"Okay, I'll be your safety man." James snuggled in and almost immediately started snoring lightly.

Sex always had that effect on James. He was asleep within minutes when they were done.

But he always held her tightly.

She had a few hours until she had to be up for work.

She'd make her decision tomorrow.

## Chapter 3

*It'll be fine.* Kate needed the positive self-talk. She was on her way to Randall's office to discuss the role. She wore her pink power shirt, complete with lampshade pleated sleeves. She could be going out dancing or to an important meeting.

Her nerves crackled as she walked down the hall, the jitters of anticipation tingling in her blood. To be a successful Chief of Staff, you had to be completely in sync with your boss. Her success would be entirely tied up with his. If he did something dumb, she would go down with the ship. *Stop the negative thoughts,* she said to herself. This isn't Darren.

Outwardly, Kate was optimistic. People loved that about her. They also hated it about her because she was always so damned cheerful. But inside, her thoughts often went to the negative.

She saw what others didn't. She could predict consequences for most actions four or five steps out. It made her sharp. It made her fierce.

It made her a pessimist.

She hid it well in most circumstances, putting on a bright smile for the rest of the world. Only James, her dearest James, saw the real her. That's why she needed his optimism at home.

Randall waved Kate into his office and she took a seat.

"Give me one minute to finish this email." He went back to rapid typing and muttering to himself as he re-read his words.

Randall had set up his desk perpendicular to the table so he could stay in his fancy executive ergonomic chair and swivel toward his computer or his guests. The huge glass table struck Kate as ostentatious for the size of the office. She couldn't tell if his chosen layout was efficient or designed to intimidate.

She went with efficiency. Either way, Kate didn't get intimidated easily.

With his attention on his monitor, Kate had a chance to study her potential new boss. He was probably about her age, maybe a little older. He was starting to go bald but tried to hide it by pulling his graying black hair forward over his forehead. He wore thick black glasses that accentuated his closely set brown eyes. Kate thought new glasses would make him look less severe. He wore the typical male executive wardrobe at LampLight – a dress shirt with khaki pants.

Luckily, Kate had never found a causal or even correlated relationship between an executive's ability to dress and their leadership capabilities.

Kate had plenty of interactions with Randall in her time on the global monetization team in group settings. He certainly kept his distance from the hoi polloi, but had always been respectful and had a lot of good things to say about her work as well as her attention to diversity and inclusion. This was her first one-on-one with him.

"Thanks for your patience." Randall swiveled toward the conference room table. "Has Julia talked to you already?"

Clearly, he wanted to jump right in. Kate wasn't sure how to play it. Should she feign ignorance so she heard it directly from Randall or would that get Julia in trouble for not briefing her? Kate chose a light version of the truth, already playing the politics.

"Yes. My understanding is you're not considering me as Julia's backfill and instead have a different job in mind for me." *Darn it.* Kate chastised herself for letting her frustration at not getting a shot at Julia's role slip into her answer.

Did she imagine his annoyance? "That's not exactly how I'd put it." Randall leaned back in his chair and steepled his fingers. "Aidan is moving on. I need a new Chief of Staff. That's not public knowledge yet, but I trust you to keep it to yourself."

"I see." Kate nodded confirmation that she could be trusted.

"The work you've done with the global monetization team has been nothing short of amazing. I think you'd make an excellent Chief of Staff for me. What do you think?"

Kate knew he wanted her to be elated and jump at the chance. She chose the path of full disclosure. "Randall, I'm really flattered you think so highly of me. It's nice to hear." Kate paused to let that sink in before continuing. "I was a Chief of Staff previously, and it didn't work out."

"Because of them or you?"

*That's a cheeky question,* Kate thought. "He left the company. Remember Darren Blake?"

"Oh yeah." Randall held up his hand to demonstrate height. "Short guy. Brown eyes. Good laugh."

"That's the one. He went over to CloudFire when he didn't get the Corporate Vice President role he wanted."

Randall flashed her a smile. "That's not a problem because I already have my dream job."

Kate heard the red flag. People in their dream job never called it their dream job, and execs at LampLight never settled for their current position – they were always striving for the next one. Something wasn't quite right. But it wasn't bad. Just something to note.

"That's great to hear." Kate tucked her concern in the back of her mind and pressed forward. "But I learned what I need from the job. Do you mind if I share that?"

"I thought I'd be the one setting the rules, but go ahead." Randall tapped his fingertips together.

*Red flag number two,* Kate thought.

"Okay. Three things. The first is that I need to be your thought partner. Strategy has to be a big part of the job rather than just ghost-writing emails and taking notes. I'm not good as a purely behind-the-scenes kind of girl."

"I see." Kate couldn't read his face. She waited for him to say more, the seconds ticking by in an awkward rhythm. When he didn't say anything, she continued. "The second is that I want to be placed in a senior leadership role with a promotion, after I do the customary two-year stint as your Chief of Staff."

"I would prefer three years." He looked at her over his glasses.

*Three years, not two?* She kept her face bland. "And the third is that if you decide to leave the company, you have to tell me on the down-low before it's public. I plan on staying at LampLight for the long-haul. I would need time to plan my next move. It was no fun to find out my boss was leaving the day before he told everyone else."

"You want to do strategy, you want me to place you in your next role after three years, and you want advanced notice if I leave. Those all seem reasonable to me."

Kate fixed him with a penetrating stare, trying to judge his sincerity. She didn't break the gaze even after it started to feel uncomfortable. Kate nodded her assent. "Then we have a deal. I'd be happy to interview for the role."

"Interview? You just did. I choose my Chiefs of Staff."

"Oh, I see. Then, um… when would you like me to start?" *What was she saying?* She had thinking to do. Why did her mouth betray her? Why did her brain get caught up in the moment?

"Aidan informed his new boss he'd need a month of transition time. I expect you to start working with him when he's back from a short vacation to learn the ropes. Julia told me there's a succession plan in place. I want you to be fully in your new role by the end of October."

That was only three weeks. And she had a week-long vacation planned in two weeks. She had a succession plan, but her preferred replacement, Susan, didn't believe she was ready yet.

Kate and Julia would help Susan get ready in a short amount of time because Kate knew she could do the job. Susan just needed the opportunity. And maybe a little advocacy. Kate could provide both.

Randall looked at the door and raised his eyebrows. *Time for Kate to leave.* "Okay, thanks Randall. I look forward to working with you."


KATE WAS PERPLEXED by what had just happened. Hiring rules at LampLight were very tight - at least three candidates for every open role. How was Randall allowed to ignore those rules? And what about those red flags?

Randall didn't do quarterly one on ones with underlings like other leaders. He was too busy for that. Kate didn't really know him all that well on a one-to-one basis. His public persona was good – always talking about diversity and inclusion and the importance of prioritization. And he had fired Jeff, the horrible former vice president of sales, for poor behavior. He wasn't afraid to take action.

It would be okay. She would work hard, be his strategic thought partner, and get her next great role in three short years.

If it all worked out as planned, maybe she could even pull her retirement date in and get started on her author life.

*Yeah, it would be a great career move.* It didn't align one hundred percent with her own career plan, but this one was better as it cemented an advocate and sponsor for her.

She wouldn't get to the next level without that.

She was in.

## Chapter 4

Kate shared her decision with James that night at her birthday dinner. "Congrats, Katiebug. It sounds like a great opportunity."

"We'll see. I have some reservations, but I don't see how refusing the job helps me meet my financial goals."

James wrinkled his brow. "Don't do it just for the money."

"What other reason is there? Oh yeah, fame. *Fame* and fortune. Why do you think I beat myself up so hard at work? I want to retire from corporate life. I'm forty-six today and want to be done at fifty-two. You know that."

"Yeah, I know that's our plan, but I don't like seeing you stressed. It's not worth the money."

"Maybe not to you, but the harder I work, the faster I can be done. You actually like your job. It's different for you."

"And I choose to not be on the fast track," James reminded her. "I like helping others be successful rather than being in the spotlight."

Kate pointed her fork at him. "You'd make a great Chief of Staff."

"Yeah, except that I'd have to be a full-time employee of LampLight. No thank you. I'm not dealing with the politics, the stress, and the anxiety. I'm good right where I am as a contractor for them instead."

"Are things good? How was work today?"

"The usual." James managed the designs for Lamp-Light's hardware business including the computer-aided design specs and the security of that highly confidential information. With partners and vendors working on various components, security was critical, and credentials were tightly managed. He worked about thirty hours a week, but also had to be on call almost around the clock in case something was needed.

It worked for him because he had flexibility to do other things that he enjoyed like motorcycling, fishing, and mountain biking.

"You got your job without an interview, too didn't you?" Kate tucked her tongue into her cheek and dipped her spoon in the tiramisu.

James worked very hard, but he owned his own company and had a lucrative LampLight contract. Tim, the guy who paid his contract, just happened to be a friend that James had helped get a job at LampLight in the first place.

James' position was secure. Kate was more than a little jealous at times about how easy James had it for what she thought of as a lot of money.

Kate had never been in a situation like that. Before LampLight, she had selected a few bosses because she knew them before she worked with them, but life at Lamp-Light seemed to rarely be about choice – more like reorgs and people moving on.

She wondered wistfully what it would feel like to choose her boss. She could this time, she guessed, but was quickly reminded that she didn't really have a choice.

You didn't say no to opportunities like this at Lamp-Light. If you did, you'd be labeled as an under-achiever and never get to the next level. She had to do what she could to maximize her earning potential.

"It's time to open your birthday present." James set a medium-sized box on the table.

"Thanks, sweetie."

"Don't thank me yet."

She opened it only to find another box inside. She opened that box and found another small one inside of that.

She opened the final box, getting nervous because it was ominously shaped like a ring box.

As she opened the jewelry case, a beautiful sapphire and diamond ring sparkled at her.

Shock overpowered her. She had no time to mask her first reaction. "What the fuck is that?"

"It's a ring." He sounded sheepish.

"Yes, and it's beautiful. But what does it mean?" Kate had a sinking feeling about James' intentions.

"I don't know. What do you want it to mean?"

"Don't give me that. What does it mean?" Her tone grew more emphatic this time.

The tentative nature of his voice was in direct contrast to the near panic Kate was feeling. "It's a promise ring?"

"Really? A promise ring? What, are we in high school or something?" Kate was incredulous, but at least she had gotten her emotions under control and had a joking tone back in her questions.

"Okay. It's a commitment ring."

"A commitment ring? But we aren't gay." The teasing continued.

"Fine. You won't like what I want it to be." James sounded hurt.

"Try me."

"I want it to be an engagement ring." Hope lit in James' hazel eyes.

"I know." She kept her gaze steadily on his.

"Then why did you torture me?"

"Because I wanted you to own it." Kate paused and took a breath. "We have to be honest with each other. You can't just slip me a ring without being clear about what it means."

James took her hand. "I know I've asked you a million times. I want to be with you, and I want everyone to know you're off the market. People our age who've been together for five years get married."

"I don't want to get married." Kate felt it all the way to her bones. She loved James, but things were fine the way they were.

They had fallen into a nice routine. He had moved into her condo in Seattle about six months after they started dating. They were very connected emotionally, but if she was ever done, she could ask him to leave her house.

She had kept her finances separate and he paid rent. Easy peasy if she ever wanted out.

"I was afraid you'd say that." The dejection was clear on James' face.

Kate knew she could erase his hurt by agreeing to marry him, but she just couldn't do it. She flashed back to her parent's kitchen again and the financial trap marriage represented. "How about if I wear it on my right hand?"

"That's fine, as long as you wear it." James perked up a bit. "Maybe I can convince you to move it to your other hand over time."

"Thank you. I love it." Kate leaned over the table to kiss James. She poured the love she felt into it.

She truly loved him. She just didn't want to marry him. Too many horror stories. And she had too many years of living on her own to make room for another person. "Ready for more tiramisu?"

"Yeah. And there's more to your present."

Kate batted her eyelashes at James. "More than your undying love?"

"You already have that." He quickly recovered his upbeat nature. Kate hoped the dejection had passed. "I've made all of the plans for Maui, but before I commit, I wanted to run them by you."

"James, I spend all day, every day at work making decisions. It's really nice to have some made for me. I'm sure whatever you picked is great."

James smiled. "Ocean view room in Ka'anapali. We fly in on Saturday afternoon because I know you like to have time to pack when you aren't feeling work pressure. We'll fly back the following Sunday morning so you'll have time to catch up before Monday morning." Kate smiled, encouraging James to finish the description. He knew her very well. "I rented a convertible and scoped out snorkel rental locations. I think that covers it."

"I love it. And I love you. Sounds like you thought of everything."

"I try, my love. I try." Kate tried to read James' face, but all she saw was an expression that didn't match his words – melancholy and wistfulness. She hated being the cause of that look on his face, but she had to stand firm on the marriage front. "It'll be great to squeeze this vacation in before you officially start the new job."

"It feels a little uncomfortable heading out while I have to transition my team, but I think we've made the right call. If I don't take the break now, who knows when we'll be able to get away."

KATE LAY awake in bed that night, listening to James' light snoring. Her mind was picking apart the whole marriage discussion.

Again.

She thought about Greg, her first long-term relationship. They had been together over ten years, but he really wanted to have kids, and she really didn't. He thought he could change her mind, but it just wasn't something Kate was willing to consider.

When she was a kid, Moaning Marilyn had cursed her with children just like her. Kate thought she was a pretty good kid who stayed out of trouble. Her mother certainly made it sound like having a kid like her was a fate worse than death.

Just in case Moaning Marilyn was right, she preferred to not tempt fate.

She wasn't going to give up control of her time to focus on someone else's needs full-time. She and Greg had ended things amicably and still spoke about once a year. He was up to three boys last time she got an update. *Could be more by now*, she thought with a shudder.

The marriage issue had caused her to walk away from a relationship before. Well, that was really over the kid issue. And James was clear he didn't want kids. He just wanted her. But could she end a forty-six-year run as a single person?

Her personal life was the way she wanted it. She was too set in her ways. She had to have control over her life. She could live with someone but not want to get married. That was okay. James loved her and things could stay the way they were.

But getting married was important to James. Very important. It wasn't kind of her to keep that from him if that's what he wanted.

What if he left her because she wouldn't marry him? Would he do that? Was that a good enough reason to get married?

She wanted to be with him. She could picture a long future together. Did that mean they should get married?

She had to stop swirling on this and get some sleep. She would be telling her team about the manager change the next day.

"THANKS FOR JOINING ON TIME EVERYONE." Kate's direct reports were assembled for their weekly team meeting. Half the attendees were in the room and the other half participated virtually.

Kate decided to start with the good news. "Packed agenda today, but first, I want to share some positive feedback I received from the leadership team in Europe. Vittorio, your work closing the agency deal in Italy is the largest deal we've ever had in Western Europe. And you helped them agree on terms that'll keep that relationship in positive margin territory for the foreseeable future. They said it couldn't be done, but the way you held the line in the negotiation was beautiful, absolutely beautiful."

Kate didn't have to ask her team to congratulate Vittorio – they all just started clapping and rejoicing his win. She felt the warmth of pride that she had pulled this global team together and led them through the transformation from individuals to a high-performance team. She would miss them.

"Thank you, Kate. We couldn't have done it without your coaching and guidance. I went through some dark times in the last few weeks, but since you believed in me, I knew I could do it."

Kate couldn't help blushing. "Aw, thanks, Vittorio, but this is your doing. I was in the background."

Kate saw the way Susan narrowed her eyes at her, like she knew something was up. "There's something else," Susan said. "And it doesn't look like good news." Kate wished Susan wasn't quite so perceptive. "Spill it, boss."

"Okay, now that we have celebrated Vittorio, I have some news."

"Bad news?" Susan quipped.

"No, not bad news. I think it's good news for all of us."

"Whenever someone says that, it means bad news," Ben added, flashing a mischievous smile in his video feed from Cape Town.

"I'm trusting you with some information that's not public – please keep it in the family." The team knew that meant not to talk about it outside the team. She had built a trusting, supportive, and safe environment and no one would out her secret. "Randall has chosen a new Chief of Staff-"

"And it's you." Susan finished Kate's sentence for her.

Kate nodded. Everyone jumped in with congratulations and a round of woo hoos. "Thanks everyone, yes it's me. Which means you'll have a new manager."

They immediately sobered.

"We knew this was too good to last." Veronica, the latest member to join the team, joked, but her tone was good-natured. "Just my luck to finally get onto this team and have you leave."

"There are several great candidates for my backfill because we've done excellent succession planning. Julia will definitely backfill my position and life will be good."

"Congrats Kate. This is a great opportunity for you." Susan pointed her finger at Kate. "But you're irreplaceable. Nice try."

KATE WAS in a good mood when she walked up the stairs to her Seattle condo.

"Hey Bug. How's my sweetie?"

"I'm tired, but I shared the news with my team. It feels good that the cat is out of the bag."

"Secrets are always hard to keep, especially when you're so close to your team. Has Julia shared her bombshell with the team yet?"

Kate shook her head. "We decided I would share my news with my direct team and that Julia would make her announcement next week. That gives me some time to convince Susan to take on the acting lead role for my team and influence Florence to interview Susan for the full-time role."

James squinched up his face. "That all sounds really complicated."

"Just a few pieces that have to fall into place. The stage is set for Susan's success." Kate took a moment to send good thoughts to the goddess of succession plans for support. "How was work for you today?"

"Today was not a good day." James' tone turned serious. "We had a bit of a shake-up ourselves. My team is still intact, but the higher ups have brought in a new operations team to streamline how we work. They came from Lamp-Light's customer support team and are all about process. Process, process, process." James grabbed a piece of cheese for himself and sat down at the table with a beer. "We had a team meeting today where I counted the main guy saying 'efficiency gains' complete with air quotes twelve times." James rolled his eyes.

"What do you think that'll mean for you?" Kate had an uneasy feeling about this. James was not a process guy – he was more about relationships and the fastest way to get things done. Well, except when doing dishes.

"Nothing. We keep to ourselves on the hardware side. They'll have plenty of opportunities for 'efficiency gains' in other parts of the business." James made very sarcastic looking air quotes as he said it. "Want to hit the Trattoria?"

"Sure." Kate chose to not share her concerns. James would be fine and didn't need her filling his head with a bunch of what ifs just because that's how her brain worked. "We can spend some time not talking about our jobs and instead finalize our plans for Maui."

---

## Chapter 5

---

Kate dug her brightly painted toes into the warm sand on
the beach in front of their hotel. She sipped a Mai Tai
from her "coffee" cup under the striped umbrella she and
James had rented for the day. She had just come back from
a quick snorkel and settled down with a book.

"You know I'm not good at sitting around." James had
snorkeled with her but didn't love it as much as she did.
She knew from experience that his desire for her not to
snorkel alone outweighed his dislike for the activity.

"What do you want to do instead? We have all week."
Kate smiled at the thought.

"I've done some research. You like to relax and read. If
I do that, I might go insane. I found a dirt bike ride up in
the West Maui Hills that sounds interesting. I'd be gone all
day tomorrow if I did it. I don't love that we'd be spending
time apart, but I'd be back for happy hour. Is that okay?"

"James, that sounds magical. I feel bad because I know
you get bored easily. If I had a whole day to rent the
umbrella again, alternate between snorkeling and reading,

I would have enough relaxation to jump back into activities. I'll only snorkel where other people are. We could hit the rum distillery and the blown glass place on Wednesday, drive around the island on Thursday, and then have another relaxing day on Friday."

"You're the best. A less amazing partner might've been angry."

"Good thing you don't have to experience that." Kate took another sip of her fruity drink.

James was clearly excited about his new plan. "Mind if I go back to the room to lock in the dirt bike ride for tomorrow and make a few dinner reservations?"

"Go for it. We can regroup for happy hour. I'll be right here." Kate turned her attention back to her book. It was nice to be taken care of and have a partner who shared the load.

AFTER KISSING James goodbye in the morning, Kate started with macadamia nut pancakes and coffee watching boats bob on the water from the lanai of a beachfront restaurant.

She walked along the boardwalk back to her hotel, her floppy hat protecting her pale skin from the sun. She rented an umbrella and a chair, set up in the sand, and alternated snorkeling and reading.

All. Day. Long.

IT WAS ALREADY three in the afternoon. James would be back soon for happy hour. She'd enjoyed her day of solitude on the beach and appreciated that James was out entertaining himself.

They could each do what they wanted. This was a partnership. Honest. Independent but also together.

She should marry him.

*Where had that come from?* Kate thought she had already worked through this. It was just the booze, sand, and relaxation talking.

Or was it? It would make James happy. Kate's head fell back against the towel she was using as a pillow. She sipped the rest of the Mai Tai she had hidden in a carton of papaya, orange, and guava juice. *Was she drunk?* No. It had taken her all day to work through the carton and she had plenty of snacks. She knew better than to drink and snorkel.

Was she punishing James for how other men had treated her in her long dating life? Her friends seemed to get lost in making their partners happy. She was a pleaser, and knew she could fall into that trap. She had watched her friends' divorces. Even her mentor Julia hadn't escaped a punishing divorce that left her broke. Then there was Greg and the whole kids thing. And her parents.

But James really wanted to be married. He'd been married before and it had ended amicably. They mutually agreed they'd grown apart. He didn't have the typical baggage of previous marriages.

She felt selfish because she was making a decision completely based on what she wanted.

What about what James wanted?

*James could take care of himself,* she reminded herself.

She shouldn't get married to make him happy. That was obvious.

But when she took a step back, maybe being married wouldn't be so bad. James just wanted to be with her. They had a great thing going. They cared a lot about each other. And the sex! Five years in, they were still lighting up the sheets, and the shower, and the kitchen table. Kate smiled thinking about their sex life.

Why shouldn't she marry him? If the main thing holding her back was concern about money, they would continue to have separate finances, and he would sign a pre-nup. They didn't always hold up in court, but again, James was a stand-up guy. She couldn't imagine that he would try to go against a document he had signed.

What's the worst that could happen?

He could steal all of her money.

*Oh, Kate, stop being melodramatic.* It was only money, and she could make it back again. Ha! Could she?

She was spiraling. Time to put the Mai Tais away. She'd spent thirty years saying she didn't want to get married – that it was her choice not to.

Now it was a frequently repeated story she told herself. But was it what she really wanted? It would certainly make James happy. He would lose that hurt look on his face whenever she said she wasn't going to marry him. She pulled herself back from what James wanted. She knew what James wanted.

*What did she want?*

She decided to talk to the only person who knew what it was like to live with her and want to be married. Greg.

He was somewhere in Oregon last time they talked. It wasn't too late to call.


"TO WHAT DO I owe the pleasure?" He answered on the first ring.

"Hey G-Man. I have a question for you. Got a minute?"

"Yeah, I'm at a soccer game, but as long as I yell something encouraging every few minutes, they won't notice I'm not watching. What's up?"

"There's this guy."

"Yeah, Jim Bob or Jimmy or Shames."

"Ha ha. It's James, and you know that.

"What did he do now?"

"He wants to get married."

"Oh." There was a beat of silence. It took a moment for Greg to speak again. "What'd you say when he asked you?"

"I didn't exactly answer. I just told him I don't want to get married. I figured that you of all people would know what it would be like to be married to me."

"Kate, I know what it's like to live with you and be part of your life. I can tell you it's amazing. I wouldn't give up my kids for anything and I know we made the right choice, but it would've been the perfect world if you'd wanted the same things I did. You're loving, and kind, and giving. Maybe a little too nice sometimes. He's a lucky guy."

"Thanks Greg. But do you think I'm marriage material?"

"Uh, yeah. Definitely. But you have to want it. Don't

do it for him. If you'd given in, we would have gotten divorced by now or you'd just be miserable with three kids. Does he want kids?"

"No."

"Do you love him?"

"Yes."

"Ouch. I'm a big enough man to admit it hurts a little to hear you say that so emphatically. Hang on."

Kate heard Greg pull the phone away from his ear and put his hand over the microphone. "Way to go River!" She felt bad she had touched a nerve. "I'm back. Where were we, oh right, you love someone else."

"Sorry."

"Don't be sorry. Be glad we can still talk like this." She heard his chuckle and could picture him kicking the grass with his toe like he did when he was embarrassed.

"You think maybe being anti-marriage is just a story I tell myself?"

"I always wondered if the kids thing was the only reason we didn't make it. I loved you almost enough to give up on my dream and marry you anyway. But I'm glad we both stuck to our guns. Only you know what's deep down in your heart. Hang on." Kate heard the muffling and yelling again before Greg was back on the line. He clearly took sideline encouragement seriously. "For what it's worth, I think you'd make a great wife. And I'll come to your wedding and cheer you on if you decide to go for it."

"Thanks Greg. That helps." Kate felt warm and fuzzy that Greg thought she'd make a good wife. She wasn't sure. She was a good cohabitator, but she liked her own space and ability to call the shots. "What's new with you?"

"Time to send another baby gift. Sherrie is seven months along. It's a girl this time."

"Oh Greg, congratulations! How wonderful to get the little girl you wanted."

"Sherrie won't let me name her Kate, but I'll try for a middle name."

Kate chuckled. "I'm glad things worked out as they should have. For both of us."

"The game's ending. I have to run. It's my turn to take the crew for ice cream."

"Parenting suits you, Greg. Talk to you next year."

"Or sooner. I bet there'll be a wedding."

They were both laughing as they hung up.

Kate looked out at the water. She watched tiny boats bob on the waves.

She wanted to be happy. She wanted to feel settled. She wanted a foundation. She wanted someone who would cook for her and care for her and plan vacations. She wanted someone with a job who could support himself. She wanted someone who craved her company but could also spend time on his own or with his friends so she could have quality alone time without recriminations. She wanted a compatible sex partner, one who found her sexy and irresistible.

She had all of those things in James. All of them. And with a pre-nup, she felt financially protected.

The decision was actually pretty easy.

*Fuck it.* She'd do it.

•   •   •

ONCE SHE TOLD James about her idea, she knew things would move quickly and she would be married as soon as the officiant was available.

Kate packed up the accoutrements from her day on the beach, let the attendant know she was finished with the umbrella and chair, and went back to her hotel room. After a shower, she set up her laptop on the lanai with the gentle ocean breeze flapping the edges of her hat.

She switched from Mai Tais to water. She needed to be fully sober for what she was doing.

She opened a new document and began the detailed process of writing a pre-nuptial agreement. She covered each topic as unemotionally as possible. Separate finances. No community property. Each person left with what they brought to the relationship like cars, furniture, and art. James would continue to pay rent, but it would not contribute to equity in her condo. Kate would keep all of that since he had moved into her place and the mortgage was in her name. They would purchase things as individuals to keep ownership lines clear.

She added a signature line and re-read it. Lock-tight. She should probably have a lawyer look at it, but it was James. He wasn't out to screw her.

Next up, she researched how to get married on Maui. Aside from funny t-shirts that said "Just Mauied" on them, she also learned the hotel had an officiant on staff and there was an online process for applying for a marriage license. All you needed was a driver's license.

Kate hadn't heard from James yet. She knew it would take an hour to get from the West Maui hills back to the hotel, so since he hadn't called yet to say he was on his way, she had time. She headed down to the business center at the hotel to print her protective document.

She watched the printer spit out the two-pages. Was she moving too fast? Had she really thought this through? Her friends were always telling her to be a bit more spontaneous and stop over-analyzing every decision. But wasn't this the kind she should over-analyze?

Julia deposited the document in their room and headed out to the shops to buy a dress. She hadn't thought she was getting married. She didn't have anything appropriate.

She was able to walk to a shopping center from the hotel, and she was just looking for a simple sun dress – they were all over the island. It shouldn't be hard.

She was in luck. She found a flowy red dress made of a nice cottony drapey material with a built-in bra that showed off the girls while not being too clingy. She refused to wear Spanx on the beach.

She found a big, floppy red hat with white stitching to complete her ensemble and proudly carried her bag back to the hotel. She was really going to do this. And if James wasn't interested after all, she still had a pretty new dress.

# Chapter 6

"I wish you a long, and happy marriage. Mahalo." The officiant stood in the sun, her long black hair lifting in the breeze as she smiled at the happy couple. They had just had their first kiss while the witness, also supplied by the hotel, blew celebratory bubbles through a purple plastic wand.

"Mahalo. Thank you Becca." James and Kate shook hands with the officiant. "And thank you, Pamela." Kate shook hands with the witness after she put the wand back in the bottle of bubbles.

"I'll go click some buttons to get the license filed." Becca made typing motions with her fingers. "You'll be able to print it by tomorrow."

"Mahalo nui loa, Becca." James had been practicing his Hawaiian. Kate smiled at his desire to be polite and respectful.

He looked handsome in his white linen shirt and light tan shorts. He didn't need to go shopping for the perfect Hawaiian wedding ensemble.

"Maʻalahi wale." Becca said. "And the best part is you get a free drink in the hotel bar." She pulled a coupon card out of the book she'd been using during the ceremony and handed it to Kate. "Hoʻomaikaʻi! That means good luck."

James and Kate laughed at the commercialization of eloping in Maui as they looked at their free drink card. "Might as well use it. Come on, wife." James held out his hand for Kate's.

She felt the warm sand on her feet as they walked to the hotel bar.

CHAMPAGNE IN ONE HAND AND JAMES' hand in the other, Kate and James watched the waves from the beach-front bar. "You're stuck now." James' eyes crinkled at the corners when he smiled at her.

"You're the one who's stuck. You have to deal with all my high maintenance and control issues. No take backsies!"

"You? High maintenance? That's hilarious." James turned to face her. "The only thing I have to overlook is the way you load the dishwasher. I'm pretty sure you're perfect in every other way."

Kate rolled her eyes. "Your lovely hazel eyes just turned a darker shade of brown indicating how full of shit you are, Hubs." Kate blinked her eyelashes at James several times in mock innocence. They laughed together.

"Hubs?"

"Yeah, I'm trying it out. Short for 'husband.' It's a lot to get used to."

"I like it." There was the smile Kate wanted. She knew he would be happy being married.

"Do you think anything's going to change now?" Kate spoke before she could think.

"Katiebug, I basically cried tears of joy when you told me you'd changed your mind. I immediately ironed my linen shirt even though I knew it wouldn't last." James gestured down his long torso at the wrinkled shirt. "The shirt, not the marriage." He laughed at his joke. "I signed the pre-nup and we were on the beach before the ink was dry. What're you afraid of?"

Kate didn't want to tell him she was afraid of losing control. That made her sound shallow and immature. She didn't have to lose control just because they were married. She had a voice. She had opinions. It would be okay. "I guess I'm most worried that being married will ruin our sex life." She went for the joke.

"Oh shit, I didn't think of that. What'd you say we take the party upstairs and find out if it's still good even after being married for forty-five minutes?"

"What if the magic's gone now that we're hitched?" Kate's lips thinned to a straight line. "You're right that we better investigate. See if we can revive our sex life if things have already gotten dull." Kate laughed. James did not. "Hey – now that we're married, you have to laugh heartily at all of my jokes. Heartily." Kate repeated the last word for emphasis, poking James' chest with her finger.

"Your wish is my command. Now let's get upstairs." James left a tip for their free drinks. Kate appreciated that, even though she was already distracted thinking about what was waiting for her for the next hour... or two.

## Chapter 7

Her first few days back in the office went by in a blur of transition planning. Susan was the obvious candidate. She was smart, savvy, clear-speaking, and fun. Not to mention her in-depth knowledge.

There were other candidates and there would be an open interview process, but Kate was pulling for Susan because it would be fabulous for the team to have the continuity and an excellent step in Susan's career. Kate knew that mentoring women was important but that advocating for women was even more important.

She wanted to help Susan get this job – not just advise her how to do it. Advocating required action, not just advice.

A stickler for fairness, Kate reviewed the other candidates on her succession plan. They were all excellent. Each brought different strengths to the table.

Even after the objective review, Kate knew that Susan was the best choice. Florence would be busy onboarding

Julia's replacement and wouldn't have as much time for onboarding Kate's replacement. The team needed someone who could hit the ground running and grow in the role.

An incoming instant message interrupted Kate's train of thought. It was from Randall.

My office

She supposed she was being summoned. She jogged up the two flights of stairs to his office, took a moment to catch her breath, waved to his admin Sheila, and waited by the door.

"Come on in. We have work to do."

Aidan was seated at the conference room table. Kate sat across from him and opened her laptop. "So you're the one he tricked into taking my job." Aidan jerked his thumb in Randall's direction as he laughed.

"Guilty. We should spend some quality time together now that we're both back from vacation. Congrats on the new role. It sounds great." Kate meant it.

"Sorry to interrupt, but we have a pressing situation." Randall disrupted their joviality with a serious tone. Kate was still getting to know Randall. She made a note that he was not chit-chatty. "The Customer Advisory Board is in March in Brussels. We planned to hold it at the launch of the new Customer Experience Center, but I was just notified by those idiots that the opening got pushed out for nine months. What do we do now? We have less than five months to replan the whole thing."

"For fuck's sake, I won't miss this." Aidan muttered

under his breath so only Kate heard as Randall strode to the white board and wrote "options."

Kate had an idea. "Do you think they'd have an occupancy permit and would just be finishing details? Customers might like a behind-the-scenes-welcome-to-the-sausage making experience of the unfinished space." Kate was met with two unblinking stares. "It shows that we have our challenges as a company, too – makes us seem more approachable, more human."

"That's good, that's good." Randall nodded and captured the idea on the whiteboard.

"We could cancel." Aidan was clearly done with this job.

"We can't cancel, Aidan – the twenty-two leaders have already committed." Randall shook his head at his departing Chief of Staff. His disrespectful tone made Kate uncomfortable. He was probably just stressed.

She tried another option. "We could move it to a hotel nearby and take a tour of the partially finished space – use it like a final feedback session on the set-up."

"We won't have time or budget to incorporate their feedback." Aidan's tone was dismissive.

"Yeah, but they don't know that." Randall wrote that on the board. Kate felt uneasy again. They shouldn't lie to customers.

"We could move it to the Amsterdam office. Pretty close to Brussels." Aidan suggested and Randall captured that.

"What if we asked a client in Brussels to host us, at our expense, on their campus?" Kate was on a brainstorming tear.

"A logistical challenge for sure, but another great idea." Randall beamed at Kate. She felt herself blush at the praise. She was always good at ideation and was glad to have been invited to this impromptu brainstorm.

"That'll be a nightmare." Aidan wasn't convinced. "Why not get the European Union to host us?" Kate caught the sarcasm in Aidan's tone.

"It doesn't hurt to ask." Randall missed that Aidan was joking.

"Kate, can you check with our political action committee and see who we're friendly with at the EU offices?" Kate knew it was a long shot, but she wanted to show she was game for a challenge.

"Of course. If we don't ask, it definitely won't happen." Kate was caught up in the excitement.

"Kate, I love the optimism and creativity. Keep it coming." Randall smiled again. It made up for her earlier discomfort.

"Absolutely. It was my International Relations degree kicking in." Kate wasn't sure why she felt like she had to drop her credentials like that. Probably trying to curry favor with Randall. Something about him made her want to impress him so he didn't lump her in with the "idiots" as he liked to call people he didn't agree with or like.

"It sounds like the two of you have enough ideas to get started. Write up a proposal for the options and start working through the details. We need a new plan ASAP, like tomorrow."

Aidan jumped up and Kate followed suit, reading the room. She followed Aidan to his office. Would she get this cushy office two doors down from Randall when Aidan moved out? It had a great view of the Cascade mountains and would be beautiful on clear mornings.

"Well aren't you just a little miss goody two shoes with your brilliant ideas." Aidan's Irish accent made it difficult for Kate to discern if he was joking, intimidated, or some of each.

"Easy, killer. I was just trying to be strategic."

"I get it, but here's the thing. You're going to have to tamp down Randall's enthusiasm a lot. He gets these hare-brained ideas, like hosting our event at the European Union's headquarters, and then you have to back him away from it because it'll never happen."

"But what if we could make it happen? We're Lamp-Light after all."

"You're not hearing me. YOU would have to do all that work. And when things aren't perfect, YOU will be the one running through the streets of Brussels at 2AM looking for just the right tech gadget that Randall wants to give away because he changed his mind on the plane."

"Oh." Kate still didn't understand. She liked aiming big and being creative.

"Let's get down to business and just say that legal stopped us from pursuing the EU angle. That always works with Randall. He thinks the legal team is a bunch of losers – his words, not mine."

Kate thought that was awfully rude. "Okay." She was still feeling the thrill of being in the middle of a strategy session for the biggest customer advisory meeting of the year. She set her concerns aside and got down to work on the plan.

IT WAS ALMOST like she had three teams in her new role.

First, there was Randall and Sheila – the most important team as a Chief of Staff. Sheila was Randall's always stressed and super sassy administrative assistant. They had shared many an eye-roll over the years because they both had a low tolerance for bullshit. They'd be just fine.

Then Randall's direct reports. She'd be responsible for staff meeting agendas and prioritizing initiatives for that team.

Then there was her team of direct reports that supported Randall. She studied her org chart. She knew a few of them already.

Frances led the executive communications team and was responsible for making sure Randall had his talking points for each meeting. She also liaised with the teams who managed the accounts that Randall was the executive sponsor for and for ghost-writing his blog posts. She had a team of three people.

Louella led the events team. Kate wondered why Randall required five people just to run events, but it was too early for her to question scope. Louella had a team of four people.

Jason and DeShawn rounded out her direct reports and were responsible for executive analytics. They provided the numbers and insights Randall required to stay informed about what was going on with the business.

The full team of eleven people was much smaller than teams Kate had managed in the past, but she was comfortable with the reduced number because it was a high impact team.

From what she knew of them, they seemed to operate in silos. She would fix that. And she could dust off her team-building exercises to get them working together better.

Her excitement continued to increase at the thought of a new set of challenges. She had to admit she had started to get a little too comfortable in her old role, assuming she would keep going up the ladder and lead the monetization team. She needed to branch out and get back into the broader business of LampLight.

As with every new team she joined, she started by learning as much as she could on her own, studying LinkedIn profiles, company intranet sites, and previous all-hands presentations to get a feel for the team. That helped her hone her questions so the new team didn't have as much of an onboarding burden.

Aidan had already told her a lot, too. Kate also liked to do an intro session to set the tone for her transparent approach. It took some teams a little time to get used to it, but it almost always brought teams closer together.

She would invite a colleague to gather questions from the team before the meeting. The rules were simple – ask anything you want, no matter the subject. Then, the colleague would interview Kate and ask the questions.

This created a super safe environment because the questions were all asked anonymously. They could connect as humans without any fear of discomfort. Kate remembered one new team meeting where she had almost started a riot when she said that she loved Weird Al Yankovic. That was not popular. But she was who she was!

Most questions were more serious. She was once asked about her policy on firing people. She gave a completely honest answer about her belief that great people sometimes get into the wrong role and that her preferred approach was to match people with roles they love. Of course, she would fire people, but only after trying to work it out together. The team appreciated her transparent answer and brought it up years later.

She would ask Dave to do it. He was Florence's Chief of Staff and had been mentoring Kate ever since Julia had hooked them up. He'd be perfect.

---

Chapter 8

---

Kate prepared for her team building meeting. She decided on three exercises to help the team get to know each other as people. She had noticed a lot of siloed thinking and lack of collaboration, and she was determined to fix it.

The first captured peoples' values. In Kate's experience, most interpersonal relationship issues at work stemmed from a mismatch in values. Once people understood each other's values, it often created a common language for them to speak and uncovered hidden communication issues.

Homework item number one was to review a list of thirty-six values and have each person narrow them down to twelve, then six, then three. The top three would be presented to the team.

She pre-empted the most common question in her email instructions, adding that people could add any other values they liked if they didn't see theirs on the list. It was funny to Kate how many people needed permission for simple tasks like that, but experience showed at least two people would ask.

The second was a simple overview - just four questions, but it required a lot of thought and revealed a great deal about each person. Kate typed up each question in her email:

1. What are you like at your best?
2. What are you like at your worst?
3. What's your preferred communication style?
4. What's your superpower?

Just for the heck of it, she added a fifth question because this team had worked together for a while. She bet they thought they knew each other.

1. What's something few people know about you that you'd like to share?

That should make for some good conversation. If they couldn't connect as humans, then they would never be a cohesive team.

Kate's stomach grumbled, reminding her that it was lunch time. One good thing about this new job was that when there wasn't some big emergency, which could happen at any time, she had more flexibility in her schedule.

She had learned the hard way what happened when she packed her calendar and then there was an emergency. It made for a very rough day.

She dealt with it by blocking time on her calendar just

in case she needed it for a Randall emergency, or "Randergency" as she liked to call it. Her friends knew she might have to bail at the last minute, but they were trying to have lunch once a week in the center of LampLight's campus.

Today, it looked like the coast was clear to hop a campus shuttle and head to the new building where they had just opened a cafeteria with multiple food stations. Melanie and Lesley would meet her there.

Julia introduced Kate to both of them. Lesley had started out as a career mentor for Kate and when their first year of mentorship was over, they stayed friends. Melanie was one of Julia's besties. After Julia and Kate ran into Melanie in a campus café and had lunch, Melanie and Kate had become friends. Both of them attended Steak and Bourbon.

KATE FOUND them just getting in line for Thai food, talking energetically. Melanie was a bundle of energy and people couldn't help but get caught up in her optimism. "There she is!" Melanie's always smiling face seemed even brighter today. She handed Kate a tray, her manicured nails clicking on the plastic surface.

"What'd I miss?" Kate accepted the tray and got behind them in line.

"Lesley was just telling me about her Saturday night date. It wasn't good."

Lesley leaned in close, her long brown hair falling forward with the movement. "Good enough that I still slept with him, but not good enough to see him again." She leaned back as Melanie and Kate laughed. "More fish in the sea."

"Hope he was worth the effort," Melanie raised her eyebrows in anticipation of Lesley's answer. She gave them a face that said perhaps not.

Kate perused the digital menu and chose *pad see ew*. "How'd you meet this one?"

"Another dating app find. I mean, he might be an okay back-up plan for a Saturday night, but he just didn't have the mental horsepower I need in a partner. He seemed like he fell in love with me on sight which was weird."

"I can't blame him for that, I kinda did, too." Kate laughed.

"But that was because you recognized my immense mental capabilities." Lesley emphasized her appreciation by poking her receipt at Kate. "Thanks for making my point."

"Quick updates everyone. Kate, you first." Melanie gestured at Kate with a pink frosty nail.

Kate knew the drill. Bullet point overview so everyone got a chance to talk during their short lunch break. "New job is good. Randall is treating me well. I miss J-Money. James brought me flowers for no reason, the sweetie."

"Nice update! Sounds like married life is treating you well. We'll come back around on the new job front. I remember when I stopped working for Julia. It was tough, but then we became better friends. You know she's a stickler for fairness. Melanie. Go."

"One of my peers, Scary Gary, decided to present our project without me in the meeting and has now taken all of the credit for the work."

"Dumb ass. Hope your boss knows who did all the heavy lifting," Kate interjected. That was technically against the rules of bullet point updates, but she was feeling rebellious, and the situation required it.

"Yes, and she's rectifying it. Hubby is good. Dog is good. Lesley. Go."

"You just heard about my date. Yuck. I recently watched *Shaun the Sheep* with my nephew. Better than a lot of movies I've seen lately. I'm thinking of no longer dyeing my hair. I'm taking input."

"That's a bold move. I really thought that was your natural color."

"It is, well, it was, but I've been pumping it up a little. Looking at my roots, I think it's all gray now."

"I say go for it. I just did this blond thing and am not looking forward to going back every five weeks to get it touched up." Kate ran her hand down the back of her short pixie.

"But it looks so great. I love you as a blond. Do you find that you're having more fun?"

<hr>

DAVE SAT at the front of the room, looking dashing as he always did in his bespoke tailored suit. He had dressed up for the occasion, even for him. "Kate, I've collected a bunch of tough questions from your new team. Are you ready?"

"Yes. And don't hold back."

"Girl, you certainly don't need to tell me that." The ribbing was good-natured. "I'm going to start with a heavy-hitting question, and we'll go from there." Kate braced for the first question. The stakes were high since she wanted to develop a good first impression with her team. "Dogs or cats?"

The team laughed and Kate relaxed. "Dogs. Sadly, I live in a condo in Seattle, so I don't have room for a dog. Someday, I'd love to rescue a dog from the pound."

Dave cocked an eyebrow in a fake show of seriousness. "Is that answer okay for the team, or shall we stop now?" More laughter floated up from the group. Dave was the perfect choice for this. "Next, a real question. Why did you take this job?"

"Full transparency, I was asked to take the role. It wasn't on my radar because I've been a Chief of Staff before and I didn't love it. Randall is a different kind of leader, though. I'm enthused about the opportunity. But I'm not a career Chief of Staff. My next job won't be as a Chief of Staff which means that in three years or so, one of you might be stepping into my role."

"I'd call that transparent." Dave looked at the team and nodded his head a few times. "Welcome to working with Kate, everyone. She calls it like she sees it."

Kate saw nods of acknowledgement from the crowd. It was a bit risky to say she would be out of there after her allotted time, but anyone who worked with a Chief of Staff knew these were steppingstone positions.

"Next question. What're you like at your best?"

Kate thought a moment. "Strategic. Directed. Caring. Global. Customer-focused. Sometimes too nice according to my friends." Kate tended to talk in bullet points. She found it efficient.

"I can attest to that. I've seen you do just those things, even under pressure."

"Aw shucks, Dave." Kate grinned and pretended to be embarrassed.

"How about at your worst?"

"Okay everyone, awareness is the first step, right?" There was some nervous laughter. "When I'm stressed, I can be flippant and sarcastic. My impatience shows and I stop reading cues effectively in my desire to get something done." The room was silent for a bit. Kate hoped they appreciated her honesty. "I'm working on moving from self-awareness to self-management." Kate tried to lighten the mood with humor.

"I've seen that first-hand, too." Dave looked at Kate's team, his tone turning serious. "One of the great things about Kate is that she takes feedback really well. When I've followed up with her when she wasn't at her best, she's taken it with grace and made changes."

Kate read the assessing stares from her team and noticed some people were smiling. She hoped she was getting through to them with this approach.

"Moving on, what's your management philosophy?"


THE TEAM MEETING was a smashing success. She was tired after her day-long meeting, but the energy from the day coursed through her.

She loved this job. The team responded really well to the session with Dave and the team-building exercises. Many of them commented they learned things about each other and were closer as a team. They had brainstormed ways to be more effective and came away with a concrete action plan.

She was on her way.

At the Trattoria that night, Kate shared her success story with James.

"That's great, Katiebug." James spoke around a mouthful of garlic bread. "I'm glad this gig is working out for you. You deserve it."

"Thanks. I have to say I'm pleasantly surprised. It's different than my last Chief of Staff gig. I mean, Randall is no saint, but he listens to me. And the team! It felt like I was introducing some of them to each other even though they've worked together for a few years. Randall and Aidan never gave them projects to do across teams, so they work in silos. I've already made progress connecting them and creating more of a team vibe."

"I knew you would. Your teams always love you."

"Thanks."

"Break it up love birds, your food is here." Eve winked at them as she approached with steaming plates of pasta. "Careful, the bottom plates are hot." Kate and James pulled back from each other as Eve carefully maneuvered the plates to the table. "Enjoy."

"Thanks, Eve." James and Kate spoke in unison.

They dug into their dinners. "Sounds like you made a great decision, Katiebug."

Kate smiled in agreement.

## Chapter 9



Kate's concentration was pulled away from her conference call by an IM from Randall. She explained to the attendees she had to run and hoofed it up the stairs, glad she was wearing comfortable yet adorable shoes. These were bright pink ballet slippers.

She was four weeks into her new role and loving it. But she hadn't moved into Aidan's office yet so she was getting her steps in every day.

"You rang." Kate tried an Addams Family Lurch joke. Randall laughed.

"What took you so long?"

"I'm still in my old office. Aidan is moving out soon and then I'll be right down the hall."

"He should already be gone. He's already on his new team. He shouldn't be allowed to squat in that office."

"I don't mind the exercise."

"Yeah, well I do. That's my Chief of Staff's office and he's not that anymore."

Kate didn't like how Randall talked about Aidan. He had given Randall two years of service. Shouldn't that be enough to get a few extra weeks of office space?

"Anyway, I called you in here because Craig just let me know there's going to be a reorg." Craig was Randall's boss. "Our team is growing. You picked the right time to become my Chief of Staff."

Kate perked up. More scope? More responsibility? That meant even more visibility for her. This was going really well. Kate just smiled rather than interrupt Randall's train of thought. "This will all be announced in about two weeks, but we have tons of work to do before then. The bottom line is that the Industry team is moving under me."

Kate tried to neutralize her facial features. That was the very first team she worked on at LampLight ten years before.

She didn't like a lot of them. They were entitled types who thought the world should wait on them rather than do the work to grow the team and the business. Several people were still in their exact same roles ten years later. She thought it was because no one else would hire them. She kept that to herself. "That's big news. Congrats." Kate covered her true response.

"Thanks. I'm not quite ready to be happy about it myself because I'm not impressed with the leadership of the team. They seem like a bunch of idiots."

There was that word again. It was disrespectful. But she agreed. "Yeah, I get it. That's why I left the team. I didn't agree with their vision." *If you could call it that,* she thought. It made Kate feel good that Randall was being open with her. While shocked he'd be so brutal about the team, she understood his point.

"That's a nice way to put it, Kate. Could you write up a strategy for how you'd organize the industry team within the context of all of my other teams? Aidan can help you with any details you don't understand yet, but I need your thoughts on how to proceed."

Kate loved that he was again seeking her strategic advice. This Chief of Staff position was delightfully different than her last one.

Yes, Kate would have to move her regular work to that evening, but it was worth it to be in the middle of the mix.

"On it, boss. Tomorrow?"

"Yes. Thank you."

## Chapter 10

When Kate got home to her condo in Seattle, James was at the sink at the end of his dishwashing routine. He methodically rinsed every morsel of food out of the basin in decreasing circular motions. She didn't mind his rules, especially when they resulted in her coming home to a clean kitchen.

"It's my favorite person." James enveloped Kate in a warm hug and gently rocked her back and forth. She melted in. "How was work today?"

"Work. I feel like once I start unloading, I won't stop. I'll save you from today's drama."

"But I like hearing about it." James wore a fake frown. "I promise to cut you off when I get bored."

"A million years ago, in the before-James-times, I was on the Industry team –"

"I'm bored." James interjected with a laugh. "Kidding. Keep going."

"Hardy har har. You get one more of those and then

I'm cutting you off from magical stories of my high drama workday." They bantered like this a lot and Kate loved it. She felt cared for and supported.

"I'm being serious now," he said. "Go for it. And while you're talking, I'll pour you a glass of bubbly because I know you like it."

"What're we celebrating?"

"The excitement of your pending story. Go." James got a bottle out of the fridge.

Kate laughed, remarking on how good it felt to release a little tension and remember that she wasn't curing cancer.

"There's a big reorg coming, and Randall asked me to put a strategy together for what the new team should look like because of my time on that team."

James handed her a glass of bubbles. "You know where the skeletons are buried. Or are they in the closet? Or maybe they're buried in the closet?" This is how James participated in Kate's stories – always looking for mala-propisms and puns to add to the flow. Sometimes annoy-ing, today she found it adorable.

Kate watched the effervescence rise out of the top of the champagne flute as she waited for James to finish his current arc of contributions. "They ran out of room in the closet, so now the skeletons are running through the hallways?"

When James ran out of gas, Kate sipped from the cool glass and continued. "This supposedly secret re-org is already out there and the leaders on the team joining ours started lobbying me for new positions this afternoon."

"That's great!" Kate arched an eyebrow at James as her response. "Or isn't it?" he added.

"The power play is nice – I'm not going to lie about that – but I have to do a lot of pretending. Like pretending I think these people are good at their jobs, pretending I respect them, and pretending I'm listening to them."

"That's a lot of pretending."

"Yeah, and I have this crazy thing called a memory. Some of them were not nice to me when we were on the same team and now they're acting like we were always best friends. It actually makes me a little sick." Kate sipped again and sighed to release some tension.

"Why do you have to pretend so much?" James asked. "Why can't you just be honest with them about their skillset and future on the team?"

Kate almost spit out a little champagne. She wiped her lips with her fingers. "So many reasons." James set a small plate of cubed cheese with a toothpick next to Kate.

"I bet you skipped lunch and need a snack before dinner." He snatched the plate away as Kate reached for it. "Or better yet, you should keep drinking on an empty stomach. You'll get drunk and I can take advantage of you."

"I'm not that much of a lightweight, buddy. Put the cheese back and I bet you'll get lucky even when all of my faculties are still in fine working order." Kate loved this banter. It made for a lovely transition from work to home while letting out some of her frustration. "First, I'm now representing Randall. Anything I say will be picked apart and searched for hidden meaning or commitments. I spent the afternoon on a proposal, but Randall and I haven't talked about the final org yet. It feels like lying, but I have to say a lot of things like 'what do you think' and 'uh-uh' and 'say more about that' instead of sharing my opinion. It feels like lying, but that's the gig."

"That sounds frustrating."

"Yeah, it is." It was nice to feel heard.

"Is that the end of your story?" James asked.

"Yes."

"And see how I didn't interrupt even though I really really wanted to?"

"Yes."

"And see the champagne and celebratory cheese plate?" He gestured at the spread.

"Yes."

"Happy one month anniversary, Katiebug!" James picked up a party horn usually reserved for New Year's Eve and blew it.

"Oh my gosh, that's right! It's been a month!" It completely slipped Kate's mind.

"I knew I'd love being married to you. The real question is are *you* happy?"

Kate thought about it for a moment as she looked into smiling and hopeful hazel eyes. "Yes. I'm damn happy." They clinked glasses. "Thanks for putting this together. Now I feel heard and loved."

"You're welcome, Bug. I love you."

"I love you too, Hubs."

My office

KATE HAD FIGURED out the routine. Steady state for about a day, then an interrupt-driven immediate Randergency deadline that started with an IM summons to his office.

Randall would make some disparaging comments about people involved in whatever situation was causing the issue.

She would come up with a solution and implement it. Then a day of calm.

Rinse and repeat.

She wondered what it was this time as she loped up the stairs. Aidan had vacated his office, and she would be moving in the next week which would shorten the commute to Randall's office.

"Ah, Kate, come in, come in." Randall was at his computer furiously typing up a response. "Just have to give Craig a heads up on a customer escalation and then we can get down to business. I can't believe the team fucked that up again. Why can't we hire effective sellers?"

Kate ignored his tirade, knowing it wasn't directed at her. Randall seemed so inclusive and kind in public. He was different behind closed doors. He hurled insults at people, questioned their intelligence, and was generally kind of an asshole.

You didn't get to the highest ranks of global tech companies by being high integrity, kind, and inclusive. *Unfortunately*. Kate was just glad she was on his good side. She wanted to keep it that way.

She took her customary seat at the table and waited patiently and quietly while Randall finished up the email to his boss. She had already learned that Randall wasn't a multi-tasker and remained quiet while he finished up. She would've had to repeat herself anyway if she chose to talk now.

She had also learned to let Randall steer the conversation. When he wanted an update, he would ask. If she brought up something that wasn't important to him in the moment, he didn't retain it and looked at her with impatience etched on his face.

Randall management was an art, but she was picking it up.

"I've looked at your organizational proposal and I like it. I was thinking many of the same things and you helped crystallize my thoughts. What about the digital advisors? Should we rearrange them by industry or keep them in subsidiary practices like they are now?" Randall was referring to the structure where people were arranged by local geography rather than by industry.

"I've thought about that." Kate leaned forward. "If we arrange them by industry, we have two issues." She counted the issues on her fingers. "One is that not every subsidiary team has critical mass of that specific skillset. And the second is that while customers want digital advisors who are familiar with their industry, they often want to hear about advancements in other industries. They want to leapfrog their competitors by leveraging strategies from outside of their own industry. If we arrange the digital advisors by industry, we may wind up with a lot of holes around the world and a team that delivers less perceived value to customers."

"That's what a Chief of Staff does right there. Those were great insights, Kate. Thank you." He smiled at her before continuing. "I knew about the critical mass issue, but I didn't think about the customer angle. Industries are converging as digital transformation takes hold of each industry – we can actually tie our strategy to industry convergence which makes staffing easier." Randall looked up at the ceiling like he was thinking. "You're an insurance company, you know insurance. But have you thought about how automakers could put sensors in cars to help price premiums based on actual performance and driving patterns?"

"Yeah, and with those sensors, a claims adjuster could look at the onboard camera and data collected to get a cost estimate of a repair without having to see the actual car. They could hire a team of adjustors in a low-cost market like Costa Rica or the Philippines and save a ton of money." Kate was on a roll, fueled by compliments on her strategic input. "The property and casualty twenty-year insurance industry veteran might not think that way, but a digital advisor with manufacturing experience could sniff out that scenario in a heartbeat."

"That's good. That's good." Randall had a way of repeating himself when he had already moved on from a concept as a way to finish his next thought before saying it. Kate read all of that on his face and learned not to interrupt. Ever the pleaser. "Add that to the document you already wrote about the re-org, and we'll present it to

Craig on Friday. Let's hope he's smart enough to get your point."

That last bit startled Kate. He shouldn't talk about his boss like that. But, Kate was very pleased with herself. She loved being rewarded for her strategic thoughts and ideas.

Randall interrupted her mini-celebration. "We're getting close to the announcement. How's the tick tock?" Randall referred to the minute-by-minute communications process for letting the leadership team, then managers, then their teams know about the reorganization. There were different messages for different teams. Carefully orchestrated communications were crucial. Kate had learned the hard way that order matters. Executives would fight like spoiled children over who got to send their email out in which order when there was hot news.

"The tick tock is about ninety percent done." It had been hard work. "Draft emails are all written, and people in the tent on this re-org have the copy in their inboxes for review. Feedback closes tomorrow and then we'll be ready to launch on Monday after any final tweaks from your meeting with Craig on Friday."

"Excellent. That's it." Kate nodded and left, as that was Randall's way of saying thank you and asking her to leave.

As Kate walked back to her office for a deal approval call as one of the last vestiges of her old job, she was filled with joy about this new one. Being Randall's Chief of Staff was different. He respected her and knew she knew her stuff.

She was a strategic advisor, and she loved it. She was able to use her influence to fix issues that she had seen around the business. She shouldn't worry about his disrespectful behavior. She actually agreed with it half the time. She just didn't have the positional power to get away with saying it.

Kate got back to her office and grabbed her headset to start her next meeting. She took a moment to pat herself on the back for taking the risk and going for this job.

## Chapter 11

Kate called James on the way home from work. The sun had set long ago, but Lake Washington still glittered from the city lights.

"Domino's pizza, can you please hold?" James often answered the phone like that, and it usually indicated he was in a playful mood.

"Nope. My order is too important."

"Okay, then, what'll you have? Large sausage with everything?" Kate pictured James' eyebrows wiggling up and down.

"Ha ha. I'm on my way home and thought I'd check in about dinner."

"All this talk about pizza has made me crave some," James admitted.

"Okay, I'll pick up a pizza on the way home if you call it in."

"Did you just leave work?"

"Yep. The bridge is pretty packed up. Friday night traffic. It might take a few extra minutes."

"Then I'll go get a bake at home pizza right now and pop it in the oven so it'll be waiting for you when you get here."

"Sounds great. I'll take the usual on my half."

"Done. Love you. And I'll still feed you the large sausage later."

"Classy." Kate enjoyed James' healthy appetite for sex. She felt a zing of excitement in her core thinking about the food and activity waiting for her at home.

The sound of James' voice was replaced with an NPR story when he hung up and the radio came back on. It was nice to not have to do everything all the time.

FORTY MINUTES of sitting in traffic later, Kate arrived at the condo and was greeted by the scent of baking pizza.

"Ten more minutes." James handed her a can of club soda. "Thought you might be thirsty."

"Tell me about your day. What's the latest on the software contract renewal?" Kate liked talking about James' job.

"The part where I'm actually negotiating the contract with CadPlay is great. We're increasing the number of users, and they replatformed on LampLight's stack, so all is good there. But get this." Kate watched as James popped up and checked on the pizza before she had a chance to do it. "The new process wonks are all over me because they entered a task in their new system that says I should be done by now."

"Except the contract expires at the end of December," Kate added. "You still have a few weeks."

"Exactly." James pointed his oven mitt-covered hand at her before pulling the bubbling thin crust pie out of the oven and placing it on the cooling rack. He motioned to her to sit down when she started to get up to get plates.

She stayed quiet while he got them out of the cabinet himself. None of these small favors were lost on Kate, but she didn't want to interrupt his flow. "They asked me to close the task and re-open a new one so it didn't ruin their average close time metric."

"But that makes no sense." Kate wrinkled her brows in confusion.

"I know, but they're trying to hit a two-week close rate on all open tasks and mine is skewing their numbers."

"How can you complete something in two weeks when the contract is still in force?"

"That's what I asked them, but they gave me the same answer of closing out the task and opening a new one with a due date two weeks out."

"But that's just wasting your time. Time that you could use to actually negotiate a better contract."

"Preaching to the choir, my love." James sliced through the pizza a little more forcefully than the thin crust required. "But that's what happens when process people take over."

Kate was mildly offended because she had been one of those process consultants in her pre-LampLight days. But she had never created additional inefficiency. At least she thought she hadn't. She refocused on James' story. "What a drag. I hate process for process' sake."

James brought the pizza to the table along with chili pepper flakes and oregano to shake on top.

Kate hopped up to grab the grated Parmesan from the fridge. "I forgot the snow cheese." Kate's younger sister Nina used to call it that when they were kids and it had stuck. "You'll get through it," she continued. "Maybe you can just stop entering tasks at all, I mean, you're pretty autonomous in your set-up. Maybe you can opt out of their processes. The thrill of being a contractor."

"Oh yeah… about that." James sat down with a thunk, his face the image of disappointment. "As part of the efficiency improvements, they're ending contracts with sole proprietorships in favor of a handful of larger vendor companies. Supposedly to reduce risk."

"They've been doing that around LampLight. I have to make some changes on my team, too." Kate didn't think it was a big deal. "That just means individual contractors move their contracts under larger companies."

"Exactly."

"Oh." Kate took a moment to let that sink in as she chewed her pizza. If James had to move to a bigger company, they'd take a cut of his hourly rate. With efficiency consultants running the place, he wouldn't be able to increase his rate to make up for the cut. "What're you going to do?"

He leaned back. "I'm going to ride it out for a while. They might start with other parts of the business, and I don't want to borrow trouble. Basically, I have two options. I can hook up with a larger vendor or I can take a full-time role as a LampLight employee."

"Interesting that a full-time role could be on the table. I would think you'd make more money in that option."

"Yeah, Bug, but it's not all about the money. I mean,

money's important – don't get me wrong – but I like the flexibility of my deliverables and time. Tim tells me what he needs, and I just do it. I don't track hours or enter spreadsheets or have to worry about performance reviews. My only performance review is my next payment. I don't want that to change."

Kate could see very clearly what would happen next. They'd offer him a full-time role and he would have to take it. If he didn't, he'd have a thirty to forty percent pay cut for signing up with another vendor. That was just how it worked. "Like you said, it could be months off. We don't have to worry about it now. And it's better than being told your contract is ending." Kate knew she would select the option that brought in the most money.

"Look at you," James exclaimed. "Pointing out the positives instead of the bad stuff. I'm rubbing off on you."

"Maybe you can continue the rubbing after dinner."

"I'd like that."


KATE LUXURIATED in bed after a particularly nice orgasm, stretching her arms over her head. "I feel really bad for women who don't know what sex is supposed to feel like. Sometimes I think I should loan you out."

James lay spent on the other side of the bed. "Five years in and still ticking." He tapped his finger on his heart before his hand fell limply on his chest. "Do I get to pick which of your friends I could help out?"

"You wish." Kate was not at all threatened by his joke. Her friends were amazing, and any guy would be lucky to have a turn in bed with them. "You're sober now, so you won't answer, but I bet if I get you tipsy enough, you'd make a list in priority order."

"Never!" James faked indignation. "I would have to be fully drunk to fall into that trap."

---

## Chapter 12

---

Kate drove up the hill toward Julia's house. Julia had made good on her commitment and had invited Kate to brunch. Kate had heard about Julia's famous brunches for a few years.

Attendees were Julia's most favorite women from around Seattle and Kate felt honored she was included in that group. Melanie and Lesley would be there, too since they were some of Julia's besties.

Kate loved adding female power to her arsenal. Hanging out with other strong, powerful women helped Kate feel at home. It gave her energy to continue to be herself and fight off negative thoughts.

She rang the doorbell even though she heard voices on the other side. Melanie opened the door. "Kate! We heard you'd be joining us. Welcome to Steak and Bourbon!"

"Steak and bourbon? I thought this was brunch. I've always been confused by that." Kate hugged Melanie and greeted the friendly yellow dog who met her at the door.

"You must be Selah." Kate scratched the dog behind the ears. "I've heard a lot about you."

"It is brunch. That's just a name." Melanie led Kate through the dining room and into the kitchen after Kate hung her coat on the rack in the entranceway. She counted eight women crowded around the island while Julia scrambled eggs on the stovetop in the center. A quick scan showed that she already knew Melanie and Lesley, but the rest were new to her.

"Kate! Thanks for joining us!" Julia sounded happy to see her. "Okay ladies, here's our newest entrant. Melanie and Lesley already know Kate, but could the rest of you do a quick round of intros while I plate up the eggs? Everything else is already in the chafing dishes or on the table."

Melanie stepped in as the resident social coordinator. "First up we have the amazing Margaret." Melanie spoke in her most official announcer voice. "Margaret hails from Boston and moved out here when Julia found her a great job." Kate watched as the heavyset brunette with thick, fabulous dark hair and adorable freckles curtsied with a flourish.

"Nice to meet you, Margaret." Margaret. Margaret. Margaret. Kate repeated the name to herself a few times to lock it in.

"Next to Margaret, we have the delightful Akiko." While her name sounded Japanese, Akiko's skin was the lovely color of a latte, and she had curly hair. Kate was struck by her beautiful smile that revealed dimpled cheeks. "She and Julia also met at LampLight."

"Now that's a funny story." Julia looked up from her eggs, pointing her silicone spatula at the group. "I was filming a training video while doing a three-day pear and apple cleanse. Akiko was the program manager. We'd exchanged a few emails about the recording, but we didn't know each other. When I stepped in the booth to watch the playback, I was horrified at how I looked."

"I believe your exact words to me were, 'girl, you coulda told me to put on some blush when you saw my pasty face.'"

"Yep, that's about right." Julia and Akiko clinked glasses next to the stovetop. "Sadly, Akiko left LampLight, but now she has her dream job as an adult learning consultant."

Dream job. Kate liked the sound of that.

"Next, we have musical diva Alex. She plays in a few music groups with Julia." Alex was tall and had long, coal black hair and tortoise-shell glasses. She waved at Kate with her champagne flute.

"What do you play?" Kate asked.

"Julia and I both play the bass." Kate was struck by the deep richness of Alex's voice. She sounded like a radio announcer.

"Oh, that's right. I always forget that side of her life since I've never seen her play."

"You should fix that. We have a concert coming up soon." Kate filed that away and couldn't help admiring Alex's velvety voice again.

"You have a voice for radio!" Kate couldn't help blurting it out.

"And a face for radio, too." Alex laughed, showing she was not offended.

"C'mon Al, you're gorgeous and you know it."

Melanie dismissed Alex's self-deprecating joke. "And speaking of gorgeous, Beautiful Brie is next. She's a radiation oncologist – did I get that right?" Brie nodded. "Her husband Colby used to give bass lessons to Julia's partner Rob. Rob asked Colby out for a beer after a lesson, he brought Brie, and love between Julia and Brie was born."

Brie wore the most beautiful set of flowy silk garments Kate had ever seen. Her left arm had an entire colorful sleeve of tattoos. "Welcome to the group, Kate. Strap yourself in." Brie's blond hair fell over her eye as she laughed.

"Did I hear Brie and Colby?"

"Yep. It was a match made in cheese heaven. Our cats are all named after cheeses, too. We have Camembert, Roquefort, and Velveeta."

"Does Velveeta count as cheese?"

Kate looked at the petite brunette who asked the question. She looked like a body builder.

"Close enough," Brie declared. "Process Cheese Food didn't fit on her tag."

"The questioner of the provenance of Velveeta is the gorgeous Gertie. She's a lawyer whose husband is one of Rob's best friends."

Kate sensed a kindred spirit in Gertie. They were both small in stature, but Gertie held herself like a tall diva. Kate wondered if she could pull off the same vibe. Gertie was totally ripped. She must do more than sit behind a desk as a lawyer.

"Don't let the cute name fool you. I'm a right bitch." Gertie cocked her head as she said it and looked at Kate with her piercing blue eyes.

"Should I be afraid or impressed?" Kate asked with a nervous laugh.

"Yes." Gertie let that one syllable hang in the air.

The ladies burst out laughing. "Stop hazing the new girl, Gert!" Margaret joked from across the kitchen.

"You already know the lovely Lesley. Her story is like yours. She used to work for Julia and now they're besties."

"That's right, I jumped the line between co-worker and friend and have never looked back." Lesley's big brown eyes telepathed empathy. "I fanaticize about working for Julia again someday. She's an amazing boss."

"Yeah, and she just dumped me." Kate made her face into a pout.

"It'll be okay. It means we get to come to brunch. But she does kind of ruin you for other managers."

"I'm right here and I can hear you," Julia reminded them.

Melanie moved on. "And last but not least, the angelic Angela." She paused, looking thoughtful. "You know Ange, I don't know how you know Julia." Melanie looked at Angela to explain.

"My husband used to play in a community orchestra. They did a gig at the Ballard Locks for July Fourth a few years ago, and I went. He introduced me to Julia and the rest is history." Kate tried to shake hands with the stunning black woman with long locs and bright red lipstick next to her, but Angela moved in for a hug. "I'm a hugger."

"Did you say you're hungry? Let's eat. To the dining room!" Julia grabbed the bowl of eggs and led the way.

They all took turns going through the buffet line. Kate was blown away by the entire scene. Nine fabulous women from different backgrounds sharing a meal on what looked like Julia's grandmother's china. Ten if she included herself. The food looked scrumptious.

"No pressure, Kate, but since you're new, you get to pick the first topic."

"Oh, um…" Kate wanted to impress this group of women with something witty and thought-provoking, but she blanked in the moment. "Why do you call this group Steak and Bourbon?"

"Ah, a bit of history." Julia gestured dramatically with her silver fork. "When I joined LampLight, I kept meeting fabulous women and wanted to bring them together. Lesley, Melanie, Margaret, and Gertie were the very first group about four years ago. When I called to invite Gertie to dinner, I asked her what women eat. Gertie, do you remember what you said?"

"Of course. I told her I didn't know what *women* eat, but that I like steak and bourbon."

"I loved that." Julia smiled at the memory. "I liked the power of steak and bourbon. None of this 'ladies who lunch' shit. So that's what I served the first time. Then, it moved from a dinner thing to a brunch thing, but we kept the name. We do this every month or so."

"To Steak and Bourbon!" Melanie raised her glass, and the rest followed suit. Kate hoisted her mimosa made with blood orange juice she had mixed at the extensive mimosa bar.

"There are three rules for Steak and Bourbon." Julia looked at her friends. "Ladies?"

Brie held up one finger to show that it was rule number one. "What happens at brunch stays at brunch."

"Two." Lesley piped in this time. "If you don't like it, don't eat it. Nobody's going to check your plate or ask questions about why you didn't finish something."

"Three." Angela put up three fingers as several attendees said "Don't feed the dog from the table" at the same time. Selah looked up and thumped her tail at the group.

"Got it. Confidentiality, picky eaters are okay, and don't teach the dog to beg."

"You catch on quickly!" Alex gave her an approving nod.

Julia had fabulous taste in friends. Kate already loved this group of women and was happy to be included. She basked in the strong female energy and leaned back in her chair, ready to hear what would happen next.

---

## Chapter 13

---

"I kind of froze in the moment." James paced the living room carpet, walking around the border of the rug over and over as he talked, an indication of his agitation.

"What happened?" Kate was on high alert. She had learned the pacing routine was not a good sign.

"I thought I had more time. I honestly hadn't thought about it much."

That was a clear difference between James and Kate. Kate had been thinking about James' job a lot and the various permutations of multiple outcomes if they pushed him to convert to a full-time role, ended his contract, or forced him to sign on with a different vendor company.

"Tim sat me down and gave me the whole 'it's not you it's me' thing about being pressured by the new process efficiencies. As a result of a security audit, the decision was made that a contractor can't be in charge of managing security on designs and only a full-time employee can do it."

"There goes your contract." Kate moved into problem-solving mode. "But you have plenty of other skills that could add value to the team."

"Yeah. He went on to say that my bill rate is way higher than the other vendors on the team."

"Because you're worth it."

"Okay, but there's no budget to just move me to another vendor company because then they'd be paying me AND paying for a full-time employee to do my current job."

"That's just smoke and mirrors. Tim has more power than that if he really wants to help you."

"I would think so, too, but he was pretty upset. He said the only option on the table was to convert me to a full-time employee."

"Okay, that's not ideal, but you could take it and then look for something else."

"I guess, but here's the kicker. They have to convert me at zero additional cost to them, which when you subtract the cost of benefits and other stuff, comes to about half of what I'm making. And I'd have to do forty hours a week in the office."

"That's bullshit. What were they thinking low-balling you like that?" Kate's unfairness monster was rearing its ugly head.

"I know. Tim was really bummed, but I think his hands are tied."

"Do you want to go above him and make your case?"

"I really don't. It's no fun anymore with all the changes. They're going to break up the team into what they call functional groups, like what we did before was dysfunctional." James paused to laugh at his joke. "So we'll all be moved around. I won't even be in the same building with most of the people I've worked with for years. No more lunches and hanging out."

Lunches and hanging out had rarely been a regular part of Kate's jobs, but James was different. He liked helping others be successful rather than being in the spotlight. She knew he wouldn't advocate for himself, and it wasn't her place to storm into Tim's office and tell him to try harder. "What're you going to do?"

Kate and James were different in that regard, too. For Kate, money equaled security, but for James it was there to be spent. Kate had certainly opened up her purse a lot more than she used to once she had started dating James. The huge, extra stock grants Julia and Florence had given her in the last two years were vesting nicely and it calmed her to look at her increasing balances.

"I don't know." James sounded dejected. Totally unlike himself.

Kate loved solving problems. "What if you got another job? You have a marketable skillset."

"I know. It's just hard. I've been doing this for nineteen years. There aren't that many options in Seattle for design shops. People who've left LampLight's devices team have terrible things to say about the other companies around here."

Kate had a hard time believing that. "You can do more than manage designs. You're a program manager. You could manage any kind of program."

"Yeah, but where am I going to find a job that gives me the flexibility of my current role? I like being able to work remotely or do a motorcycle ride when I feel like it rather than being chained to a desk forty hours a week."

"I think your run in a comfortable job is over. That was a pretty sweet gig. I'm not surprised LampLight couldn't keep it going."

"Thanks for the support." James' eyes flashed with anger.

"Sorry. That came out wrong. I guess I've been a bit jealous of your work situation."

"Jealous? Of me? You're the one who wants to be in the spotlight and move up. And that's what you have. You also have the stress and pain that goes with it. I don't want any part of that."

"Okay. Let's just dial it back. I'm trying to talk this through with you. When do you have to make a decision?"

"By the end of the week, according to Tim. But Lamp-Light always takes longer to get stuff done than they think. I bet I have about a month."

"Okay, then come up with a plan and let me know what you decide."

KATE RACKED her brain for a solution while she made dinner. They had started talking immediately when Kate got home from work, and having an intense conversation was not a good idea when she was hungry.

She put on some Chick Corea fusion jazz and got down to business making dinner. She put oil and a spice rub on the pork tenderloin and put it in the pre-heated oven. She moved on to prepping the Brussels sprouts. She could have this meal on the table in forty minutes flat.

Kate pondered the options while she chopped off the stems and peeled back a layer of little leaves. With the promotion and stock awards Julia had given her, she and James were in the thirty-six percent tax bracket.

If they hadn't gotten married, this would be much less complicated.

If James took the job, after funding his retirement account and paying taxes, he would only be pocketing about fifty thousand a year. It didn't seem worth it to Kate for him to toil in a role he hated and work more hours for less money. Especially when her quarterly stock vest was way more than that.

Part of what she loved about James was that he was a productive member of society and supported himself. He was not threatened that she made more money than he did, instead, he just enjoyed it when Kate offered to pay for something that was beyond his reach.

She set the table and opened a bottle of wine to let it breathe.

They could afford it if he took a break from work. She could float him for six months or so while he figured something else out. He could take some time to regroup and figure out what he wanted to do next. He would be free to join her on business trips and take advantage of free hotel rooms around the world when she traveled for work.

It would just be a temporary thing until he figured it out. She was glad she could give him this time. He had put up with a lot, sticking with her through the trials and tribulations of her last five years at LampLight.

Late nights, early mornings, canceled dinner plans, rescheduled vacations. He had paid his dues for her, and it was time to support him. That's what you did in a good marriage. You didn't yell at your spouse to be a stand-up guy and pay-off the house. You supported him how he needed it.

The timer dinged, indicating that the pork was done. She took it out to rest while she tossed the Brussels sprouts in balsamic vinegar. James came into the kitchen at just the right time to pour them both some wine.

Kate made a quick pan sauce and threw in a dash of the red wine she had opened. She thought about how nice it was to have him in the kitchen helping her out and just generally being a supportive presence. She put the steaming plates of pork tenderloin and vegetables at their customary places at the table. James set her glass of wine nearby.

"Did you have some time to think?" Kate added a dash of salt to the sprouts.

"Yeah, but I'm not very comfortable with the answer."

"Let's talk it out." Kate placed her napkin on her lap and took her first sip of wine. The rich Malbec tasted like a mouthful of raspberry jam – in a good way.

"I know I don't want to be an employee of LampLight even if they offered me a better package." James speared a sprout and brought it to his lips, munching thoughtfully before continuing. "I also don't know what I want to do instead."

He gestured with his fork like he was making bullet points in the air. "I have a lot of options, but I also have a long list of requirements like flexible working hours and the choice to work at home."

"What if you took some time to explore what you

really want to do?" Kate's words hung in the air. She let the silence sit, knowing James was considering her question rather than ignoring her.

"I thought about that, but I don't want to be a leech. You already bring in more money than I do. I don't want to make the imbalance worse. You married an employed guy, and I know how important financial stability is to you."

"I appreciate that. What if we put a timeline on it, say six months."

"Katiebug, That's a lovely offer, but I would really have to think about it. On one hand, it sounds like a brilliant escape route. On the other, it feels like a hand-out and charity. I'd hate myself."

"The fact you'd be uncomfortable with it is encouraging."

"Um, what? You want me to suffer?" James looked confused.

"Sorry – that came out wrong. I mean if it was doable but uncomfortable, you'd stay on target and get another job. It might not be an ideal one, but it'd be something. And then you can figure out what's next after that."

"This feels like dangerous territory, and I don't get why you're pressuring me to quit. I could just suck it up and take this job."

"No pressure from me – it's just an offer of help. An offer I wish had been available to me when I was stressed about LampLight a few years ago. I would've taken it in a heartbeat."

"Really? Would you?" James' skepticism was clear in his voice.

"Okay, maybe not, but I would've really appreciated the offer, and it would've lessened my stress knowing I could've just walked out at any time." James knew Kate well and understood she could never walk away from money like that. Money was security, and she needed to have it coming in, even at a reduced amount.

"I'll keep thinking about it."

"Sounds good."

"And by the way, I was so into our conversation I forgot to tell you how good this dinner is. You spoil me, Katiebug."

"That's the point." They smiled at each other over their wine.

## Chapter 14

"It's official! I got the job!" Kate was delighted Susan landed the role as Kate's replacement. *Finally!*

As weeks had passed, Kate became more and more concerned they wouldn't pick Susan and had kept telling herself large companies move slowly.

Kate knew Susan would be a great leader for the team and would put her own stamp on the strategy. She tingled with the feeling of accomplishment. Kate had served her team well and had a successor in place who would continue to steer them to even more greatness. Thank you, Julia and Florence!

"Oh, Susan, I'm thrilled for you!"

"Thanks, but I'm scared. I don't know who Julia's replacement will be and I'm not as good at the people stuff as you are. Everyone freakin' loves you. Such huge shoes to fill."

"Don't try to do it my way. Your way is different. And it'll be better than how I did it." Kate meant it. She fully believed in Susan's ability to take the team even farther than she had. "It's never fun to take a job without knowing who your boss is going to be, but you're amazing, Susan, and any manager will see that. Julia asked me to participate in the interview process. They'll have to get through me to get the job as your manager."

"Okay, that makes me feel better about my direct boss, but with Julia leaving too, that's a lot of change."

"Which is why you being a stalwart, kick-ass diva will have even bigger positive impact on the team. Your steady leadership and calm demeanor will guide them through the chaos. And I'm not going anywhere. You can always come to me or to Julia with any questions. Or even if you just need some support."

"Now you're going to make me cry. Thanks Kate. I wouldn't have gotten this opportunity without you, and you're right. I'm going to nail it!" Susan banged on the desk with finality. "Oh shit," she said looking at her watch. "I'm late for a meeting with Marketing."

KATE RETURNED to the project she'd been working on when Susan interrupted her with the great news. She'd been eyeballs deep in a people review spreadsheet she had to fill out about her team and their individual performance.

She and Aidan had met earlier that day to ensure his feedback from the first part of the fiscal year was captured. It was important they got full credit for their work before she got there. She wasn't sure how much Randall was involved in the day-to-day workings of the team, but it didn't seem like he knew them all that well.

Kate's protective team instincts were on alert to ensure the team's impact was fully understood. This was core to the manager/employee relationship and building trust with her team. Positive impact equaled stock grants and bonuses in the year-end review. This was only the half-year review, but it still set the stage for fiscal year-end ratings, raises, bonuses and stock.

LampLight required managers to hit a bell curve for performance and rewards. Each team was funded to award the standard bonus amount to each person on the team. Some people were highly rated and some had to be on the low end to hit the distribution curve.

The pool of money was then distributed according to the curve. Every extra dollar above the target given to a highly-rated person had to come from taking a dollar away from a lower-rated person. It was a zero-sum game.

Kate sighed as she looked at her model. Good people she would be happy to hire again and loved having on the team had to be on the bottom.

She had some tricks for getting her team what they deserved, and they worked every year she had been a manager. Since her manager also had to hit a distribution curve but had their entire team to work with, Kate took the opportunity to battle it out with her peers.

She came to people review meetings armed with data and impact statements about the great work people on her team had done which was usually enough to keep them off the bottom rung when her manager finalized the distribution curve for their larger team.

She already knew who would be at the top of her team's performance list. Frances on the executive communications team, DeShawn on the analytics team, and Shana from events were consistently fabulous team players who always went above and beyond.

The tricky part was figuring out the lower performers. This truly was a team of high achievers anyone would be lucky to have. On a different team, Bernardo and Penny would've been in the middle of the pack, but with this group, they fell to the bottom. Jason was just above them.

Bernardo and Kate had talked about how he could increase his impact, but she had never questioned his capabilities. He had a lot going on at home. But Kate couldn't let that color her performance ranking. It had to be based on specific impact and deliverables. He was the lowest performer on the team.

Aidan had agreed with the stack ranking but also shared Kate's agita about having to put strong performers at the bottom of the performance curve. *That's the game*, Kate muttered to herself as she saved the spreadsheet and sent it to Lorna in HR.

Lorna would run the meeting the next day and wanted everyone's spreadsheets by close of business today so she could collate the results.

Kate would do her best to represent her team at the performance review meeting the next day. She was hopeful she could argue effectively enough with her peers to get Randall to move people from other teams lower and protect her team.

It was tough to argue against Kate when getting money for her team was on the line.

She looked at her watch. It was time for her to have one of those "meetings about the meeting" she hated, but that was the job. She swallowed the bitter pill of wasting time. You'd think she'd be used to it after several weeks on the job. She started to unclip her laptop from the docking station so she could head to the meeting.

An incoming message flashed on her screen.

My office

*Looks like the meeting about the meeting will have to wait.* She sent a quick note to let them know to start without her as she walked to Randall's office. It only took thirty seconds to get there these days.

"What can I do for you?" she asked the top of Randall's head as he bent over his laptop.

He answered without looking up. "Cancel tomorrow's people review and make it a series of one-hour meetings with each of my directs."

"Okay. When would you like me to reschedule the people review meeting for? The reviews have to be completed by December fifteenth."

"Don't reschedule it. Just convert it to one on ones. Like I said."

"I'm sorry, I don't understand." Kate's brow wrinkled in confusion.

"We're not going to talk about all of the teams together in the performance review. It's just too time-consuming. And there's too much in-fighting. I'm going to have one on ones with each manager tomorrow and then Lorna and I will calibrate the entire team to hit the model."

Kate tried not to ogle at him. That is not how she had ever done it. She had always had the opportunity to sit with her peers, align on what strong performance looked like for the year and argue on behalf of her team.

Randall didn't seem to follow any HR rules. He would just sit with Lorna and do it? What did Lorna know about the individuals on the team? She felt a little sick to her stomach.

"That's it." He still hadn't looked up.

Kate scurried back to her office to make the changes to the meeting the next day. Everyone had already set aside the time, so it was easy to do. She took the last slot of the day because tomorrow was the Friday before Thanksgiving. Others would probably take the week off, so she didn't want to keep them too late.

She finished making the changes and checked her watch. She still had time to get to her meeting about the meeting. *Darn it.*

KATE TOOK some of the freed-up time on Friday to get super crisp on her bullet points about her team and their performance. She needed to do everything she could to ensure Randall and Lorna had everything they needed to calibrate the team properly.

She showed up at her allotted time just as Florence was wrapping up. She hadn't seen Florence much except in monthly staff meetings. They hadn't had much time to talk.

Florence saw her at the door and waved, giving her the five minutes hand gesture. Florence did not look like her usual happy self. Kate nodded her agreement and waited outside Randall's office.

Ten minutes went by. Then fifteen. Kate hoped she would get enough time to talk through her team.

Florence finally bustled out of the office and sped past Kate. "I'm late for my ride to the airport. Have a great Thanksgiving." She was gone in a flash of color.

Kate took a seat in Randall's office and said hello to Lorna.

Randall looked at Kate with tired, bloodshot eyes. "Can we cut this short? It's been a long day, and I want to get out of here for the weekend. Think we could get through your team in fifteen minutes?"

*Um, no,* Kate thought. Her plan backfired. She thought she was being nice to the team taking the last spot of the day. "I'd prefer we take the time to cover everyone. I'll go as fast as I can." She waited for Lorna to back her up. She did not.

"Let me rephrase." Randall rubbed his eyes. "You've got fifteen minutes. Go."

Kate was good at summarizing, but eleven people in fifteen minutes was tough. She provided the bullet points of high impact for her top three people, spending only two minutes on each one. Then ran through the list of the middle folks. She covered each one in thirty seconds. "It's all in the summary document I sent. But let's talk about the bottom of the list." She had reserved five minutes because this was important.

"I have what I need." Randall looked even more tired now.

"Wait, we still have five minutes to talk through the low end."

"I said I have what I need." His tone sounded impatient. "You hit the curve for your team. I'll go with what you said on your spreadsheet."

"I was hoping I could explain their work and get them off the bottom. Find someone else from your team who is actually underperforming. They're only there so that I could hit the curve. They don't deserve to be there."

"This model's a bummer, but somebody has to be at the bottom. Even rock star teams have lower performers compared to their peers. You should think about replacing your lowest performer, what was his name?"

"Bernardo Oliveira."

"Yeah, Bernardo – sounds Brazilian - with a stronger performer. It's only mid-year, not the year-end rewards discussion. Lighten up."

*What was with the Brazilian comment?* Rather than focus on that, Kate tried to get a few points across. "It's just that he's relatively new to role and with some additional guidance, he'll become a strong performer. I take my team's performance seriously. If we could just–"

"I do too. We're done here." *Dismissed.*

Kate walked slowly back to her office, deflated. Definitely one of those mismatches of values she liked to work through with her team. She'd have to address this with Randall after the Thanksgiving break. And what was up with Lorna? Why didn't she help?

# Chapter 15

"Do you have a minute?" Kate looked up from her desk Monday afternoon to see Frances in her doorway. Kate noticed that Frances was rattled, her eyes wide. "Come on in and sit down. Are you okay?"

"I'm not sure, boss. I need your advice."

"What's up?" This looked serious.

"Bernardo was just in my office, crying."

"Bernardo? What's wrong? Does he need something?"

"Oh my gosh, Kate. It's bad, and I'm not even sure if I should tell you." Frances was not her usual calm self. She looked to be on the brink of a panic attack.

"It's safe here, Frances." Kate spoke calmly and quietly to help Frances regain her composure.

"Bernardo was invited to a one on one with Randall this morning."

"Really?" Kate was surprised. "I didn't hear about that. Did something happen with the reorg communications?"

Frances shook her head. "No. Randall just called him

into his office. When he sat down, Randall started speaking Portuguese to him to start the meeting."

"But Bernardo is from Guatemala, and he grew up in Queens."

"Exactly. Bernardo told Randall he didn't understand. Randall asked why he pretended to not understand since his name, Bernardo Oliveira, is clearly a Brazilian name and asked Bernardo why he was ashamed of his heritage."

"No." Kate's heartbeat increased as she thought of poor Bernardo in Randall's intimidating office.

She and Bernardo had talked about his rough teenage years in Queens after being raised by his grandmother in Guatemala. He had escaped gang life in Queens. Most of his money still went back to his family to help them out. It was a complex situation.

"It gets worse. Randall really turned the screws on Bernardo, asking him why he was underperforming in his role and why he thought he should even be on the team." Frances took a breath. "Do you have any idea why he would say things like that? I mean, we know Bernardo is struggling a bit, but it's nothing we can't coach him through."

"Oh shit," Kate said. "We had our performance review meeting on Friday. Bernardo is at the bottom of the stack rank for our team. With the forced stack ranking, someone has to be at the bottom."

"And we agreed it was Bernardo," Frances added.

"Yeah. I tried to work some magic, but it doesn't sound like it worked. I explained that he's relatively new to role and with some additional guidance will become a strong performer. I guess Randall thought he could help out by jumpstarting the conversation."

"He definitely didn't help." Frances teared up again. "Bernardo said that he kept quiet in the meeting but told me he felt racially discriminated against. He wants to leave the team and asked me not to tell you about what happened."

Kate inwardly groaned. "You did the right thing by telling me. LampLight has a clear anti-bullying policy, and this certainly feels like bullying to me. Poor Bernardo. How did you leave it with him?"

"I was honestly too upset to think straight. I agreed to not tell you, but now I have. Can we just forget the whole thing? Just telling you made me feel better."

"Absolutely not." Kate's tone was gentle but firm. "I'd like to talk to Bernardo and make sure he's okay. I'll tell him you were acting in his best interest and following the very important policy about speaking up when you hear about bullying."

"I appreciate that, Kate. He needs help and I'd hate to lose him from the team."

"I'll ping him right after we're done." Kate took a breath. "One last question. Are you okay? I mean, that's a lot to process even though you didn't witness it."

"Actually, I'm not. You'll see how upset Bernardo is when you talk to him. I've never liked Randall. His in-your-face attitude has always put me on guard. I feel like I was caught in a blast zone. Collateral damage."

"Can you take a walk, maybe get some coffee?" Kate pushed the tissue box closer to Frances. "LampLight has an employee support system in place for situations like this. It's free."

"I'll be all right. I just need a few minutes to pull myself together."

"You're welcome to stay here while I reach out to Bernardo."

"I think I'll take that walk. Thanks, Kate. I know you haven't been on the team very long, but I trust and appreciate you. I know you'll make this okay."

Kate wasn't so sure. But she smiled reassuringly at Frances. "I've got this. Leave it with me now."

Got a minute?

KATE SENT a quick IM to Bernardo. She soon saw the bubbles on the screen indicating he was typing.

Yes

Kate was glad he responded quickly.

I know it's kind of late today, but I talked to Frances about what happened. When can we talk about it?

I left work and am now at home. Happy to talk via phone. I don't want to be on camera.

Calling now

Kate took a deep breath and dialed Bernardo's

number. She would listen and provide counsel. He needed support.

"Hiya." Kate tried to keep her tone light. "Sounds like you had a rough meeting."

"Uh, yeah." He didn't continue.

"I'd like to hear about it if you're willing to share. Frances told me you asked her not to tell me – I'm glad she did. As your manager, and as a human, she did the right thing."

"Am I going to get fired?" Fear was evident in his voice. "I'm scared I'll lose my job."

"Oh, Bernardo, don't even ask that. You're not getting fired. Period." Kate's heart broke for him. This was bad. Bernardo was a nice kid. Quiet and unassuming, but you knew there was steel underneath. For him to show fear was a big deal. "I just want to hear what happened so we can figure out a plan. You're an important member of this team. You've had a rough interaction, and I want to help you process it."

"I only want to tell this story once." It was even worse than Frances' version. "It was like he wanted me to know that he was the man and I was anything but the man. You know Latino culture, and clearly so does he – it's like his questions were designed to provoke me. Or undercut me. I haven't been bullied like that since the playground."

Kate had to control her own anger at Randall as it wouldn't be helpful to Bernardo. "My friend, I'm supposed to get all protective of LampLight right now and move into legal mode. I'm not going to do that. I'm talking to you as a friend." Kate knew she couldn't really just talk to

Bernardo as his friend since she was his boss' boss and representative of the company, but he needed a human being right now. "What do you need?"

"A new job. I can't be part of a team where the leader would treat me like that. And I can't be the only one."

Kate had seen the signs but hadn't experienced it directly from Randall. "I get it. It's awful you feel like you need to leave the team. Maybe with a little time, you'll feel differently? I would hate to lose you, but I respect your decision." Kate paused to let that sink in. "Why don't you take some time to think about what you'd like to do next, and I'll activate my network when you know. I'll help you."

"That all sounds great, Kate."

"One more thing, Bernardo. I have to report this to human resources."

"Do you really? Can't I just go get another job and fade into the background?"

"No, Bernardo. His behavior is not okay. Like you said, he may be doing this to other people, so we have to address it. LampLight has an anti-retaliation policy. You'll be fine."

"As long as I have you and Frances as the go-betweens, I will be fine. But I'm not meeting with him again, especially alone. Thank you so much, Kate. I was sitting here wondering what I did wrong, but you helped me understand this is about him. I really wanted to slug him, Queens-style."

Kate laughed at his joke sensing he was trying to lighten the mood. "I got your back, B. My next meeting with Randall is on Wednesday morning. Could we meet that afternoon, say two o'clock?"

"That works. Thanks, and good night." He ended the call.

Kate sat there looking at the screen where his picture had been. *What was she going to do?* She looked at her notes where she had captured words like scared, undercut, bullied.

She would talk to Julia. Even though Julia was knee deep in her new role, she was only a phone call away. Kate knew Julia would keep the conversation confidential, and she needed the guidance.

THEY MET AT RAYMOND'S, a bar near the LampLight campus.

"What're you going to do?" Julia dragged her hot wing through the sauce.

"I know I have to talk to Randall about this. Technically, I have to report him because an employee told me about being bullied. That's the policy."

"Are you worried about retaliation?" Julia always jumped right to the heart of the matter.

"Yes, of course. I mean, Randall and I have a great relationship right now, but I've seen how he can turn on people. Behind closed doors, he's really different from the happy, inclusive guy he presents in public."

Julia took a sip of her drink. "I meant additional retaliation against Bernardo. Interesting that your brain went to retaliation against you." Kate let that sink in. She was worried about her own neck as much as Bernardo's. That felt wrong.

"Normally, I'd go straight to HR with an official complaint, but I'm wondering if a bit of caution is in order here. Maybe I could talk to HR on the down-low without making it a huge, big thing with an official complaint?"

"You could do that," Julia looked thoughtful. "But there's always a chance that Frances or Bernardo reports it and when they say that you knew but didn't do anything, you'd be in big trouble."

"Good point." Kate revised her plan in real time. "I can tell HR I need some advice rather than calling it an official complaint. Then I'd be covered."

"That could work. Of course, HR is there to protect LampLight, not to help with interpersonal issues. That could go south really quickly."

"I know!" Kate spit out a bit of her nachos by accident. "Sorry for sharing my nachos with you. That's what I'm afraid of. Maybe I could just ignore it and report it if it happens again."

"You're kind of missing the point, Kate." Julia's tone turned serious. "Randall bullied Bernardo. That's not okay. I don't care if he was doing it out of the goodness of his heart. This is the entire problem with all of this. If you don't do something, he'll continue doing it completely unchecked in his bullshit way."

Kate looked down at her food, chastened. Julia was right. She was focused on the wrong issue. It wasn't about protecting herself. It was about making sure Randall got the training he needed and that her team knew she had their backs. "You're absolutely right, J-Money. Thanks for being my conscience."

"Hey, remember. It's just a job." Julia signaled to the

server for another round. "He can't actually hurt you." Kate wasn't so sure. "And there's an anti-retaliation policy to protect you and Bernardo."

"I hope I don't need that." Kate looked down at the table.

<hr>

## Chapter 16

<hr>

Kate couldn't shake her concerns that things were going to get ugly. She had seen Randall's behind-closed-doors volatility and now it might be directed at her. But she couldn't let this aggression toward Bernardo stand. Tuesday morning, she squared her shoulders, opened a new IM window, and pinged Lorna.

Soon, they were on a video call.

"Thanks for taking the call Lorna. I need to talk to you about something." Kate's Spidey Sense told her to tread carefully.

"If you're calling to talk about the model, please don't worry. It's just mid-year."

"No it's not that. I need some advice. An employee bullied someone on my team."

"Oh no." Lorna looked shocked on the video screen. "We just went through the training on that. How disappointing it's still happening." Lorna sounded stern. She leaned toward the camera. "You know we have a strict anti-bullying policy." She punctuated each word with the pen she was holding. "Why didn't you just report it to the Report It Today email system to start the investigation?"

Kate took a deep breath. "It's kind of sensitive. The employee doing the bullying was Randall."

"Oh." Lorna didn't seem shocked.

After that one-word response, Kate was met with silence. She let it stretch out.

Lorna finally continued. "It's probably a misunder-standing. Just Randall being Randall." Lorna shrugged her shoulders.

Kate was stunned. She couldn't believe how quickly Lorna switched from concern to dismissal. Kate's brow furrowed as she looked at Lorna and tried to steel her features into a more bland expression.

Interesting change once Lorna knew who it was.

At Kate's silence, Lorna continued. "I'm sure he didn't mean it." Lorna's tinkling laugh floated through the microphone. She leaned toward the camera, her voice softer. "Have you talked to anyone else about it yet?"

Kate experienced emotional whiplash as Lorna moved from dismissal to protection of Randall. "No. That's why I called you. I thought you could help me." *Yeah, help me. Not dismiss me,* Kate thought.

"Kate, I really think it's just a miscommunication. Go ahead and talk to Randall and then get back to me if you need anything."

"Wait, you want *me* to talk to him? I was hoping for some support from you."

"And you have it. But it's better for you to talk to him about it. You're his Chief of Staff, after all. I'm here if you need anything. Okay, bye." Kate was stuck looking at a message that said "call ended" on her screen.

*What the Hell had just happened?* She fell back in her seat. She had heard about stuff like this but had never witnessed an about-face like that first-hand during an HR complaint.

And Lorna wanted *her* to talk to Randall? *What the fuck was the point of having an HR business partner if they weren't going to help?* Kate almost screamed in frustration. Almost.

*Talk to him herself?* He was her boss, after all. Lorna had a point there. She could handle this. She would just push down her anger and protective feelings for Bernardo and have a rational conversation. She could be rational. Really.

She was glad she had an evening with James before she had to have the conversation with Randall in her weekly one on one the next day. At least she'd have two days off for Thanksgiving after that.


"IT'S EVEN WORSE than I thought it would be," Kate lamented to James at dinner that night. "And I'm stuck in the middle of it. I was ready for the meetings about the meetings and the background work. But emotional babysitting and having to lecture my boss about appropriate behavior? Why did I take this job?"

"Because you wanted a chance at upward mobility, a promotion, and more money." James ticked off the very items Kate said she wanted.

"And I still want those things," Kate admitted.

"Then you have to go in there and tell him he was a total dick. Maybe he'll take it well and appreciate your candor."

Kate looked at him with a baleful expression, her eyes unblinking.

"Yeah, long shot," he continued. "But you know I find it physically painful to not believe the best of people."

Kate rolled her eyes.

"Oh, don't be like that, Katiebug. It'll be okay. And you'll gain his respect by speaking up."

She didn't agree, but it was too late to go back now, and having the conversation was the right thing to do. Her personal integrity wouldn't allow any other response.

"Okay, topic change." James beamed at her. "Where am I taking you out for dinner Saturday? Date night!"

"I have to get through Thanksgiving first. And by Saturday, I won't care what you feed me as long as I didn't have to cook it."


KATE REVIEWED her conflict management training before her one on one.

Don't say this would be a difficult conversation – that ensured it would be just that.

Don't be accusatory – that would create conflict.

Don't ask questions that start with "why" because that could make him feel defensive.

Don't give into your own negative thoughts about the situation – that will make you too transparent.

Seek to understand before being understood.

Kate was fed up with the conversation with Randall before she even got started. But she knew she had to do it.

Her heart beat quickly and she tasted metal in her

mouth from the shot of adrenaline she experienced as she approached Randall's office.

She knocked lightly on the casing of Randall's door, uncharacteristically holding herself outside of the office. "Hey Randall, I'm here for our one on one."

"Yeah, come on in, but I'm afraid I'm going to have to cut this short. Craig is raking me over the coals again for the growth numbers and scheduled an impromptu meeting. I need you to get the latest numbers from Jason and I'm out of here at noon to start my holiday." He turned back to his computer and kept typing.

"I know that's important, and I'll get right on it, but I need to talk to you about one thing first."

Randall looked up from his computer with what Kate read as shock since she didn't jump right into taking action on his request. "What now?"

"It's kind of sensitive." Kate had practiced her wording to be as bland and non-confrontational as possible. "I heard you had a meeting with Bernardo on Monday." She took her usual seat at the table.

"Yeah, and?" Kate was not going to back down even with the angry impatient glare Randall shot her way.

"What was your intention in the meeting?" It was the safest way she could think of to start the conversation.

"My intention? What do you mean?" He turned up the snark.

"Well, it sounds like things didn't go very well and I was hoping to understand what your goals were."

"I don't need to explain my goals to you." Snark factor up to six.

"No, you don't, but Bernardo is very upset and since

he's on my team, I want to understand what message you were trying to land so I can help coach him. I also want to provide you with some feedback about the impact your comments had on him."

"He's an idiot. I wasn't impressed." Snark factor eight.

"Okay, wow. Uh. He's not an idiot." Kate was shocked at his harsh tone and defensive demeanor. "He's a hard worker with a lot going on and he just hit a rough patch. Ease up."

"Don't tell me how to treat my employees. I can say whatever I want whenever I want. Period. Now, could you get me some coffee? Cappuccino, two sugars. And those numbers."

Kate's forehead wrinkled and her neck cracked from the awkward way her head turned at the affront. "No, Randall, we're going to spend five minutes on this." Kate knew she was angering him, but he had no right to be such a jerk. The coffee powerplay was a little over the top.

"Fine. Two minutes. Your time starts now. Tick tock. What do you have to say to me?"

*Why is he so angry,* Kate wondered. "Randall, I'm trying to help a bad situation. You bullied him." Kate gave Randall a penetrating stare showing she meant business. He finally gave her his full attention.

"Who have you told?"

*That was his first question?* Not, is he okay? Or tell me more. "I spoke with Lorna yesterday to get her guidance on how to handle this."

"And she told you to report me?"

"No. Randall, you're missing the point. I'm not reporting you. I'm trying to talk to you about it. Bernardo feels bullied and like you don't want him on the team. He said you spoke to him in Portuguese and wouldn't stop even after he told you he didn't understand."

"That isn't bullying. That's bonding. I picked up a decent amount of Portuguese when I led the sales team in Brazil. His last name in Oliviera, for fuck's sake. He's Brazilian and he should be proud of that. It's a great country." Randall shook his head. "Idiot," he said under his breath.

"Except that he's not Brazilian. He also said you asked him why he thought he was equipped to be on this team. What was your intent there?"

"My intent? Stop with the consultanty-HR bullshit, Kate. You're the one who said he was at the bottom of your team's stack rank. I was just trying to help you by helping him make the decision to leave the team. End of story. I'm done talking about this."

"Randall, I'm not trying to make you angry. I want to untangle this situation."

"What do you want me to do, apologize?" Snark factor ten. Kate wasn't sure it could go much higher. "Fine, I'll have another one on one with him."

"No, Randall. Bernardo doesn't feel safe meeting with you unless someone else is there."

"Oh great, he wants witnesses."

Randall's face suddenly changed. Kate sensed that he finally saw how bad this was. *Maybe.* "What do you propose?" Snark factor back to four.

"I'll share our conversation and explain you were trying to bond with him."

Randall looked almost repentant. *Almost.* He sighed

and shook his head. Was that remorse Kate saw? "Let me know after you talk to him."

Kate hoped she had finally gotten through to him.

Then he spoke again, shattering that hope.

"Great. Thanks." Back to snark factor ten. "Now, could you go get me those numbers and the coffee?" He gave her what her grandfather would have called a shit-eating grin, his eyebrows almost meeting his hairline.

"No problem." She heard her own snark in her one-word response, but it was too late. She walked out of the room. Before she could let her reaction out, she asked Sheila if she had time to get Randall his coffee.

"Sure. Um, Kate, are you okay? You look a little shell-shocked. Want to talk about it?"

Kate didn't want to unleash on the innocent Sheila.

"I'll be fine. I have to get some growth numbers for the Big Guy. Gotta run."

Kate stormed back to her office, anger almost boiling over. How could he be so insensitive? She knew he could be a jerk, but she didn't expect him to be mean to her. She got that he was angry, but shooting the messenger was not okay.

Kate continued to fume as she dug through the Excel pivot tables to find the latest numbers for Randall. She had built him a dashboard with everything he needed, but he still wouldn't self-serve.

She clipped a screen shot, pasted the link and the screenshot into a new email. She provided the information to Randall along with some quick insights about what they were doing to fix the problem and progress since the last query from Craig on this exact topic and hit send on the email.

As per protocol, Kate then sent an IM to Randall telling him that the information was in his email inbox.

Now she could give her full attention to the situation with Bernardo and what she should do about it. Her first step was to take a quick walk to clear her head. That would give her a chance to think.

_______________

## Chapter 17

_______________

Clearing her mind took a bit longer than expected. She checked the time and saw she was almost late for a candidate interview. Randall decided he needed a second admin to help Sheila. Who did interviews on the Wednesday before Thanksgiving anyway? Oh right, Randall.

Kate headed down the corridor to the conference room where the first candidate was waiting. Peering through the small window, she could see Sheila wrapping up her interview. She waited patiently outside. Her cell phone buzzed with a text. It was from Randall.

> Do you have those numbers yet?

> Yes - in your inbox and sent via IM. Can answer questions after the admin interview

She had sent all of the requested information to Randall via email and sent an instant message but didn't text. Three channels seemed a bit extreme, even for him.

Sheila opened the door with her usual high energy.

"Hey Kate! Feeling better? Anything new?" She was subtly asking if anything had blown up while she was in the interview. They both knew that Randall's favorite word was "now."

"All good. Just the usual. Putting the F-U-N in dysfunctional." Kate and Sheila shared a laugh as Kate headed into the conference room.

"Amanda, this is Kate, your next interviewer. You're in good hands."

"Nice to meet you." Kate took a seat across from the candidate and wondered if she always looked surprised with her eyes round like saucers or if it was the result of her conversation with Sheila.

"You too." Amanda shifted in her seat.

"Can I get you anything before we get started?" Kate liked a human-first approach.

"Nope, I'm good. My first question is why I should take this job.

*Whoa, easy killer.* Kate found it odd and a bit alarming that Amanda would jump in like that but also admired her confidence. "We'll get to that," Kate said. "But first, why don't you fill in a few questions about your experience."

Kate got the conversation back on track with a few pointed questions about Amanda's background before turning to Amanda's original question. "I like candidates to understand the day-to-day situation on the team so that if you were offered the job, you'd come in eyes wide open." Kate thought it best to be transparent.

Amanda leaned back in her seat and folded her manicured hands in front of her on the conference room table. "Okay, tell me."

"It's fast paced. It's go go go from the moment we get here to when we leave. You get used to it, but I underestimated the time pressure Randall puts on the team. Being able to prioritize your work and help him feel heard while you decide the best course of action requires confidence and the ability to push back."

"Push back? Wouldn't I mostly be scheduling meetings and managing his travel?"

"Yes. As with a lot of executives, Randall likes to tell people he'll meet with them, but it's our job to then suss out who he actually wants to or needs to meet with and who he was giving lip service to. Then it's up to us to explain that Randall can't meet. Have you experienced that type of environment before?"

Kate knew she was taking a risk by being transparent with her, but Amanda was an experienced admin. She had probably seen it all before.

"So, he's a big baby?" Kate didn't stifle her laugh in time but recovered quickly. "No. Amanda, not at all, it's just that he can sometimes have happy ears about the amount of time he has for one on ones with people."

Kate really didn't like this candidate. She didn't seem to have the ability to take things in stride and go with the flow.

"Okay, I get that, but you still haven't answered my question. Why should I take this job?"

Kate didn't want her to take the job. "It's a highly visible position with an agile team who has fun together." Kate thought she had given a good answer without actually saying anything. She was done with this interview. Amanda was not a good candidate.

Amanda rolled her eyes. "In other words, it's random and ambiguous."

"No, it's actually a lot of fun - it's just that there's a certain amount of churn that happens as priorities shift, but that's just the nature of executive leadership teams at LampLight, or really anywhere in Corporate America."

*Can anyone say no hire?* Kate thought.

They just looked at each other. Kate waited for a follow-up but didn't want to invest any additional time in this candidate. "Okay, then. Thanks for your time. Sheila will be in touch with any next steps." Kate stood and offered her hand to Amanda for a goodbye shake. "I'll walk you out and you can leave your visitor's badge with me."

As soon as Amanda was past the reception deck, Kate raced back to her desk to make sure Randall had everything he needed. She was relieved to see all was quiet.

He had already left for his holiday break. *Onto the next challenge*, she thought. She put her interview feedback in the tool and recommended against hiring Amanda. Then she tackled her next open item of closing the loop with Bernardo.

She quickly forgot about Amanda and her poor interviewing skills.


"THANKS FOR COMING BERNARDO."

"I was nervous coming to your office, I don't want Randall seeing us in here together."

"He's already gone for the day and I hope you can leave right after this, too."

"Phew."

"Okay, let me dig in. I talked to Randall. He's sorry things didn't go well." She didn't think that was too much of a lie. She sensed some discomfort and perhaps even some remorse in his tone during the meeting. "I'm not defending how he went about it, but I do believe Randall thought he was being helpful. Clearly, it landed completely wrongly, but he was trying to bond with you."

"It sounds like you're defending him." Bernardo sounded incredulous. "What, did he get to you, too?"

Kate tamped down her own feelings about Randall. "I'm not condoning his behavior. He was a jerk. Initially, he didn't think he had done anything wrong. I was glad I walked him through how I saw it. I'm hopeful he learned something."

"Yeah, well, I hope to learn what it feels like to get a new job. I can't work for that guy anymore. I've lost all respect for him."

"I get it, and I hate that you'd leave the team over this. I also know that if you don't respect your boss, you have to go."

"But I do respect my boss. And my boss' boss." Bernardo was emphatic. Kate smiled. "It's the people above you who are the problem. All the way up. I see the way Craig talks to people. It's not my thing."

"Well, that narrows down your job search at least. To get away from Randall and Craig, you'd have to join product marketing or engineering."

"Who do you know in engineering who needs my help?"

"Every Corporate Vice President has an executive

communications person. It's up to you to pick a few who you respect. Meanwhile, I'll work my network to see who's moving on from a comms role. You'll get a new job quickly." Kate hoped that was true.

As Bernardo started talking about the kind of new manager he wanted, Kate kept turning his comments over and over. Yeah, Craig was a tool. And she'd seen a few red flags from Randall but thought if she stayed on his good side, things would be okay.

She might not be there anymore.

But Randall had to understand she was trying to help. He was oblivious to the impact of his behavior. Kate was helping him see it. Randall himself had used the same argument – that he was just trying to help.

He couldn't use that to excuse his own behavior and then not understand Kate was trying to do exactly the same thing. It was pretty simple, really. It would all blow over.

"I TALKED TO HIM." Kate reported to Julia via video call later that day.

Julia's face showed concern. "I thought you were talking to HR."

"I did," Kate confirmed. "And they told me to talk directly to him."

"That's unexpected." Julia's brow wrinkled. "Wonder why they wouldn't help."

"Beats me, but I did it, and the conversation felt really yucky, like something shifted in the power dynamic. He went from disbelief to anger to repentance to dismissal.

The repentance part was the shortest. I wish the whole thing hadn't happened."

"At least it's behind you now. You did the right thing. We'll help Bernardo get another job and it'll be over."

"You're right, as usual, J-Money. Can't wait to see you at the next Steak and Bourbon."

"Thanks Kate. Too many holiday commitments in December, so no brunch until January. In the meantime, have a great Thanksgiving!"

$$\rule{6cm}{0.4pt}$$

# Chapter 18

$$\rule{6cm}{0.4pt}$$

Thanksgiving was Kate's favorite holiday. She loved gathering her friends together for a huge meal. Her family was all back East, and they had a strict no-travel-during-the-holidays rule. They typically celebrated the holidays in July when airfare back to Chicago was cheaper.

James' brother took his wife and kids to Hawaii every year for Thanksgiving and both of his parents had already passed away. Even before she was with James, Kate had started the tradition of inviting single friends to share the holiday.

Over the years, a few co-workers from other countries started participating as well. Kate enjoyed introducing them to the American holiday.

There would be twelve people this year.

She motored around the kitchen on Wednesday evening chopping vegetables, making desserts, and generally having a great time. Every time thoughts of Randall, Bernardo, or Frances came into her mind, she pushed them right back out again. She was not going to ruin her favorite holiday worrying about work.

She used her great-grandmother's recipe for pie crust. Making pastry calmed her. The way the ingredients seemed like they wouldn't come together and were suddenly perfect spoke to her every time she made a pie. It was kind of like life. She loved the feel of the soft dough in her hands as she formed the balls and started rolling. Apple, pecan, and the traditional pumpkin were on the menu. The pressures of LampLight fell away as she worked.

SHE SLID the final pie into the oven and surveyed the damage. Dirty pots, pans, and bowls were everywhere. The counters were littered with powdered sugar, flour, and unidentified globs. High on the excitement of prepping for her favorite meal, she attacked the dishes and had the kitchen spotless in less than an hour, just as the last pies were coming out of the oven.

Kate had meticulously mapped out what she needed to get done this evening and had an hour-by-hour schedule for the holiday. She was on-track.

Next up was table logistics for how they would fit twelve people into their condo.

James was already trying different configurations with their folding tables. "How's it going in there?" she called out to him as he fiddled with the arrangements.

"I would say that it was very *charitable* of you to give me a task."

Kate groaned at the pun and came out of the kitchen

to give him a hug and a kiss. "Really? You got a chair and table pun in there? How long have you been working on that?"

"A while." James wiggled his expressive eyebrows at Kate. "It was better than my first thought."

"Which was?"

"Asking me to help you arrange furniture was a very moving experience."

Kate groaned again.

"What're the chances you're all caught up and we can get a work-out in before we pig out tomorrow?"

"I'm tired enough. I can't imagine hitting the elliptical right now."

"I meant the kind of work-out where we lie down a lot." James rubbed his hands up and down her arms.

"Oh, well I always have time for that."

James took her hand and led her to the bedroom.

KATE POPPED out of bed raring to go at six the next morning. No alarm needed! She padded down the stairs to begin the marathon that would get her meal on the table. Lunch was served promptly at noon, whether or not everyone was there.

By ten o'clock, pots were bubbling, side dishes were cooking, the turkeys were sizzling, and everything was on schedule.

Folks started arriving around eleven-thirty, and she was ready to go. She wished her job could be like that. Good preparation, solid execution, on-time deliverables, and success.

Putting the apple pie into the oven to warm during lunch, Kate took off her apron, ran her hands through her short hair to fluff it a bit, grabbed a bottle of wine, and joined the party.

The laughter and chatter soon bubbled up from the happy crowd as the wine was passed around the table a second time. Kate was filled with warmth as she looked around the table of people eating and chatting. She had a moment to relax before getting up to bring the desserts out of the kitchen. She needed this.

WITH ALL THE leftovers packed up and sent home with her friends and one of the turkey carcasses bubbling in a stock pot, Kate and James assessed the wreckage. The kitchen was a disaster zone.

She had about three hours of clean-up to do, but another successful Thanksgiving was in the books. Everyone had been laughing and talking when they left with their doggie bags of leftover sandwiches or even full meals.

"The Thanksgiving Queen strikes again!" James congratulated her. "Can you take a break before we tackle the dishes?"

"Sure." She joined him on the couch which was shoved into the corner to make room for the tables. "Ross and Marcus really appreciated the invitation this year. They had no plans and then you casually invited them like it was no big deal. It was to them. Thank you, Katiebug."

"The more the merrier." They smiled at each other and enjoyed their wine.

"To our first Thanksgiving as a married couple. I hope there are forty more." James clinked his glass to hers.

"I like the sentiment, but I doubt I'll still be doing this at eighty-six."

"You don't know that."

Kate wondered what life would be like if she made it to eighty-six. Would she be a famous author? Or would she just be sad she hadn't gone for it?

She remembered her grandmother saying that fifty to sixty-five were the best years of her life. Her kids were launched, she had some money, and she was healthy enough to travel. Maybe the best was still ahead of her.

"If I sit here much longer, I won't get back up." Kate let out a groan as she stretched her arms over her head.

"Then let's get to it." James joined her in the kitchen with a stack of towels to dry the silver and china. She switched on her cleaning music soundtrack and approached the kitchen.

And she still had the long weekend to not think about work.

Or so she thought.

SHE MADE the mistake of checking her phone on Friday. Six texts from Randall starting with a request for information and ending with an emphatic "where are you?"

*Um, enjoying my holiday,* she thought. She IMed him Friday afternoon.

Sorry for the delay. I had a bunch of people here for the holiday. What can I do for you?

You can answer me when I contact you

Kate didn't want to dignify that last comment with a response. She wasn't going to apologize again for not being available on a holiday.

I'm here now

Craig ripped me a new one on Wednesday. Get with your friend Florence and write up a plan for how the advertising team is going to help the Industry team get in front of Chief Marketing Officers. The sooner the better. No later than tomorrow morning.

On it

She had no idea where Florence was. Kate only knew she had raced to the airport last Friday. She sent a text.

Hey Florence. Randall wants us to write a strategy document for a meeting with Craig on Monday. I know it's a holiday weekend, but are you around?

Kate didn't wait for Florence's response. She had a lot of ideas about how to do that so she could get started on her own.

She was about three pages into her Word document when James popped his head into her office. "Everything okay in there? I can hear you angry-typing from downstairs."

"Yeah, just another Randergency."

"Is it going to take long? It's a holiday weekend."

"I know. I'm sorry. He's mad I didn't respond yesterday. I'm going to crank this deliverable out and send it to Florence for review."

"It's her holiday too."

"Technically, she's French."

"Yeah, but I mean that she gets the holiday off."

"I know. But it's about her business, so I don't want to just go it alone and speak for her."

"Okay, see you downstairs when you're done. Love you."

She got back to work. One hour became two. Two became three. James returned with a piece of leftover pie and a cup of coffee. She was deep into it, so he just left them next to her.

She still hadn't heard from Florence when she put the final touches on the document. She had taken it as far as she could go. She sent it to Florence via email and texted again to tell her it was waiting for her.

SATURDAY MORNING KATE still hadn't heard from Florence. She had to decide what to do. Should she make Randall even angrier by missing his deadline, or should she run the risk of sharing the document and having Florence be mad at her?

If she outed that Florence hadn't seen it yet, Randall might be mad that Florence wasn't willing to interrupt her holiday. She didn't know where Florence was. Should she cover for her and say she was in Fiji or something and didn't have a signal?

None of the possibilities seemed like good ideas. She didn't want to lie, but she also wanted to protect her former boss' boss.

She decided a version of the truth was best.

She crafted an email saying that Florence was out of mobile range and that this was as far as she'd gotten. She explained that she would rather get him a draft and change it after Florence's review than delay sending it to him for comment. She thought that was the best of both worlds.

She never heard back.

## Chapter 19

Monday morning, she was at her desk bright and early in case Randall had questions before his meeting with Craig. She had put on additional armor that morning – a bright yellow shirt and pink pants with adorable green ballet flats that made her feel powerful.

She hadn't heard back from him or Florence for the rest of the weekend. She was on edge, waiting for him to arrive at the office.

She received the instant message she had learned to dread.

My office

She headed to Randall's office.

"How'd your interview with Amanda go?" he asked. No "hello" or "how are you?"

Kate had to think back. Last week seemed like three years ago. "Oh, I didn't care for her. She had gaps on her resume and her questions showed she doesn't have what it takes to do the job and roll with the punches."

"Punches? Don't make us sound violent, Kate." Randall seemed annoyed.

"Oh, okay, um sorry." Kate blushed. "It's just a turn of phrase."

"Yeah, well I don't like it. I'd hate for us to be viewed as bullies." *Ouch.* "Amanda told Lorna you were very negative toward her and you called me a big baby."

A shot of dread zinged through Kate's chest. "Of course I didn't say that."

"Then why would she say you did?"

Those had been Amanda's words, not Kate's. "I have no idea why she'd come away with that notion." Except that she did know. She felt like she'd been set up.

"She told Lorna you said the team was dysfunctional and you'd been brought in to fix it."

Kate was fuming. And embarrassed. "I'm not sure why you'd believe I said those things. You know me. I'm really positive. I told her that priorities change and we need to be agile." She had made that joke about putting the F-U-N in dysfunctional. *Oops.*

"Well, Amanda refused the job, so you're now responsible for finding me a better candidate."

"Refused the job? I recommended against hiring her. My feedback's in the tool."

Randall's lips pressed into a thin line. Understanding flashed through Kate's mind. Amanda must be connected to Randall and he had already given her the job. Why even bother to waste people's time on interviews?

"It doesn't matter now because she said no. Get me the list of candidates."

*Okay, Sarcasm Man.* It mattered a whole lot to Kate. Why was he taking Amanda's word over hers? Why was Lorna carrying tales to Randall? Why didn't Amanda listen to Kate when she tried to correct the candidate's negative perception? *None of it made any sense,* she thought.

"Okay, but…um."

"Spit it out."

"Did you have a chance to look at the document I sent you on Saturday for your meeting with Craig today? I worked really hard on that."

"He canceled the meeting."

"Oh." Her eyes darted back and forth as she tried to figure out what to say next.

"Why do you have to be so dramatic? I asked you for a simple document and you delivered." Kate looked down at her shoes. "And what the heck are you wearing?" Her head snapped up to look at him. "In order to be successful at this company, you really need to be more bland. Less drama, less energy, less color." He waved his hand at her dismissively indicating her wardrobe.

She thought she looked nice. Vibrant and professional. A power ensemble that helped her feel good. "Thank you for the feedback," she said, looking down again. Fighting more would not help her, even though she wanted to scream.

"That's it." She looked up to see Randall shaking his head at her, a look she read as disgust on his face.

She plodded back to her office. All of that work. For

nothing. Did he still need it? Did she have to track Florence down? What the heck was going on?

He was wrong. She had a right to exhibit her personal style. She could talk how she wanted to talk. She could dress how she wanted to dress, as long as it wasn't low cut or see-through or something else inappropriate.

Where had the Randall she had known before gone? His treatment of her was scandalous. Randallous.

He would now be known as Scandall. Maybe that would dimmish the strength of his voice in her head. She sighed and got back to work.

She tried to hail Florence one last time when she got back to her office. She wanted to make sure Florence was good with the content as the subject was likely to come up again. This time, Florence answered her phone.

"Kate. How are you? How was your holiday?"

"Great, thank you. Did you see my messages?"

"Yes. I called Randall on Saturday and we talked through it. I added a few details to the brilliant document you created. He sent it to Craig who told him he loved the plan and we should implement it. The meeting was canceled because we didn't need it. Randall said he'd follow up with you so I could get back to my holiday."

"Okay, that's great to hear. Thank you."

"He didn't tell you, did he?"

"He's busy. I get it." Kate took the diplomatic path. She was a consummate Chief of Staff after all.

"I'm so sorry, Kate. I should have closed the loop. I really thought Randall would. I was with Clarisse in Cabo and she was pissed that I even looked at my phone. You know how spouses get when you work on vacation."

Not really. James had been super understanding and brought her pie, for fuck's sake. She had to remember to thank him again. "It's fine." Kate kept a cheerful tone. "Did you have fun?"

"Ooh la la, it was amazing. And I got to work on my tan. Now it's back to the cold, rainy, Seattle weather. Au revoir."

Kate just stared at her phone. *What the fuck?* Why was Scandall messing with her? The emergency weekend assignment and then calling her a bully? And then not giving her the context for why Craig canceled the meeting? It was great news when Craig did that because it meant no questions! She nailed it. That was a huge success.

Kate decided to focus on that instead of the lost holiday time and the worrying about Florence and her reputation.

All in a day's work as a Chief of Staff.

## Chapter 20

My office

*Here we go again*, Kate thought. What could it be this time? A broken fingernail? A change of font? Ever since their chat about Bernardo three weeks before, Randall had become completely different. He picked on every single thing she said and cut her out of important discussions.

"Where's the latest agenda for next week's leadership team meeting?" he demanded.

"In the folder on the share site called Leadership Team Meetings with next week's date." *Just like they always are,* Kate added to herself.

"I can't find it. Send me the link." Kate dutifully opened her laptop and brought up the file. She IMed the link to Randall and waited while he looked at the document. "What's this section you're leading on titles?"

"Our title taxonomy has gotten out of control. There are almost six thousand people on your team after the reorg, and we have 231 distinct titles. Some are segments of one, others have five people, and some have hundreds. It makes career path management, calibration, and goal setting difficult. I have some ideas to share with the group about how to streamline titles for improved efficiency and people experience. I thought we were supposed to be working on that across Craig's team."

"Sounds like waste of time." *Was it a step up or a step down to go from sarcastic to dismissive,* Kate wondered.

"How would you like to use the time instead?" Kate had learned not to push back when he changed his mind and to just adjust her approach. It was very much against her nature, but she needed to be successful in this job to get what she wanted out of it.

"How about we talk about something important, like next year's scorecard? We have to make sure we're measuring the right things. There are only six months left in the fiscal year."

"Are there new priorities you'd like us to drive next year? That would be a good place to start to determine new metrics."

"That would be a good place to start." Randall mimicked Kate in yet another dismissive gesture, turning his mouth downwards and moving his head back and forth as he spoke. "Obviously, Kate. So why don't you take the document I just wrote about next year's strategy and come up with some metrics for the group to discuss?" He tossed a printout across the table at her that bounced off her chest.

Kate was momentarily stunned. Had he really just treated her like that? "Okay Randall. I'll put some thoughts together and update the agenda." She kept her tone light. "Anything else?"

"Yeah, can you get me a cup of coffee?"

She swore he did that to alpha roll her and show her who was boss. Chiefs of Staff don't get coffee. "Sure, Randall. I'll make sure you get a cup of coffee." Kate picked up the document, walked out of the office, and went directly to Sheila's desk. "Coffee for the boss, please. Thank you." She smiled at Sheila before heading back to her office to process her new assignment.

Was he messing with her? Trying to make her quit? Or was he really just an asshole? He certainly had assholic tendencies before, but this was way over the top.

Her strategic assignments and respectful interactions were gone, replaced with this vitriolic attitude, mocking, and under-cutting.

He had written a new team strategy without her. Even though she was supposed to be his strategic right hand. *What the fuck?*

Kate decided she was being too sensitive and took a deep breath. Randall was probably under a lot of stress and needed help with the scorecard. He had just forgotten he asked her to fix role taxonomy. That was all.

She would make the best of it and keep plugging. Kate dug into the new team strategy to capture her thoughts for how to effectively measure progress.

---

THE LEADERSHIP TEAM assembled around the white conference room table at a fancy hotel north of the Lamp-

Light's campus for their last leadership team meeting of the calendar year. Outside, Lake Washington sparkled as the yachts bounced on the small waves caused by the breeze. Even in December, boats could stay in the water in Seattle because of the mild winters. *What was it like to have enough money to buy one of those?* Kate's mind wandered from the current conversation about hiring a new Corporate Vice President. Her session on metrics was up next. She pulled her focus back to the meeting.

"We'll table that for now and move on to our next topic. Kate, what's next on the agenda?" Randall had started taking every chance he got to treat her more like an admin than a Chief of Staff.

"Metrics for fiscal year 2018." Kate remained upbeat and smiled at the audience even though a collective groan rose from the group.

"That's a pretty heavy topic right before lunch." The leader of the industry team rolled her shoulders as she leaned back in her chair. "Can we at least get a coffee break before we dive into that?"

"The faster we get through it, the faster we break for lunch. Mind if we proceed?" Kate was determined to add value and keep the group on track. She heard mumbles of agreement. "I hope you all had a chance to read the 2018 strategy memo—"

"Really Kate. Hope is not a strategy." There was that rude tone from Randall again. "Everyone has read it."

"Okay. Let's dive right in." She continued, unruffled. "It's highly disruptive to the field to change metrics. We need a compelling reason to add a new one, and we should end up with no more than seven to help the field prioritize. I have a few ideas on the next slide and then we'll open it up for brainstorming and discussion."

Randall interrupted. "Why don't we hear from the group before you share your ideas, Kate. The leadership team should set the metrics, not the Chief of Staff."

*Was he purposefully baiting her?* He had asked her to prep a list of potential metrics to share with the group based on the strategy document. And now he wanted her to shut up?

"Sounds good." Kate tamped down her anger. "Who'd like to start?"

"I'll take a crack." It was the industry lead. "Growing our industry-led solutions is core to our strategy. I'd like to measure how many times a packaged industry solution is sold."

Kate captured that on the whiteboard. Soon, there was a list of twelve new metrics in addition to the seven already on the current scorecard. Everyone had shared what they wanted to add.

It was time to narrow the list. "Okay team, we can track and report on all of these metrics even if they don't make it onto the scorecard." She thought that was a diplomatic way to say there were too many metrics. "We should pick the top two or three that best represent our strategy to add to next year's scorecard."

"We have to have revenue from product support on the list. If customers don't buy support, they won't get the full value of our solutions."

"Thanks Jim. Any other ideas?" Kate looked at the attendees for input.

Randall jumped in. "Kate, I don't know what your goal is here. We can't have twelve new metrics. Let's just pick the top two or three and be done with it."

Kate's face burned. She had just said that a minute ago. She blazed ahead. "Let's vote on the top metrics. Everyone gets three votes. Let me know when you're ready to start voting." Kate stood poised with the marker in hand, once again feeling passed over and insignificant.

She was so tired from putting everything she said through a tight filter and still getting it wrong. She had to figure out a way to fix this with Randall and get through this difficult phase. Maybe if she apologized, they could get back to the way things were before.

She had to make this job work. She just had to, or the last ten years at LampLight would've been for nothing and she'd have to start over somewhere else. That would push her goal out. Again.

<hr>

"THAT'S RIDICULOUS." James was clearly enraged at Kate's story. "When do you just get the fuck out and leave this company?"

"It's not worth leaving over. I just wish it was like it had been before the Bernardo thing."

"Katiebug, he's messing with you. My team is messing with me. We should both just quit."

"Whoa, Hubs. What happened at work today? You're taking this pretty hard. Is something up?"

"Yeah." James scratched his head. "I got the ultimatum. I have to make a decision by the end of the week."

"Well, it's been longer than the week Tim originally gave you. I guess we should feel lucky."

"Nothing about this feels lucky. I just want to leave."

"Then leave. We'll work it out." Kate wanted to make the pained expression on James' lovely face disappear. Things were not great at work with Randall's recent attitude change, but it would blow over. She'd be fine. They'd be fine.

"Are you sure sure sure it's okay for me to take a six-month break from working? We don't talk about it much, but I don't have a lot of savings. You know I like to live. I spend almost all my paycheck on my car payment, rent here, and my hobbies. I'd have to immediately start using your money."

Kate's heart froze. She felt physically frightened by that. She didn't know he didn't have a cushion.

Did this change anything or was she still committed to the outcome? "How do you envision it working?" She used the question to give herself time to get her reaction in check. "It would freak me out to just hand over my credit card."

"Yeah, I don't want that either. But I don't want to have to ask permission to spend money. For this to work, I have to have some degree of freedom." James must have seen the look on Kate's face as she figured out he was broke. "This is so embarrassing."

"Don't be embarrassed, James." She thought he should be just a bit embarrassed. He'd been working at Lamp-Light for twenty years. "I just didn't know. I mean, I knew you weren't rolling in it, but I didn't know you didn't have any savings."

"It sounds so harsh when you say it like that. I prefer to call it 'living well in the moment' rather than broke." He smiled his warm smile at her and she relaxed.

"Can you tap into your retirement funds?"

"I don't have much in there either."

"Right." Kate chose not to press him further. She had known he didn't have a large nest egg, but she didn't know it was zero.

In her zeal to write a pre-nup, she hadn't bothered to ask about his finances because she was focused on protecting herself. She figured he had assets worth protecting, too. "Well, let's do some math and figure out a plan. Maybe I could pay you a salary each month. I mean, it's only for six months, right? I would have to cash out a little stock each month to cover it because our expenses would outstrip my salary."

Kate felt the discomfort creep up her spine as she said the words, but she had already committed to the plan in principle. She couldn't back out now when James had finally come to the conclusion he should leave. She had the money, and it would only be for six months.

"You would do that? It would solve a lot of problems."

Kate loved solving problems. "Yes. How about five thousand a month? You'd have been paying thirty-six percent of your salary in taxes anyway this year since were married. And you won't pay rent while you're out of work, so that's basically a replacement of what you were making." Kate wanted James to feel empowered during this period rather than emasculated.

"That would be amazing, Katiebug. I'll spend it wisely."

## Chapter 21

She had most of the week off since LampLight basically shut down between Christmas and New Year's for everyone who wasn't closing a big deal by the end of the calendar year. She would be on call but could take it easy.

Craig was happy with progress on the Industry integration, so Randall had calmed down about that. She would pop the title taxonomy back onto Randall's radar in the New Year and get to work on execution. She wasn't psyched about working with Lorna from HR on that, but maybe it would be a chance to build an ally once Lorna could see that Kate really was doing a good job. She might need the help someday.

She pushed thoughts of work away as she drove across the bridge to their condo to start her vacation.

She and James would spend Christmas Day with James' brother and his family. Christmas Eve was just for them, and she wanted to make it special for James. It was his last day at LampLight.

She hit the very busy grocery store on the way home

and had everything she needed for dinner as well as the ingredients for the sweet rolls she was taking with her to her brother-in-law's house.

At home, she pulled out the wrinkly piece of paper that contained her paella recipe. It was dog-eared and had splashes of what was probably saffron and wine on it.

As she built the layers of paella, she thought about what she should do about Randall. She recalled a story that Gertie shared at Steak and Bourbon when they were discussing the best work advice they ever got. A wide-eyed Gertie just starting out as an associate at a Seattle law firm had asked a senior partner how to be successful. Her answer had been that she had to "eat a lot of shit." It had worked for Gertie as she was now a very successful lawyer in her own right.

Kate was certainly eating a lot of shit. A bad attitude from Randall, being relegated to scheduling and admin tasks because she was cut out of strategy, being told to not be herself.

She had toned down her wardrobe and tried to always speak in an even tone with bland vocabulary. She was a mess from the constant need to keep a strong filter locked in place, second guessing and replaying every interaction with Randall's leadership team.

It was exhausting. But the pressure was on to get through this assignment and make the best of it. She signed up for it and knew it could be awful. She just had to eat the shit and get through it.

But for now, she could eat a wonderful Christmas Eve meal with her husband.

She tried to push the work thoughts out of her head and focus on the task at hand for a second time.

After adding the final ladleful of chicken stock, she checked the cooling chocolate cake. Cool enough to frost. She covered the cake in buttercream made with peanut butter. Two thirds covered, anyway.

She thought that chocolate and peanut butter were two great tastes that tasted nasty together, but it was James' favorite flavor combination. She compromised by gluing the layers together with chocolate buttercream, frosting one big slice with chocolate and covering the other three-quarters of the cake with the peanut butter frosting. It made for a funny looking cake but a happy couple.

A part of the cake had stuck to the pan, so she put extra chocolate frosting on that part. No one would ever know but her that the frosting covered a mistake. She wondered if there was such a thing as Randall Frosting, something that would make her seem alright to him if she just covered herself with it. A new attitude? A new wardrobe? A new personality? With a heavy sigh, she forced work thoughts out of her head. Again.

With her cake frosted and her paella simmering, Kate wrapped the presents for James' family. She and James decided not to exchange gifts this year to save some money, but they had still bought gifts for their families. She took a moment to appreciate the array of wrapping paper, ribbons, tape, and boxes laid out on the table. She loved wrapping presents.

As she carefully cut the paper and folded the edge over to get a straight line, she smiled to herself at how much it pleased her to make it perfect. Perfect. She loved perfect.

She could accomplish it with wrapping gifts and paella. She wished she could get there at work. She would settle for acceptable. She didn't need to love her job. It was called work for a reason. But it needed to be bearable.

When had her standards dropped so low? Did she really just think that a bearable job was enough? Where had that adorable optimistic version of herself gone? The one that believed in herself and built her career? What was she doing just playing the waiting game. That was not enough.

She reminded herself that she had a job to do, a husband to support, and a commitment to a role. Someone had to pay for the presents James had picked off his family's wish list.

She would get through it. And she would stop letting her thoughts ruin the Zen of wrapping presents. She focused on what was in front of her, rejecting her ruminations about work... for the fourth time since her vacation started.

Kate looked at the neat stack of wrapped presents. Their red, white, and green festive paper increased her holiday cheer. She congratulated herself on a job well done. At least she could wrap presents well.

JAMES CAME in with a rush of cold air from outside.

"Right on time," Kate said as she glided over to give him a welcoming hug and kiss. "Merry Christmas Eve and happy last day."

"It smells great in here!" He sniffed the air with appreciation. "Is that delightful smell what I think it is?"

"Paella."

"Thanks, Bug. I love your paella."

Kate separated from their hug to go back to the stove to take the paella off the heat. "That needs to rest for about fifteen minutes. We can open the wine and start on the salad. And of course there's dessert."

"I thought you were dessert," James slipped his arms around her waist while she stood at the stove.

She liked that he was in a good mood. Perhaps he was feeling happy about his next chapter. She hoped so. "Ha. You'll like this dessert better." She pointed at the strangely frosted cake.

James' eyes got round like saucers. "Could that be an appetizer instead?"

Julia laughed. "Why don't you grab two wine glasses and meet me in the dining room?"

"On it. And I'll bring the salad."

They sat at the dining room table which Kate had already set with her Christmas dishes - blue rimmed plates with cartoon snowpeople and Christmas ornaments hanging off their twig arms. She enjoyed sharing her silliness with James.

"How was your last day?"

"Good. The contracts have all been signed by the year-end deadline. I closed out the deliverables on my contract, and I'm done. Done. Done. Done." He raised his glass and Kate clinked hers to his. "I spent the morning with my replacement showing her the ropes. I offered to be on call for a few days in case she needs anything."

"That's kind of you."

"I worked on that team for a million years. I can't just

walk away without being helpful." Kate knew so many people who could. She admired James' integrity. "How 'bout you?"

"I've got a couple open items for Randall, but nothing major. I'll just keep one eye on my email to be safe."

"Randall who?" James laughed at his joke. "C'mon, you're on vacation. Any chance the paella is ready? This salad is great, but it doesn't compete with paella!"

"Sure, it's probably rested enough."

Before Kate could get up, James was at the stove scooping steaming helpings of the saffron infused rice, chicken, and shrimp onto her Christmas dishes.

"THAT WAS REALLY, REALLY GOOD." James wiped his mouth on a napkin. "I love the crunchy bits from the bottom of the pan."

"The socarrat." Kate spoke with dramatic flair. She could be herself with James. "It came out better than usual this time because I resisted the urge to stir while the rice was cooking."

"I have an urge to stir." Kate raised one eyebrow at James' comment.

"Want dessert?" she asked.

"Yep." James stood up and took Kate's hand. But rather than leading her to the kitchen for a slice of cake, he took a left turn up the stairs.

"I thought we were having dessert," Kate asked with mock indignation.

"We are. And then we'll have the cake." They climbed the stairs to the bedroom.

Chapter 22

A refreshed Kate with a new attitude about making the best of her job showed up on January second, ready to keep her head down and do the job.

First up was gathering feedback on the effects of the industry team reorganization.

The industry team was in the new configuration, largely based on the strategy Kate had written up for Randall before Thanksgiving.

That was the good old days before he relegated her to being his glorified admin.

The organization was arranged into industry-specific teams along with a central shared services team that supported all of the industries. Some of the leaders on the team did not like having to share their resources with the centralized team. Kate wanted to hear and address their feedback. She was convinced it was the right approach but wanted to be open to it if something really had to be tweaked.

She had learned that explaining why decisions were

made was the best way to get people on board. Once they understood why, they could get behind the strategy. And, if they disagreed with the conclusion, they could go back and revisit the strategy behind the why.

The group assembled in the conference room with a few people joining virtually. They could all see each other on the big screen.

"Thanks for coming, everyone. Happy New Year. I've heard there are some issues with the organizational changes, and I want to have an open dialogue about what's going on so we can address your concerns or jointly agree on a new plan."

"Sounds good, Kate. Where's Randall?" Christos led the Manufacturing team. His expressive, bushy eyebrows went up and down as he asked the question.

"He's not attending today. I'll take any changes we agree on to him for approval after the meeting." Kate's Spidey Sense tingled, like he wouldn't listen to just her. She set the chip on her shoulder aside and kept going. "Shall we dig in?"

"Sure. I don't see why I had to give up half my team." Anita led the Financial Services team. "I was already understaffed."

"Okay, let's tackle that one." Kate remembered all too well how secretive and credit-hogging the industry teams were. She had to break down those silos to get people working together. "There are a lot of solutions that can be used across multiple industries. If we all work in our industry silos, we don't share the base solutions. We lose speed and agility."

"We share," Christos interrupted.

"Yeah, we already do that without the cross-industry team." Anita sounded like she was priming for a fight.

"Oh, that's great to hear." Kate kept her voice light, hearing Randall's feedback to not be negative in her head. She knew Anita's comment was patently false. "Can you tell me about a few of the solutions that started in one industry and were shared with others?" Kate thought that was better than pointing her finger at Anita and yelling "liar" like the old woman in *The Princess Bride*.

The room was silent. The mood turned awkward.

Florence jumped in. "We shared the advertising effectiveness dashboard to see if other industries could use it." She was trying to help, and Kate appreciated the olive branch.

"Awesome. Was anyone able to leverage that?" Kate tried to keep her tone innocent and looked around the room.

"I couldn't use it. Manufacturers don't do advertising." There went Christos' eyebrows again.

"Not in the traditional sense." Kate tried to sound understanding. "But manufacturers spend advertising dollars on trade funds management. They need to know what works and what doesn't. Did your team have a chance to assess it?"

"No. Like I said, it's not relevant for us."

He was wrong. Dead wrong. But she wasn't going to argue with him. "Any others?"

The meeting went on like that for another twenty minutes. Molly, the leader of the cross-industry solutions team, did her best to keep suggesting solutions that her team had in progress, citing the names of people on the industry-specific teams who were advising them. But the leads just kept blocking and saying that the solutions were irrelevant.

Kate wanted to change course. "It doesn't seem like we're getting anywhere with this discussion. Christos, Anita, Florence, and others, how would you like this to work?"

"I want my team back." Anita sounded emphatic.

"Me too," Christos added.

Kate thought that Florence and Molly did a good job representing the alternate perspective that sharing and leveraging each other's work was a good thing.

"Could we take one more crack at trying to leverage some cross-industry solutions?" Florence was really helping Kate today.

"Fine," Anita said. "I'll let the experiment run for a few more weeks before escalating to Randall." Christos nodded his agreement.

"Great, thanks. And we don't have to escalate. We can just talk through it again. Maybe you'll have some additional ideas and input the next time we get together."

Kate tried to celebrate the small success. Christos and Anita had dug their heels in, but Jim from the media team, Kelly from the retail team, and John from the public sector team were onboard and agreed with Florence and Molly.

Kate closed the meeting with an agreement to get back together in three weeks to check on progress.

Then she was off to a meeting about a meeting to help do the background work necessary for Randall to be successful in a presentation the following week.

KATE JOGGED over to Randall's office. She hadn't seen him in the two days since they returned from their holiday break. "What do you need?" No chit chat or small talk anymore. No inquiries about his holidays. All business. Just like he said he wanted it. It felt kind of mean to Kate, but she was trying to be the Chief of Staff he wanted.

"I don't *need* anything," he snapped at her. She had said the wrong thing. Again. "What I *want* is for you to explain why we have so many standard titles. I just got my ass handed to me by Craig's Chief of Staff because you haven't cleaned that up yet."

Kate flicked him a baleful glance but chose to keep her mouth shut rather than pointing out that he had removed that exact subject from the last leadership team agenda. She kept her tone neutral to avoid any additional controversy. "What would you like me to do about that?"

"I pay you to think. Not just take orders. Aren't you the one who says that you're so *strategic*?"

"Lorna and I have everything documented. We just need to execute the plan."

"There you go again with violent language. Why can't you just *implement* the plan. Fix it and get back to me when it's done. That's it."

"Yes, sir." Kate backed out of the office and into Florence.

"Oh, excuse me, Florence. I didn't see you there." Florence's response was covered by a yell from Randall.

"And don't call me 'sir.' I hate that. It sounds like you're talking to my father."

"Sorry."

Kate pushed past Florence and headed back to her office. She dusted off the slides she had prepared for the last leadership team meeting and the plan she had created with Lorna. She edited the document to say "implementation plan" instead of "execution plan."

She wanted to review the changes with the leadership team prior to rolling them out, but with Randall wanting the work done immediately, she would have to push ahead. She would probably get yelled at for not gathering enough feedback.

She couldn't win.

SHE WAS FINALIZING the email to the team with the implementation plan when she heard someone at her door. "Florence, how nice to see you. Sorry for almost running you over earlier."

"Yes, you seemed like you were in quite the hurry to escape from Randall's office." Florence adjusted the colorful scarf at her neck.

"No, just busy." Kate loved Florence and knew she wasn't in a good place when she found herself fibbing to her former skip-level manager.

"Is everything okay in your new role?"

"New? It's been a few months already. It doesn't seem new." Kate tried for the deflection.

"Kate, I'm serious. Are you okay? Randall seems to be picking on you. Is something not right between you two?"

Kate was highly embarrassed that Florence had noticed. She needed advice, but didn't know the dynamics of Florence and Randall's relationship. In her old role, Kate wouldn't have hesitated to ask Florence for help. But Randall's feedback made Kate doubt herself. Florence was technically her peer, and she didn't want to create an awkward situation.

"I know that look, Kate. You can talk to me."

"I'm good. I've just got a lot to deal with for Randall. I'm trying to be who he wants me to be." She felt the last several weeks of hurt and indignation start to bubble up and tried to tamp it back down.

"It's best to just be who you are. Let me know if I can help."

Florence was gone in a flash of color, her French perfume lingering in the doorway.

Could she talk to Florence? Things were just so weird. She didn't know if it was a good idea or not. She needed allies but what if it backfired like talking to Lorna in HR?

Even before she took the job, she knew that being a Chief of Staff was very isolating. Kate was alone and she had to keep her head down.

Especially now that she was the sole bread winner.

# Chapter 23

"Roast chicken with Brussels sprouts." James set a plate in front of Kate when she got home late from work. She was getting used to having James take care of everything for her.

She had never had a house husband before. Her laundry was done. The house was clean. The pantry shelves were stocked. He made dinner. The nineteen fifties started to make a lot more sense to her. James, on the other hand, seemed kind of quiet and withdrawn.

"How was your day?" Kate picked up the fork James had set on the table.

"I went for a long walk this afternoon and witnessed an accident. A guy just changed lanes right into a kid on a motorcycle over on Virginia Avenue. I helped her pick up her bike, retrieved her center stand from the intersection, and got her bike to the curb. She was pretty shaken up, but okay. Her bike was still operable. Good thing she had crash guards."

"Geez, that's no fun. Nice of you to stop and help her."

"That's what I do. I was just coming back from taking the guys out for a happy hour when it happened. Marcus, Trevor and Ross say hello."

"It must have been nice to see them." *Taking the guys out for a happy hour? Why was he paying for their drinks?* "Tough way to end the afternoon, though."

"I'm ending the evening with you, just the way it should be." James grinned at her, and the problems of the workday faded away.

"Can I talk to you about something?" James asked.

"Sure. What's up?" Kate didn't like how uncomfortable he looked.

"When we talked about me taking a break from work and you replacing my salary, we missed something. I want to be able to do things for you, like fill your car with gas, replenish household supplies, or buy dinner, but that's not covered in the money you give me."

"You bought those things before though."

"Yes, but hear me out. You were with me, and you often paid. Now, I'm doing those things on my own to make things easier for you." He had a point. When they hit the store, Kate usually paid. And for gas for her car. And for groceries. She got what he was saying.

"Do you want to track everything you spend and give me a bill for the stuff that was for me?"

"That sounds like a lot of work." He clearly didn't like that approach.

"Yeah, and I don't need more administrative work when I have my hands full at LampLight. What if I added your name to one of my credit cards?"

"You would do that?"

"There'd be rules." Lots of rules, she thought. "Let's talk about them." Kate took a moment to chew while she thought. "You would use the joint credit card for household items. You would use your own credit card when purchases were just for you, like going out with the guys for happy hour or gas for your car."

"That's pretty clear. And I know it's a big request. Thanks for being cool about it."

"It makes sense. Let's run it that way for a while and see how it goes. I can take you back off once you're working again." Kate couldn't read James' expression.

My office

KATE WONDERED what she had done this time. Randall rarely summoned her to his office anymore unless it was to berate her for something.

She contrasted it to how she felt when she went to meet with Julia in the good old days. That seemed like a lifetime ago, but it was only four months. She walked rather than ran to his office and stood at the door until he beckoned to her to come in.

"What the hell did you say to Anita and Christos? I had one on ones with each of them and they both told me you were awful to them in your feedback meeting. That you said they shouldn't talk to me."

Kate didn't have any more fight left in her. "We went over their feedback on the new org structure. You know they don't like it. We had what I thought was a healthy discussion about it and agreed to keep in on the rails for three weeks to see if we can make progress that satisfies them."

Old Kate would have burned with indignation that he would call her on the carpet for doing her job. New Kate just took it.

"Why do you have to be so disrespectful to everyone?"

"Disrespectful? Did you hear from other meeting attendees like Florence, Molly, Jim or Kelly?"

He just glared at her. Deflated, Kate stopped defending herself and just took the beating. She was rude. She was awful. She didn't listen.

Why couldn't he see she was leading instead of caving and that Anita and Christos just didn't like having their toys taken away and were having a tantrum? "I need my Chief of Staff to be gluing the team together. Not tearing them apart when I'm out of the room. You better shape up."

What could she say? She didn't want to agree with him, but she also wanted to get the heck out of his office. "Can I go now?"

"You'll leave when I'm through with you. I demand to know how you're going to change and be the Chief of Staff I need you to be."

"I'm confused, Randall. I'm exactly who I was before. And you liked my approach when I was in my previous role." She worried her lip waiting for his response.

"I guess I wasn't watching closely enough to see how you get things done. Being rude and disrespectful to get your way doesn't cut it on my team."

She went for deferential. "I hear you. I'll do better."

"See that you do. That's it."

Kate left the room, continuing to keep her head down.

She needed to take Florence up on her offer.

"YOU WERE PERFECT." Florence was rocking two scarves today. You could take a diva out of Paris, but you couldn't take Paris out of the diva. "I didn't find anything you did even remotely disrespectful, Kate. Honestly, I would tell you if I did. I would come to you first because I'm invested in your success. I'm shocked to hear this is why you wanted to talk to me."

Florence's words helped soothe Kate's nerves. "He's making me feel crazy. He snaps at everything I do. He questions my motives. It's a lot to take."

"Did something happen between you two?" Kate wanted to trust Florence, but her experience with Lorna rattled her. "Come on, Kate. It's me. We have history. I'm rooting for you. What's going on?"

"Okay, Florence, I'll tell you, but please keep this between us."

"You have my word."

"I spoke to HR about Randall for bullying a member of my team. Then I confronted him about it, and he's completely changed toward me."

Florence's face blanched. "That's terrible. How's your employee?"

"He's fine. Thanks for asking. I helped him find three potential new jobs and he's going through the interviews."

"And how are you?"

"You see how I am. I second guess everything I do. I wonder if Randall is right and I'm awful. I'm losing sleep. It's affecting my relationship." Kate sighed heavily and got her voice under control. It all had come bubbling out of her and she wanted to stuff it back in.

"It'll blow over. Just keep doing what you're doing and it'll get better."

Kate wanted to believe her.

"I'm trying." Kate felt the sting of unshed tears.

"Randall is a powerful leader." Florence shook her head at Kate. "It's not a good idea to go against him. It might have been better if you had just kept quiet about the situation."

Kate was floored. She looked up to Florence as a leader. But now she was seeing that Florence would toe the line like the others.

"What do you think I could do?"

"Stay quiet, keep your head down, and finish out your assignment. You don't want to make an enemy out of Randall. Let him think he had influenced you and that you're the perfect Chief of Staff. All will be well."

Kate hated that advice. Hated it with a white-hot passion. "Will you put in a good word for me, Florence? He listens to you."

"If I get a chance, I certainly will."

That wasn't a yes. Kate thought. "How are things between the two of you?" Kate sensed that all was not well there either.

"Let's just say I understand what you're dealing with. My new peers on the industry team are, how do you say, little brats, but they seem to have Randall's ear for some reason."

Her words spoke volumes.

Clearly, Kate couldn't count on advocacy from Florence.

She was alone.

---

## Chapter 24

---

The Steak and Bourbon ladies where just what Kate needed to pull her out of her funk. She wasn't alone. She had them.

Rule number one was there for a reason. What happens at brunch stays at brunch. They would help her.

She arrived early, craving the female energy of the group. She handed the bubbly to Julia who greeted her at the door. "So great to see you. You're the first one here."

"Hope that's okay. What can I do to help?"

"You timed it perfectly. Everything's ready to go and I was just pouring myself a glass of bubbly. Now I can have an appetizer and not feel guilty about starting the brunch without any guests."

Kate's shoulders relaxed. She already felt better in Julia's welcoming presence.

Julia held up a tray. "Try a toast point. Fig jam, French butter, and prosciutto on sourdough toast."

"Holy crap that's good." Kate talked around a mouthful of crunchy goodness.

"What's new? All good with James? Randall?"

"James left his job." It felt weird to say it out loud, like she had to explain. "His cushy gig is over, and now that we're married, it doesn't make sense for him to take a pay cut. He's going to take a six-month break and figure out what's next."

Julia's face looked grim. "Sorry, flashback. When my ex-husband lost his job, he was never the same. Don't do what I did and let it go on for almost ten years."

"I hear you, but James chose to leave, and we've agreed on six months."

"Okay, good. And my flashback is entirely about me and my ex in a different situation. I'm sure you'll handle it better than I did." Julia clinked her glass to Kate's.

"And Randall, who I now like to call Scandall, is not good." Kate took a breath. "Everything has changed since the Bernardo thing. He's rude and picky. He likes to belittle me in front of others. It's pretty subtle sometimes, but other times it's flagrant. I'm worried I have huge blind spots and really am an asshole. He's making me doubt myself."

"Stop that right now. You're amazing. This sounds like a lovely topic to talk through at brunch. Most of the ladies don't know you that well. They can be super objective. And as you have probably noticed, they don't pull punches. They'll give it to you straight."

"I love that about them." They nodded in agreement.

"We rely on each other for different perspectives." Julia continued to munch her toast point. "Like I've told you, I think of this group as my Board of Directors. I run lots of decisions past them for debate and discussion. We all do. And at the base, we have each other's backs. Because of that, we can say things to each other we couldn't hear from others. It might take a while for you to feel comfortable sharing deep dark secrets with the group, but they've already accepted you and are well-versed in problem solving."

"Yeah, I witnessed that with Angela and Brie last time."

"Yep, that's the Steak and Bourbon Way."

"Do you have any topics for your board today? How's your new gig?"

"It's amazing. So much work to do but I'm really enjoying it." Selah let out a soft bark as Alex, Margaret, and Akiko came through the door. The next session of Steak and Bourbon was starting.


"I'D KICK him in the balls." Angela spoke around a mouthful of waffles. "Randall sounds like a total turd."

"He wasn't before though. I admired him when I was lower in his org."

"Yeah, it's often easy to admire people at work before you see the behind-the-scenes version." Brie shook her head, showing she had experienced something similar.

"Scare tactics." Julia's tone was matter of fact. "He's mind-fucking you so you disappear. What a dick."

"What if it's true? I mean, I do have to be tough with people on deadlines and preparation. Have I crossed the line? Randall jumps down my throat whenever I talk now, telling me I use inappropriate and violent language." Kate waved her fork. "You know I do that. I've been known to pound the table a time or two."

"Kate, just stop." Julia threw up her hands. "You're one the nicest, kindest people I know. You know who you are. Stop listening to him. Randall's bullying you and retaliating for complaining about him."

"Hang on." Akiko had a questioning look on her lovely face. "Are you talking about Randall Cunningham?"

"The one and only," Kate answered.

"Shit, girl." Akiko's face changed to anger. "He's done this before. My colleague Brenda had a similar situation with him. All smiles until she crossed him and then it was retaliation city. I know she reported him, too. He was, of course, not investigated. I guess that's the way." Kate felt her frustration reflected across the table.

"There would be a record of that," Gertie interjected.

"Really? The manager training I took said that unsubstantiated and uninvestigated claims are not in your record."

"Not in your *official* record. But HR keeps tabs in an unofficial way in files that only HR and lawyers who subpoena them can see." Kate looked at Julia, agape. "What?" Julia shrugged. "I was investigated once. A white guy accused me of discrimination for promoting Lesley over him. I was cleared of all charges. But a couple years later, another HR person mentioned it when I fired a man. There's clearly a secret version of the records."

"That guy was such a douche, but I might be biased." Lesley chuckled and the group joined in.

"More importantly for Kate, there's a pattern, and it's documented." Gertie's tone was all business.

"This sounds retaliatory. I mean, the guy was fine until you reported him, right?" Brie summarized it well.

Kate nodded.

"Have any proof his treatment of you changed, you know, like emails or anything written?" Gertie was even more terrifying in lawyer-mode.

"No. He's too smart for that. He just treats me badly and belittles me." Kate felt small telling her tale of woe. She should be able to stand up to a bully better.

"Think anyone would testify on your behalf?" Margaret jumped in. "If I had seen anything, I would want to be named in an investigation." She wiggled her dark eyebrows. "I would rehearse my lines for the highest dramatic effect."

It was nice to laugh about the situation a bit. "I don't want to get involved in all that." *Did she?* Kate wondered.

Brie pointed at Kate with her fork. "Then get a new job. Seems pretty clear to me."

"But I just started this one, and I signed up for a three-year assignment. I can't just walk out."

"And he signed up to not be an asshole. It's not prison, it's a job." Brie wasn't going to let go of this idea quickly.

"Maybe he wants you gone, too." Akiko was right. Kate was only looking at this from her perspective. Randall probably had buyer's remorse.

"Julia, you know Randall. Florence advised me to just suck it up. What kind of risk would I be taking by bailing on him?"

Julia chewed for a moment before answering. "First of all, you wouldn't be bailing. You'd be exercising self-preservation. But I hear you. He's a pretty powerful and well thought of executive. I love Florence and owe her a lot. But I also heartily disagree with her feedback. It's time for you to take some action."

Angela jumped in. "I've dealt with people like him before. Hit him with your own manipulation tactics. Make it his idea for you to leave, like, ask him how you're doing and push him a bit until he tells you to go."

"Oooh, interesting. But what if I can't get another job on his timeline? James left his job, and I have to bring in the dough."

Nine women looked at her. Lesley broke the silence. "You're incredibly employable and you have a strong network to leverage. You'll get another job. Am I right ladies?"

A resounding chorus of yesses rang out around the table. They were right. She wasn't trapped. She had choices.

"You'll have to switch organizations and get out of Randall's sphere of influence. LampLight is a huge company, so there are a lot of options. I'll start looking into it. You should, too."

"You're in the big leagues now, Boo." Lesley nodded sagely.

Alex spoke next. "In the music world, if you cross the wrong person, you're locked out of gigs without even knowing they were behind it. You never know who's connected. Get as far away as you can."

"That's exactly what I'm afraid of," Kate admitted.

"Now that I'm out of his organization, I know a lot of really senior people don't respect him. You just have to get far enough away. We'll help you." Julia looked at the group.

"Damn skippy. Any way we can." Angela held up her glass.

"Thank you. You're right. I got it stuck in my head that this was the fastest route to promotion, and I just need to stick it out, but there's more to life than a promotion."

Kate's words sounded hollow as she thought of her dwindling savings if James stayed out of work longer than planned. "Thanks for the pep talk. Now, I want to hear an update on the latest personal ads that Lesley shared with us last time."

Lesley steepled her fingers in front of her. "Has anyone heard of a sex chair?"

---

Chapter 25

---

Kate's palms were sweaty as she approached Randall's office. She wiped them on her gray pants. She didn't like admitting defeat, but he had won.

She couldn't be the Chief of Staff he wanted. She should have known she couldn't play a background role. She should have known Randall was too good to be true.

He had told her what she wanted to hear instead of the truth. She should have listened to the voice that said he would retaliate. Executives with fragile egos didn't want powerful women around. She had experienced it before. She should have seen it all coming a mile away.

Worse yet, she did see it and ignored the signs in her zeal for the spotlight, money, and a promotion.

She heard Brie's voice in her head, shaking her out of her self-flagellation. It wasn't a prison sentence. And he had signed up to not be an asshole. It wasn't all her. He had retaliated when she had stood up to him.

The infusion of Steak and Bourbon energy filled her with strength.

"Randall, we have to talk." Kate realized she sounded like she was breaking up with him. In a way, she was.

He held up his finger and continued to type. He left Kate sitting there for several long minutes. She assumed it was to exert his power, but maybe it was just an important email. She studied the French cuff of her business-like white dress shirt.

"What is it now?" Randall's tone was short and curt.

"This really isn't working. I can't be the Chief of Staff you want. I think you should find a new one."

He sat back in his executive chair. "Kate, you made a three-year commitment to me. A lot of people would've killed for this job, and I gave it to you."

"I know. You also made a commitment to me about what the role would be." *Could he have forgotten?* "You don't have me working on strategy anymore. It feels like you've lost respect for me. All you do is yell at me."

"Are you calling me a bully again?" Randall's words hung in the air, challenging her to answer.

"Well… yeah." It was the best Kate could do.

"Takes one to know one," he spat at her. *Was this kindergarten?* "You strut up and down these halls treating people poorly, making them bend to your will, and generally being rude, but you have the nerve to tell me I'm the bully? You're one of the most negative people I've ever met." He shook his head at her. "Your behavior reflects very poorly on me. I'm tired of fielding complaints about you."

Kate fell back in her seat. This wasn't the way she thought this conversation would go. When was she rude? "What complaints?" Kate tried to keep her voice steady. Was he reporting *her* to HR?

"No way – I'm not going to play the 'he said, she said' game. You know how you are." Kate heard Julia's voice in her head and recognized the scare tactics for what they were.

She waited for him to continue. "Fine, get a new job. It'd be best for me. You're not holding up your end of the bargain." The sides of his mouth turned down even lower than before. "So don't expect any help. You're not who I thought you were. That's it."

Wow. Kate's hands shook from suppressed rage as she walked out of Randall's office. *She* was the bully? *She was the nice one, for fuck's sake!*

But at the end of the day, she'd gotten what she wanted from the conversation. She had permission to look for a new job.

She'd keep doing the best she could in her role while activating her network and finding something else.

She certainly wasn't going to walk away from all the unvested stock Julia and Florence had given her.

That would just be dumb.

JAMES WAS ready to go for their date the next evening. She was thankful he was doing a great job of keeping her spirits up and supporting her emotionally while she worked through the Randall situation.

He had continued to arrange their weekly date nights. It helped keep the spark alive and made sure they didn't fall into a rut. He drove towards Pike Place Market and the restaurant Julia had suggested.

"Do you mind if we swing by the Hard Gear shop on the way to dinner? They just released a new set of adventure hard bags that'll fit my motorcycle. They've gotten great reviews, and I want to pick some up for the Backroad Discovery Ride I'm doing with Ross and Trevor next month."

"Sure, let's go." Kate wasn't sure why the last set of hard cases she had sprung for wasn't enough. But she decided to keep it to herself. Part of their agreement was that he could spend the money she gave him on whatever he wanted.

The store was tiny but packed with tons of gadgets and gear that intrigued Kate. She wanted a moped really badly when she was a kid. The feeling came flooding back to her as she stood in the shop.

Her parents wouldn't let her get one even though her Dad had one for years. She had happy memories of sitting and watching him work on his bikes. Until one summer day.

He had the bike up on its center stand with the engine running while he adjusted something. In a sitcom-worthy series of events, he hit it just the wrong way and the center stand released. The motorcycle careened into the garage and smashed into the stack of storm windows. Moaning Marilyn made him sell the bike. If he couldn't have a motorcycle, she couldn't have a moped.

But nothing stopped her now. Except money. When James got a job again, she'd get herself a motorcycle.

James selected the gear he wanted along with a new jacket and a GPS mount. He looked so happy. "Let's get your new toys to the car so we can head to dinner. I'm hungry."

"They aren't toys, Katiebug. They're important equipment."

"Oh I know. I mean toys as in things that make you happy. I don't drop that kind of money on myself very often and when I do, it makes me happy to think about the fun I'll have with whatever I bought."

"Yeah, you really don't spend money on yourself. I can't remember a single new thing you've bought yourself in forever."

He had a point. She'd been saving money while James was out of work. "There was that new paella pan."

"I know, but you get what I mean. We aren't poor, and I'm looking for a job. We don't have to scrimp and pinch."

He was right, but she would still only have one glass of champagne at dinner. No reason to have more when she could just open a bottle at home for way less money.

THEY WERE SEATED in the window. It was a cold and rainy evening so she couldn't see very much. She bet it was a beautiful view of the Olympic Mountains on a clear day.

"How's it going day to day?" Kate asked James as she stabbed a piece of lightly dressed lettuce. He was watching a ferry all lit up on the water heading toward Puget Sound.

"All good. Why do you ask?"

"No big reason, just checking in now that you've been doing your own thing for a few weeks. I want to make sure everything's good with your new, um, situation."

"Yeah, I'm happy. I've been researching motorcycle-related jobs I could do, like design work for the big shops, but most of the work is in Germany, Austria, or Japan. They haven't started distributing that to the US, especially to locations like Washington State."

"Is that important to you? Would you want to move?"

"No, it's just one of the options I'm looking at. I used to be a mechanic. I could do that again. Ross and Trevor are looking into program manager jobs at their companies. We talked about it the other day."

"Sounds like you're exploring a lot of avenues. That's cool. Something will pop." *And soon*, she added to herself.

"Speaking of exploring, I'm thrilled to hear you're breaking up with Scandall." He had started using the nickname, too she noted. "I'll be glad when you never have to deal with him again. Wolf in sheep's clothing."

She hoped this experience would be in the rearview mirror soon, too, and appreciated James' support.

---

## Chapter 26

---

"You want that role? Easy peasy." Julia sounded so positive about Kate landing the job. She hoped Julia was right.

The role in engineering to help write the strategy and landing for a new customer management solution seemed too good to be true. It was posted a level higher than Kate, but she always liked to aim high.

She could help LampLight get off their antiquated customer contracting system while updating the approach to be harmonized across channels. It was incredibly strategic while also requiring that she dig in and get the work done.

Ideal.

The only problem was that Kate didn't know Charlie, the hiring manager. Actually, she didn't know very many people in engineering at all. But her network did. Kate didn't like asking people for help, but she knew she wouldn't get this job without some well-placed calls. A quick view of Charlie's LinkedIn profile showed they both knew a few people in finance, and of course, Julia.

"This looks like the best one out there for me." Kate didn't want to put her hopes in one job basket, but this role seemed perfect. She had applied for the role in the tool and sent a carefully worded note directly to Charlie. She knew from experience that simply asking for an informational interview would not be enough. She needed to show her interest by applying and enabling her network. Julia would help her.

"I know Scott, the guy who's currently in that role. He's moving over into marketing. I'll talk to him and get the lay of the land. I've heard great things about Charlie. I know him enough to send a recommendation for you. I'll do that after I find out from Scott what Charlie's looking for."

Kate was impressed with Julia's reach. "Is there anyone you don't know?"

"Comes with the territory when you're an extrovert, you change jobs a lot, and you interact with tons of people as part of your job. I try to never burn a bridge. Even with the assholes." Julia added that last part quickly.

"Well, unless they really deserve it." Kate poked Julia.

"Some really, really do," Julia conceded.

"Thanks for the help and pep talk, as always."


THREE DAYS WENT BY, and Kate didn't hear anything back from Charlie. She started to lose faith. She had built this role up in her head as the best option. Senior strategy positions in her area of expertise were hard to find. Especially ones working for people with great managerial reputations.

Kate busied herself with her next task. She had tried to steer clear of Randall as much as possible, but she had to get him to write the fiscal third quarter reviews for his team. The deadline was approaching, and Craig wanted them on time.

"Why don't you just do it for me?" Randall asked. "I mean, you see these people every day. Write something about them. I don't have time."

"I would need to log in as you to do that. Otherwise I wouldn't have access to the review portal."

"Be back here at noon. I'm having lunch with my wife. I'll leave my laptop logged in and you can go into the tool and write them."

"Are you going to tell people you didn't write their reviews yourself? Is this just a temporary one to hit the deadline and then you'll do real reviews?" Kate was affronted that he would trick the system like that and not give his people real reviews. Let alone that he wanted her to participate in his trickery.

"Kate, really. Just do it. Noon."

"Okay." She guessed it meant he still trusted her. She could do a lot of damage on his laptop. She could put herself up for a promotion and he probably wouldn't notice.


SHE KNEW she couldn't get through twelve people's reviews easily in sixty minutes. She sat down to craft short paragraphs about each person's contributions so she could copy and paste them into the tool. What if the team found out she was doing it? Would she get in trouble? She already didn't trust HR, but it was a direct order from her boss. She had no choice.

When she got to her own review, she didn't want to be too positive and make it look like she took advantage of the situation, but she didn't want to undersell herself either. Especially because Charlie would be able to read her reviews before offering her a job. *Whoa*, she was getting ahead of herself. She didn't even have an interview yet.

She wrote some innocuous comments about ramping up quickly in role and executing effectively. Not too glowing, but still good. Under "opportunities for development" Kate paused. She should reflect something accurate about Randall's feedback. "Kate can sometimes come across as negative and should work on adjusting her communication style." There. Not too strong, but a nod to what Randall had told her. And that was feedback for just about anyone in a tough gig at LampLight.

As requested, she was at Randall's office at noon.

"Try to be done by one when I get back. I'll need my computer for my meeting."

SHE HIT submit on the final review twenty minutes early. She could copy and paste with the best of them.

———

AS SHE WRAPPED up for the day, an email caught her eye. It was from Charlie asking her to work with his admin to get a half hour on their calendars. Woo hoo! She made the first cut.

His admin told her she was in luck and that Charlie had a cancellation the next afternoon. She jumped at the chance. Randall would just have to deal without her for a bit.

She dressed in black and white for the interview, but added shoes with small red flowers as a tiny rebellion. Bland enough for Randall but with a little of herself thrown in.

"WHO ARE YOU?" Charlie asked with a laugh. His hair was cropped short and looked like it used to be black but now had a healthy dusting of gray. He had a thick beard and kind brown eyes. He did not fit the LampLight corporate cookie cutter type for a General Manager. He oozed joviality.

Kate sensed it might be a put-on to entrap unsuspecting candidates and stayed on guard.

"Where should I start?" Kate liked to seek precision before rambling.

"We've never met before, yet it seems like everyone I talk to tells me to hire you. You even came up in my conversation with Scott this morning who has you on his succession plan. So I ask again, who are you?"

Kate made a note to thank Julia. Clearly, she hadn't just had a chat with Scott. She got him to put her on his succession plan. Amazing. "I've been with LampLight for ten years and I've had several roles. I'm strategic, optimistic, and customer focused. People love me for my energy and humor. People also hate me for it." Kate stopped to see what response that elicited.

Reading his face, Charlie seemed to be in the "people who think she's funny rather than annoying" camp.

"In those ten years, how have we not crossed paths when it seems like everyone in my network knows you?" Charlie stroked his beard.

"I'm not one to blow my own horn," Kate answered. "You've probably seen my work without seeing me." As soon as she said it, Kate realized that's truly how she felt. Julia had certainly done her share of advertising for Kate, but prior to that, her bosses had taken the credit.

"Well, let's get down to it and talk about the role. I've already got my short list of candidates, but with the pressure from your network, I decided to give you a shot."

"Sounds good. Hit me." Kate settled in for the informational interview. She knew it was informal but also understood how important making a good first impression was. She had to take someone's spot on the short list, as only two or three people ever went through the interviews for these roles, and there was usually a front-runner.

The thirty minutes went by in a flash.

"Kate, you just jumped to the top of my short list, which kind of annoys me because now I have to cut someone else." Charlie laughed.

"Sorry to put you in an uncomfortable position so soon in our working relationship." Kate quipped.

"You're smart and quick. You're humble. I like that. I'll be in touch."

Kate had a line on a job. Thank you, network!

·  ·  ·

"J-MONEY STRIKES AGAIN!" Kate called Julia to thank her for the help on the way back to her building.

"No, I just told him why you'd be fabulous for the role. Kate, your capabilities and track record speak for themselves. Stop listening to Randall. He's a total jackass."

*Easier said than done*, Kate thought. "I'm trying, but the negative voices are so much easier to listen to."

"Girl, you need to stop that. And soon. It holds you back. Things got a lot easier for me after I turned the volume on those nasty little fuckers way down. They aren't gone, but the volume is much lower, and I know that voice for what it is. Just negativity and doubt. Ignore it."

"Great advice, as usual. I'll try harder. I'll be better."

"There you go again. Just be you. Be genuine." Julia's voice got louder and louder with each sentence.

"Okay, I really hear you now. I'll take my fabulous self off to my next meeting and do epic shit."

"That's better. Knock 'em dead. And as my very favorite mentor says, 'don't let the assholes get you down.' It's a good saying."

"I always forget you have mentors, too. You always seem like you know what you're doing!"

"Smoke and mirrors, my friend. Smoke and mirrors. And confidence," she added quickly.

"Boom."

They were both laughing as they hung up.

# Chapter 27

Kate prepared for her interviews. Luckily, she didn't have to officially tell Randall she was up for a new role. He wouldn't have to know unless she made it to the offer state. Why borrow trouble or get his hopes up she was leaving if it didn't work out?

From her time selling support before her last Chief of Staff job and working for Julia, Kate knew a lot of the inner workings of LampLight's antiquated customer relationship management solution. It had been custom built over the course of forty years and was like Frankenstein – new offerings bolted on, processes that didn't match the functionality, competing quoting models, an outdated sales methodology hard-coded into the workflow, unintended inconsistencies in pricing across channels, and an unhappy user base from constant tweaks that never really solved the issues. She would inherit a crapload of problems.

It sounded perfect. She loved digging into deep operational details and understanding them better than anyone else. That allowed her to zoom out, use her pattern matching skills, and flip models around for better outcomes. She could do this job. All she needed was the opportunity!

▭

KATE WORE one of her favorite ensembles for the interviews. She needed the energy from a nice, bright color to help keep her going. The large blue flowers on a white background of the cotton dress always brought a smile to her face. She added a yellow jacket to complete the look. It was crisp and professional while also fun. It put a bounce in her step every time she wore it.

Tereza was first on the interview slate of three people. She led change management activities for partners using the small amount of functionality already released on the new customer management platform.

Tereza started out in serious interview mode. "Everyone who interviews has great stories about their successes. Tell me about a time when you managed a project that went very badly and what you did to recover." Tereza's impenetrable stare and Eastern European accent made her just a little scary.

"My projects rarely go smoothly because I deal with so many competing priorities," Kate admitted. "Here's one of my favorite recovery stories where I turned the biggest naysayer into my champion." Kate walked Tereza through the story at a high level, hitting the most important points about knowing your audience, catering your message to them, incorporating their feedback, and making progress.

"Okay, you get it." Tereza switched from interview

mode to friend mode. The conversation was much more transparent about what made the job difficult and how they would work effectively together. One down, two to go.

Tereza asked if Kate had any more questions. She pulled out her favorite wrap-up question. "Is there anything else I can share with you that would help you recommend me for the role?" Kate found it was a great way to lock in the results. It made interviewers think and react in real time. She found that if they said they would recommend her, they actually did.

"Nope. You've got my vote. Good luck with Bobby. He likes to hear himself talk."

Kate thanked her for her time and walked down the hall to Bobby's office.

TALL AND IMPOSING, Bobby gave off the vibe that he was clearly used to getting what he wanted. He was a peer of Charlie's and an important stakeholder. He jumped right into the interview. "Why are you a good fit for this role?"

That was kind of a lazy question, but Kate was ready and answered in her typical bullet point style. "I'm strategic and hate process for process' sake. I learn as much as I can and rely on data to help guide my decision-making. I'm an excellent people manager and have worked on customer relationship management solutions and quoting in the past."

Kate quickly realized that Bobby's main concern was making sure she wouldn't get in his way too much. Tereza was right – dude loved to hear his own voice.

Kate employed her favorite interview technique with people like Bobby and got him talking. It worked like a charm. She spoke for maybe ten minutes of the forty-five and had been treated to a lecture about how messed up Charlie's team was after that.

"We're running out of time. Last question?" Impatience shot from his eyes. She hoped it meant he had made his decision and was ready to move to his next meeting.

"Will you recommend me for the role?"

"Yeah, I don't see why not."

That wasn't the glowing endorsement she wanted, but it was enough. "Then I won't sell past the close. Thanks for your time."

HER NEXT INTERVIEW was with Scott, the person leaving the role.

"Kate, I presume?"

"That's right. Nice to meet you, Scott."

She took the seat across from him. "This isn't going to take long. I had a great chat about you with Julia. And then my finance partner also gave you a high recommendation. If you can get the two of them in your corner, you've got skills. They're both tough to impress."

"Thanks. I'm lucky to have worked with both of them on difficult projects. I worked for Julia until I took my current gig as a Chief of Staff."

"Yeah, what's up with the short tenure there?"

"I'll call it executive misalignment. Randall is great, but I'm meant to lead, not support."

"Good answer. I totally get it. I was a Chief of Staff a

few years ago. It sucked. All that background work and then staying in the shadows. But the Vice President I was a Chief for helped me get this role, so it was worth it. Maybe you just got to skip a step."

Their interview lasted twenty minutes.

Kate showed herself out and headed to the Café for a quick cup of coffee before her final interview with Charlie forty minutes later.

She checked her email and was delighted to find that nothing had blown up in the last two and a half hours. She'd be back at her desk in another ninety minutes or so and hoped that trend continued.

She sipped her coffee and reflected on her first three meetings. Could she really have just skipped a step like Scott said? Was she on the path to get the job and the promotion she wanted without having to do her full three year sentence with Randall?

That would be amazing. It would make it all worth it.

No red flags in the interviews which was good. Tereza and Bobby both covered the negative points of the platform initiative, but hard work had never intimidated Kate. She was up for it. And there were no easy projects at LampLight. Decision rights were always spread across multiple teams. The best strategy didn't always win. That was just how things worked, and she had learned to operate effectively within the system.

*Until Randall.* Scott had been delightful. He was a little cagey about why he was leaving, but that was understandable.

She was filled with hope as she took her last sip of coffee and headed to Charlie's office for her final interview.

. . .

HER CONVERSATION with Charlie wasn't like an interview at all. He spoke to her as if she already had the job. "I birthed all these programs and tools over the last twenty years." Charlie shook his head. "My vision is clouded when it comes time to kill them and do something different." Kate was amused that he talked about them like they were living beings. "I need your clarity of thought, strategic brain, and executional powers to fix it."

"I'm even more interested in the job after my conversations with Tereza, Bobby, and Scott."

Charlie beamed at her. "I read their feedback, and they all gave you a thumbs up. I'll be in touch after the interviews with the other candidates wrap up."

Kate had a skip in her step as she returned to her office that afternoon. Luckily, she hadn't heard from Randall while she was out. Perhaps he didn't notice she was gone at all.

KATE WAS HAPPILY REVIEWING the event strategy for Randall's all hands meeting when she heard the chime of an incoming instant message.

My office

Those two words had quickly become her least favorite words in the English language. They struck dread in her heart since she knew it wouldn't be pleasant. She tried to remind herself it didn't matter. She headed to his office.

"Do you have a new job yet?"

No preamble. No "how are you?" no nothing. Just a nasty question.

"Working on it. There are a couple of jobs that look interesting. I interviewed for one today. I'm spending some time on that, but my current job takes a lot of time, too." Kate didn't want to make things worse by not delivering in her Chief of Staff role. And she didn't want him to know she was potentially close to an outcome. She preferred to deliver it as a fait accompli once she had an offer. If she didn't get the job on Charlie's team, it could be months before she could get out of there.

"What's the latest on the Brussels meeting?"

She gave him an update on the venue, attendees, and speakers. She had made amazing progress, at least according to herself.

"That's it." He looked her up and down.

She hoped her outfit annoyed him.

She headed back to her office. The fact that he hadn't had any follow-up questions or changes to the Brussels event was a major victory. Pre-retaliation Randall would have thanked her and told her she did a great job.

She just told herself in this new phase of their relationship.

KATE WAS delighted when the email arrived from Charlie saying she was everyone's top choice for the job.

Her happiness was short-lived.

He also said he wanted to talk to Randall before making an offer. He was checking that Randall knew she was interviewing before reaching out to him.

Panic ensued.

Kate hoped they could skip that step. She thought Randall might ruin this for her. But he wanted to get rid of her as much as she wanted to leave. And she didn't have any red lights in her written review. Maybe Randall would say he was too busy to meet with Charlie anyway. Or even better, schedule the meeting and then blow Charlie off since he was more junior than Randall.

Charlie showed a lot of class by asking her if Randall knew she was interviewing before reaching out. She would do the same and confront the issue head on. She IMed Charlie.

LMK when you can chat

You got me in between meetings – calling

Kate took a deep, calming breath and answered the call. "Hey Charlie. I was thrilled to get your note."

"I was thrilled to send it." Charlie chuckled. "The team loved you. But I sense there's a problem from your tone."

"We didn't talk about why I'm leaving my current job. Let's just say I don't know what Randall is going to say about me. We aren't a good fit." She chose not to provide additional detail.

"Understood. I'd still like to talk to him. I don't know him particularly well although we've been in meetings together. As you know, this position is posted a level higher than you are now and the person leaving the role is a level higher than that. Part of my conversation with Randall will be whether or not he supports you getting a promotion on hire."

The fact he was talking about potentially hiring her filled her with joy. Perhaps Randall would be glad enough to get rid of her that he would support the promo.

Even as she thought it, she knew it was wishful thinking. But she still might get a new job. She remained hopeful. "Of course. He knows I'm looking. Please feel free to reach out whenever you like. I'm really glad I made it to the next step."

▭

"WHY SO SAD, BUG?" James noted her melancholy when she came in the door, dragging her feet.

"It was a day of ups and downs."

"Sounds like you need some champagne. Be right back."

Kate watched his retreating back as she kicked off her shoes and followed him into the kitchen. "The good news is that I'm the top candidate for the job on Charlie's team."

"That's great news! That's the most important news! Let's celebrate!"

"Not so fast there, Hubs. He wants to talk to Scandall before he decides to make an offer."

"Shit."

"Exactly."

"He wouldn't dare block you from leaving. You're worried for nothing."

"Maybe, but the role is a level higher than I am so

there's a potential promotion on the table which would mean more money."

"Money, money, money with you! Can you just focus on the fact that you nailed the interviews? I mean, I'm not surprised because you're awesome, but can we toast that, please?"

"You're right. I'm focusing on the negative instead of the positive. Cheers."

She continued to worry about what Randall would say to Charlie. He could easily block her from getting the job. Maybe, just maybe, he knew he was being harsh and critical. Maybe he would do the right thing and help her get that promotion.

-----

# Chapter 28

-----

Kate was just wrapping up a presentation for a leadership team meeting when she received an IM from Charlie.

Got a sec?

Yes

She answered the video call. "Hello Charlie. How are you?"

"I'm fine. I just spoke to Randall." Kate chose to stay quiet. Would her worst fears be realized, or did he go easy on her? "What's up with that guy?"

Kate chose again to be quiet, not wanting to give anything away since she didn't know what he had said. When Charlie continued, Kate let out a shaky breath. "I just have one question. What did you learn from this experience?"

It was a great question, and she wanted to unleash about how awful it had been. But she knew she had to play the good corporate citizen. She started talking before she knew exactly what she would say. She hoped that by the end of it, Charlie would have what he needed. "I've learned to listen more and talk less. I've learned to check in with people before, during, and after meetings to ensure everyone feels heard. I've learned that sometimes the best thing to do is keep your head down and live to fight another day."

She hoped it was enough to combat whatever Randall had said to Charlie.

"Those are all good lessons." Charlie nodded at her through the screen. "But I have to say," Charlie paused before continuing. Kate's heart clenched. "That dude is crazy. He spent our time together telling me how awful you are." Kate again chose to be silent. Better to be mysterious than a raging screamer.

"Am I out of the race then?" Kate dreaded the answer.

"Thanks for the direct question. I have to think about it. I never make people decisions quickly. This is an important position, and I need someone I can trust in this role. It's too important to waste time on miscommunication and bad attitudes."

Kate didn't know if Charlie meant Scandall's or hers. "I understand. It's a tough spot to put you in. I really want to work for you and kick ass in this job for you and the team. I think I'm the right choice. I respect your decision process and look forward to hearing your answer."

"Thanks Kate." She sensed his discomfort. "I'll get back to you soon."

Kate's head dropped down and she contemplated her shoes. She was shaking. She had held it together during the call, but the stakes were high. There were no other jobs she wanted, and she had to get away from Scandall. She could only imagine what he had said about her.

Why would he ruin her chances like that? He said he wanted her gone. She was trying to get gone.

This clearly damaged her shot at the job, let alone the promotion. If Charlie still offered her the role, she would be doing the work of someone two levels above her. Even though Scandall talked shit about her, she should still get a single level promo out of it. Right?


KATE PUT on a happy face and went to her team meeting. They were putting the finishing touches on the Customer Advisory Board final agenda. Construction was far enough along they were able to get an occupancy permit even though the entire building wouldn't be complete. She was able to get the team to ensure that the largest conference room was up and running and that the Industry Discovery Center had four different industry demos.

Yes, the team would have to step over some wires and see empty walls, but the members of the advisory board had jumped at the chance to provide feedback.

Kate planned to take a couple members of her events team with her to Brussels to help manage the actual event. Everything was clicking along.

"I can't believe you pulled this off." Louella, who ran the events team, beamed at her. "The presentation monitors are so cool. I got the training on how to use them in case the onsite team has trouble. Randall's going to love it."

"I'm pretty excited about it, too." Julia looked at

Frances. "Are all of the attendee details ready for Randall to review? He'll want to spend time with those files on the plane over."

"Yep. Ready to go."

Ling-Fei jumped in. "Kate, I have to say that this is the smoothest this has gone in the four times we've run the Advisory Board. You're help with the detailed planning and consensus from the team has been great. And using your connections to line up the speakers made it so easy."

"Thanks Ling-Fei. That's what ten years at this company and a strong network can do. Everyone in Europe is excited to make this launch successful. They were happy to participate."

"Take some credit, Kate. This isn't how it used to be. I'm glad you're here." Shana, Dale, and Geoffrey from the events team nodded their agreement.

Everything was good to go. They even had some buffer with three weeks until the event. She finally had a win. She felt the love and support from her team. She would miss them if she got the job.

***

KATE HAD JUST ABOUT GIVEN up hope late Friday afternoon when she hadn't heard anything from Charlie.

She wrapped up her latest Randergency about the tagline being wrong on the jackets he wanted to give to the Customer Advisory Team participants. He wanted "#bettertogether" instead of the phrase Better Together. Seriously?

This was what Aidan warned her about. The change

would add three thousand dollars to the event budget and add a week to the turnaround time, but Scandall would be happy.

She should be doing strategic work, not administrative bullshit.

The ring of a video call interrupted her lamentation. She almost ignored it because it was four thirty on a Friday, but guilt stopped her. She was glad it did. It was Charlie.

"I have good news and bad news."

*Shit*, Kate thought. That's exactly how Julia had started before she dropped a bomb on her. "I'll take the bad news." Kate prepared herself for the letdown of not getting the job.

"Well, it doesn't matter because it's the same news either way. The bad news is you're going to have to deal with my special brand of humor every day. The good news is the job is yours if you want it."

"That's all good news!" Kate's heart jumped to her throat and lodged there. She was surprised she could talk around it. "I accept."

"Hang on, there buckeroo. With the input from Randall, I won't be able to get your promotion on hire."

*Fuck.* There was bad news. "Oh." Kate tried to keep the disappointment out of her voice. "No wiggle room on that?"

"None. After I did the right thing by letting Randall know I would be making you the offer, he went to my boss and told him not to promote you."

"Wow. He really hates me." She couldn't believe he did that. What a tool.

"Yeah, but like I said, that dude is crazy. That kind of

behavior is unhinged and unnecessary. I'm psyched to have you on the team, and I have no doubt we'll get you that promotion soon."

"Thanks Charlie. Again, I say even more emphatically, I accept."

"Yeah, you'll be great and worst case, you get away from that guy."

She laughed. It felt good that she could. "Have a great weekend Charlie. We can start transition planning next week."

"You bet. Have a great weekend."

Kate's emotions swirled. Mortification and embarrassment mixed with elation. Saved by her solid interviewing skills and her network. And Charlie.

She was impressed he bucked the system and hired her anyway. From what she knew of Charlie, perhaps that's *why* he hired her. He struck her as pretty anti-establishment.

But whatever the reason, she had her ticket out of Scandall's team. She would focus on that instead of the lateral move.

▭

"I DID IT." Kate couldn't contain her excitement when she called James. "I got the job!"

"I knew you would. You're amazing." James was always in her corner.

"Thanks. Can we celebrate tonight?"

"Of course. I'll make dinner and pick up tons of

champagne. The good stuff. When will you be home?" James' reaction was perfect.

"The usual time, maybe seven."

"Uh, Katiebug, I'd like to remind you that you just got a new fucking job. You don't owe Scandall McShittyPants anything. Leave now. Please."

"That's not how it works. I can't just abandon the team. But I'll compromise and leave now. I don't have any more meetings, just work to do. See you closer to five thirty." James had a positive influence on her.

"That's my Katiebug!"

## Chapter 29

Kate waited until Monday to share the news with Scandall. She was not looking forward to telling him, but she knew he couldn't hurt her anymore. Charlie had probably already told him anyway.

"I'm glad you took me seriously and found a new role."

*What the fuck, dude?* Kate had come to him with it. But she remembered Angela's advice about making it Randall's idea to smooth the transition. "Yes, thank you," was all she said.

"I assume you'll give me the customary month of transition time for a Chief of Staff role?"

"I was hoping for two weeks, actually." Scandall had such a way of making her feel small.

"One month is customary in high profile roles."

"Okay, one month." Kate wasn't looking forward to telling Charlie there would be a delay, but what else could Randall do to her? He had already stripped her of her promotion opportunity. She just had to make it through a month. "Do you have any successors in mind?"

"Tons. Here's a list." He flicked something off his sleeve. "Vet them. I want you to identify the top three candidates by tomorrow morning. And talk to them to make sure they want the role. Add others if you have someone else in mind."

*What, and trick someone in her network into taking the role?* No thank you. "Ah, Randall, I don't think that's the best idea given how this ended. I'll talk to Marianne on the Talent Acquisition team. I bet she has a solid list of candidates."

"Fine. I don't care how you do it, just get me the list. And needless to say, we won't be needing you in Brussels for the Advisory Board meeting. Cancel your trip."

She was looking forward to a trip to Brussels. But getting out of Scandall's sphere of influence was better than revisiting a city she had already been to a few years before.

The self-satisfied look on his face suggested to Kate that Randall thought he had won.

And she was happy to let him think that.

"Louella, Frances, and Ling-Fei will nail it." She left his office with a smile on her face.

***

"YOU'RE LEAVING US ALREADY?" Frances' tone bordered on whining. She knew more than most about why Kate was running from the team, but they had kept the situation with Bernardo quiet. Frances' look communicated a lot.

Kate bet that Frances would leave soon after her.

"What happened to three years?" Jason asked.

"That was my plan, but Randall and I decided this role was not a great fit. He needs a different type of Chief of Staff." Kate thought that was the safest route. Not better, just different.

"Sucks for us. We had just broken you in." Louella put a fake pout on her face and crossed her arms.

"There are a lot of great candidates already coming forward, and I'll invest time in their onboarding to help them. You'll be in good hands."

Bernardo followed her out of the conference room.

"Got a sec boss?"

"For you, of course. Why don't you join me in my office where we won't be overheard." Kate headed down the hall to her office and closed the door. "What's the latest on the job search? I sent that recommendation you requested."

"Yes, thank you. And that's what I'm here about. I got the job."

"Yay!" Kate raised both arms over her head. "You did it! Congrats!"

"It was all because of you."

"No, Bernardo, it was because you're a strong and capable team member with an impressive track record. Don't let the last couple of months change that." Kate needed to follow her own advice. "When are you starting?"

"Frances has been great about it and knows I need to get out of here, so it'll be two weeks."

"Makes sense."

"She'll announce it later today, but I wanted you to hear it from me and to thank you again for your support. I wish every boss was like you. High integrity and not afraid to stand up for people. I'll carry those lessons with me."

"Thanks B," Kate said. Her eyes started to sting with unshed tears. "That means a lot to me."

"If you ever need anything, please just let me know. I don't know how to repay you."

"Easy. Just put this behind you and focus on being your awesome self."

Kate dialed into her next call with a boost of positive energy from her conversation with Bernardo. She was glad they were both escaping.

▭

"YOU WANT TO DO A TRANSITION REVIEW?" Kate was shocked. It really annoyed her since Scandall hadn't bothered to do any sort of review in the five months she'd been in role. Should she remind him that he made her write her own third quarter review? Why did he suddenly have an interest in doing one?

"And I want your new boss to attend."

*Red flag.* "Okay, I'll work with Sheila and Charlie's admin to get that set up."

"Soon."

"Yes, soon."

Too soon. Through some miracle, they were both available the next afternoon. What a way to end the week.

She figured it would just be a check the box exercise that HR was making Scandall do since she was starting her new job two weeks later. It was just policy that her new manager would join her. She should stop thinking the worst. Scandall was just following the rules. *For once.*

Kate distracted herself from her near panic by focusing on her plans for Saturday and James' birthday. She wanted something positive to look forward to rather than her transition review on Friday.

SHE HAD WRITTEN up her part of the review, explaining the great work she had done, and the high morale score she received from the team. Typically, the manager filled their part out and shared it before the meeting. When she had asked Scandall for it, he had ignored the request. Another indication this was a check-the-box exercise. He was travelling, so it was a virtual call.

Kate dialed into the call and saw that Lorna from HR was the line, too. That was weird. But perhaps since things had gotten ugly with Randall, Lorna was there to protect her or at least to witness things so they didn't deteriorate further. Charlie joined next. The three of them chitchatted until Scandall got on the line.

"Let's get started." He was all business when Charlie tried to joke with him. "Kate, I've been highly disappointed with your performance in this role."

Not a good start.

"You've been rude and caused problems since the very beginning. People repeatedly come to me and tell me you talked trash about me, the team, or them. I don't understand how you got to where you are in this company with the way you treat people."

Kate was stunned. This was nothing like what she

expected. So different than the feedback her team had just given her. Wanting to defend herself, she instead stared at Charlie on the video, looking for clues about how he was taking in the information. His face was bland. Randall continued to berate her.

"As a result of this pattern of poor performance, I've given you the rating of Poor for this period."

Kate was floored. That rating made her ineligible to change roles. He was trapping her on his team. Even more retaliation.

"I hear your feedback, Randall." She tried for calm. "Is there anything I can say or do to change that rating? As you know, I can't take the new role with that on my review."

"Absolutely nothing. You deserve this bad rating." His words were cold.

Kate's heart pounded even harder in her ears. She couldn't believe this was happening. If only she could rewind the clock five months and stay in her old role. Now her only choice was to leave the company and walk away from her lucrative future stock vests. Why would he do this?

Charlie's soothing voice filled her headset. "Randall and I have discussed it, and we've agreed to bend the rules. I'll work with you on this feedback and am confident you'll be able to address it."

"Thank you for believing in me, Charlie."

Kate couldn't remember very well what happened after that. Her mind was reeling.

·  ·  ·

AS SOON AS the call was over, Kate called Lorna.

Lorna answered on the first ring. "I figured I'd hear from you." Was that victory Kate heard in her tone?

"I just want to understand what happened. I won an award for my hard work and collaboration last year. After a manager change, I'm suddenly a horrible bully? Randall changed toward me after he and I talked about the situation with Bernardo. This feels like retaliation."

"No, Kate. This is deserved. Randall and I are aligned on this poor rating."

"But this came out of left field. No warning, no conversation, just a terrible review."

"Kate, that's not true. Your anger issues were outlined in your last review. And I quote 'Kate can sometimes come across as negative and should work on adjusting her communication style.' It's right there in your last performance review."

Kate's words had been read back to her. "But I wrote that myself. Randall had me write everyone's reviews. He didn't write that!"

Kate was met with silence on the other end. It stretched from long to awkward.

"I think we're done here. I hope you take this feedback seriously and improve."

And with that, Lorna dropped the call.

Kate just sat and stared at the empty screen.

She shouldn't dwell on the negative thoughts about what had just happened. But it was so easy. Easy to wallow in the terrible things Randall had said. What if even half of them were true? Did people hate her? Was she a bully? Did she have such a huge blind spot that she just didn't see it? She knew she could be tough, but a bully?

Another video call came in. It was Charlie.

"Wow, that was a lot. What the Hell happened between you two?" Kate took a breath to answer but Charlie interrupted her. "On second thought, I don't want to know. Your job is to take this experience, learn from it, and move the fuck on. We have work to do."

It really was that simple. Charlie believed in her. That's what mattered now. She had a few months to prove herself in her new role before bonuses and additional stock grants would be awarded. She had time to make this right.

▭

KATE TRIED to get her shit together on the drive home. She was going to have to be super careful for the next few months to ensure none of this feedback popped up again.

She called Julia and was grateful when she answered. "J-Money, it was terrible. I don't know up from down anymore." Kate relayed the story of her transition review.

"Sounds like retaliation to me. And Lorna didn't help you? This shit runs deep at LampLight. How do they explain your amazing performance for the last several years if you're such a tyrant?" Julia's indignation felt like a balm on Kate's frazzled nerves. "Listen to me, Kate. It's them, not you. Just because they say it doesn't make it true. Are you listening? You. Are. Amazing."

"Thanks J-Money, but it doesn't feel like that right now. I'm second-guessing everything I say and constantly reviewing how I could do better. It's exhausting."

"Don't give into their bullshit. You're a strong leader. Your style and approach have brought you success. You are kind and inclusive. Don't doubt yourself. Really."

"It's so much easier to listen to the bad stuff, Jules. Maybe I should just leave."

"Don't do that. You just got this fabulous new job with an amazing manager. Charlie had his one on one with Randall and listened to that vitriolic bullshit Randall spewed about you, and he still wants you on his team. He knows it was total crap. Trust him."

"You're right," Kate wasn't so sure. "You're right," she said with firmness. "I just have to set this aside as a learning experience and give it my all in my new role."

"And get that itty bitty shitty committee in your head to shut the fuck up. Don't listen to them. Listen to me and your successful history to date."

"Okay, I hear you." But Kate didn't. Perhaps these were real issues that no one had bothered to point out before. Maybe they were the real reason she was behind on her career plan. Maybe she was awful and not cut out to be on the senior track at LampLight. Maybe she had wasted the last ten years.

No! She wasn't going to give in to that. If she were giving advice to someone else, she would tell them to forget the negativity and move on. She had to follow that advice.

"What's the plan for kicking ass in your new job?" Julia mistook Kate's silence for acceptance.

"My first step is to learn as much as I can. It's a complicated mess right now and I can't fix it if I don't understand it."

"Good point. Sounds like you're on a solid path. You've got this."

Kate tried to heed Julia's words for the rest of the drive. As she swirled on the negative feedback, one key message kept floating to the top.

She was free and starting her next job.

The Scandall nightmare was over.

## Chapter 30

"Happy birthday," Kate murmured when James woke her up early the next morning.

"Thanks, Sleepyhead. I feel a little bad waking you up, but I'd like to exercise my birthday right of acting on morning wood. You up for it?"

Kate felt James' readiness on her leg. "Sure. And I can already tell that you are."

They got down to business.


"I'M GOING on a motorcycle ride with the guys later this morning." James handed her the soap in the shower.

"I know. Can you be back by five?" Kate tried to sound casual. She was all but bursting with her secret about that evening, but she was trying to play it cool. "That's when we'll have to head downtown for our private birthday dinner."

Kate had arranged a surprise party with a bunch of James' friends. He loved to sing and there was a direct correlation between how much he had to drink and how comfortable he was singing. She wanted to combine drinking and singing for maximum party fun for James.

Twelve of his friends were joining them at a new private room karaoke bar in Seattle. She had done it in Hong Kong a couple of years ago on a business trip and thought it would be right up James' alley.

"Are you sure you don't want to ride on the back of my bike and then go to the Trattoria?" James asked. "No reason to spend extra money on me." Kate appreciated his conservative approach given his work situation.

"No. You go have fun with your friends. We have the dinner reservation. Let's just go." Casual, casual, casual.

"You're right. YOLO!" James perked up. "Or in this case YOTFEO!"

"Yacht fee oh? What?"

"You only turn forty-eight once. YOTFEO!"

"You get to be extra corny on your birthday. Well done."

"Thanks. I think I'll pop a few more jokes before I'm done." James nodded his head up and down to collect Kate's adulation for his pun.

"I'm all ears for your next few jokes." She threw back.

"Oh, double score – you saw my corn joke and raised me! You are amazing, spelled A M A I Z I N G."

Kate groaned and handed back the soap. "Aw, shucks."

James narrowed his eyes. "There's a kernel of truth in what you say."

Kate gave him the last word. If she didn't, they would go on for hours.

"TREVOR, Ross, and I planned a motorcycle trip while we were riding today. We're going to trailer our bikes down to California and then start in the Redwoods. We'll be gone for about five days"

"That sounds fun."

"Yeah. We'll rent the trailer from Ross' friend. We'll take camping gear since we'll be off the beaten path a lot. It should be warm enough to go camping unless we're in the mountains."

"Do you have dates in mind?"

"I have the most flexible schedule, obviously. Ross and Trevor are locking down dates they can get away from work. I have some shopping to do. My camping equipment is pretty old and not small enough to fit on my bike with all the tools and other off-road supplies. Those new hard cases I got will be perfect. Thanks again. You're making my life really fun."

"Right back at you." They smiled at each other.

Kate wondered how much it would all cost. It sounded like a lot. But he hadn't asked for more money, so she guessed it fit into his monthly payment. She wouldn't bring it up unless he asked her to pay for it. No reason to borrow trouble, especially on his birthday.

"I think we've eaten everything we're going to eat."

"All right, birthday boy," Kate said, tossing her napkin beside her scraped-clean plate. "Want to take a walk?" She had to waste a few more minutes before the party.

"That sounds nice."

"Let's go down by Cal Anderson Park to see if anyone's

playing bicycle polo." That was the best excuse she could come up with to head to the karaoke bar.

They were in luck. Two teams were going at it, performing impressive ball-handling stoppies and pivot turns as they passed the ball and scored. Kate checked her watch – almost eight o'clock. James' friends knew to be there before eight so they would get there before he arrived.

"Hey, the car is the other way," James said as Kate walked toward the Rock Stage.

"I know, I just wanted to check this place out." She spoke with nonchalance to hide her growing excitement. She sent a quick text to Trevor so he knew they were almost there.

"That band is pretty bad for this neighborhood," James said over a particularly shaky rendition of "Summer of '69." There were speakers on the outside of the building that the people doing karaoke inside had turned on so everyone in the street could hear them.

"I'm pretty sure those are amateurs, not performers. It's a karaoke bar."

"Really? Why are you heading for the door? You know I love to sing, but I'm not doing it in public. Everyone will laugh at me. No way."

"Relax, I have it covered." Kate led him through the door.

They were greeted with wall panels painted matte black and bright flashing lights. Kate gave her name to the host, and they were whisked off down a dark hallway with doors on either side.

The host stopped at last door. They could hear "Time

Warp" from the Rocky Horror Show bleeding through. Kate was happy to know that at least some of James' friends were already in there having fun.

Kate maneuvered to be behind James. When the door opened, James' friends yelled "surprise" as he was ushered into the room.

All of his closest friends were there cheering for him. He grabbed a seat on the u-shaped leather couch surrounded by people he loved. He accepted a beer from Marcus.

His friend Deb had already figured out the music player and was teeing up the next song. There were two microphones in the room. Deb had "You've Lost that Loving Feeling" starting as she handed James a microphone and gave the other to his friend Ross. Too startled to put up a fight, James started belting it out as the crowd went wild.

"You got me. I'm so surprised!" James hugged Kate when he finished the song. "And you got me tipsy enough at dinner that I'll actually sing. You're the best."

At the end of the evening, they walked back to the car hand in hand. Kate didn't have anything to drink after dinner so she could drive them home. "That was a great time, Katiebug. Thank you."

It made Kate happy to make James happy.

## Chapter 31

"Okay Kate, let's talk about this first meeting with my boss." Charlie was helping Kate prepare for a strategy debate with his boss Dan. She knew him only by reputation.

He supposedly loved math, liked to oversimplify things he didn't understand, and wanted everything to fall into nice, neat boxes. Not exactly how these programs worked.

"The Kilimanjaro team is trying to launch a new product that doesn't fit any of our existing pricing models or tools." Charlie referred to the code name for a new cloud security offering that was being launched soon. "We literally can't quote it the way they want to. And if we can't quote it, we can't contract it. And if we can't contract it, we can't charge customers for it."

"Where do we come in?" Kate was ready to start problem solving.

"We have to figure out a way to shoehorn it into an existing contracting mechanism or tell them they have to give it away for free while engineering builds a new tool to track usage. Then, we'll have a fight on our hands. Your job is to listen intently, capture your ideas, and keep quiet."

Kate was a little shocked at the 'keep quiet' part. Charlie continued. "You're new here, and these people are sharks. They don't get our contracting systems and don't like to be distracted with details and reality." Charlie stopped to laugh. "So let's say you're following everything, it all makes sense, and you have the perfect solution. Dan looks at you with great meaning like he wants you to speak. What do you do?"

Kate nodded her head at Charlie. "I shut the fuck up and smile at him pleasantly."

"Bingo. You've got it." They both laughed. "In a few weeks, I'll hand you the reins in these meetings and you can venture in. But this first time out, just watch."

Charlie was protecting her. He wasn't silencing her. He was giving her a chance to be prepared and to make a good impression on Dan. She appreciated Charlie's support and started to understand why the team called him Papi Chuck.

KATE HAD JUST USED her team building exercises a few months earlier and they had worked. No reason to change them this time. She asked Julia to play the role Dave previously played. She didn't want to ask him again so soon. And Julia would do a great job. Since there was no shared reporting structure, it wouldn't look weird.

Kate didn't want anything to tarnish this job. She had a lot to prove to Charlie and the team and she still wanted that promotion. She knew in her heart of hearts her perseverance would pay off.

She had a team of thirty-four people. It wasn't the largest team she'd ever managed, but it was big enough to matter even in the hugeness of LampLight.

She had six direct reports, each of whom had five or six people working for them. She had five peers who all worked for Charlie. The stakeholders in engineering and marketing were mostly new to her, but she knew the field really well and that was her superpower. She would leverage that experience to increase the agility and adoption speed of the new tools and processes.


CHARLIE WAS SET to introduce her at their next all-hands meeting. He had a weekly staff meeting and a monthly all-hands. He didn't have a Chief of Staff because he preferred to be self-sufficient.

She read through the previous all-hands deck and their fiscal year 2017 strategy. Both sets of content were pretty light. It looked like this team was mostly at the mercy of Bobby's team on setting direction and on engineering for delivering – or more often not delivering – on their commitments.

Her team felt the brunt. They had to manage the existing contracting programs while trying to move customers and partners to the new platform while it was still being constructed. In some cases, it was more than double the work because everything had to be designed twice. Plus, there was a ton of pressure from the field to make updates to the existing tools, but engineering had frozen functionality in the current platform to focus their resources on the new stuff.

Talk about a game of prioritization, planning, and back-up planning.

Kate sent the values and superpower homework to her team and forwarded the invitation to her all hands meeting to Julia. She was off and running.

JULIA SAT at the front of the room, in sight of the camera and close to the microphone for people joining remotely. "This team just got really lucky. Kate is one of my favorite people at LampLight and is famous for taking care of her teams."

Kate's new team wasn't sold yet.

"I have the list of questions from the team here and there are some doozies. Shall we get started?" Julia was good at pumping up the energy in the meeting.

"Bring it on!" Kate was ready to go. She gave the team a big smile.

"You can't actually be this happy all the time. Is it a put-on?" Julia winked at Kate as she read the first question.

"That's a hilarious question. I like to be optimistic and keep things in perspective. I've noticed a certain grumpiness around LampLight lately, and I guess I do sometimes turn up the optimism because I truly believe we can make changes if we have a positive attitude about the work we're doing."

"I can validate that, folks," Julia added. "I've worked with Kate for four years and she's like the Energizer

Bunny." Blank stares from the young team. "Rock 'Em Sock 'Em Robots? No?" Continued blank stares. "Wow, you make me feel old. I mean that she just keeps going, even when she gets knocked down. Kate is optimistic and persistent. In the most delightful way. It's not a put-on." Additional blank stares. "Mary Poppins? No? Okay, moving on."

Feedback from the team meeting was largely positive. "You're like a real human being," Tamar said as they walked back to their offices after the meeting.

"Yeah, what you see is what you get." Kate decided to just be herself instead of trying hard to be someone she wasn't. She'd rather fail as herself than go down as someone else.

"HAVE you spoken to the sales team that focuses on small business about this new program?" The team had just briefed Kate on the changes they were making to the platform to support the new small business strategy.

"No way, that's a recipe for getting our heads handed to us." Sunita emphasized her point by dragging her finger across her throat. "We finish the plan and then present it."

Kate had her work cut out for her. "I see that differently. I think we should present the end goal and the problem statement to the small business sales enablement team." She tried to read the team's faces, but all she got was blank stares with a little terror mixed in. "It's not like these issues are a secret, and they can help us craft the solution. Then, they help present it. Acceptance by the field will be easier because we developed it together. That's how you drive change."

"It sounds like a lot of extra work. And Bobby gets mad when we leak information about strategy and platform."

"Bobby is in charge of the platform strategy, not the landing strategy." Clearly, Kate had made a good enough impression on him that he supported Charlie's hiring decision. Maybe she could influence him.

She had a lot of sympathy for the team. They had been trying to figure out a way to move sellers to the new platform when it didn't do everything they needed it to do. Kate knew that was a tough place to be.

She was undeterred. "It's more work in the short-term, Sunita. It'll add an extra round of meetings to the process, but it saves time later. You don't have to sell it to the field because it was co-created. You slow down to speed up."

"Do you think it'll work?" Sunita didn't sound convinced.

"I know it will. It's how every successful project I've landed has worked. I'm not saying there isn't room for improvement, but it's always better to go with a joint solution. The field doesn't like having things done to them. They like to have a voice in the design."

"That's not the way we do it." Tamar picked up where Sunita left off. "We know they'll just tell us it won't work, so we wait until the last minute when it's too late to turn back."

"That's the way Bobby wants us to do it," Sunita added.

"We don't work for Bobby. We work for Charlie, and Charlie is good with the approach I'm suggesting." Kate was sticking to her guns. "And how's your current approach working for you? Do I recall a major initiative announced to partners being rolled back at the last minute because of major outcry from the sales team that went right to our CFO?"

"Um, yeah. That was a few months ago." Tamar looked pained at the memory.

"And they remember that project. I'm telling you, take your ideas to the field and let them kick the tires." Kate was emphatic. "You'll wind up with a better, more quickly adopted solution."

"Oh, I think I'm getting it." Kate could almost see a light going on above Sunita's head. "We still steer them toward our solution but pretend we're gathering feedback."

*So close.* "No, we actually get their feedback. People aren't dumb. And they don't like being sold to." Kate hadn't realized how sheltered from the field this team actually was. They didn't seem connected to the people who did the day-to-day work.

"I think I like the current way better." Jacob chimed in. "We hand the solution over to the team who has to land it, lead one training webinar, and wait for the results. It's easier that way." Jacob was pretty early in his career. Kate knew she could help him develop new skills.

Change is hard, Kate thought. But she found this fun. She had to inspire a different approach in this team, but she was used to resistance. She would lean in and model the behavior she wanted to see from them. "I'll run the first set of meetings and show you what I mean. Then we can regroup and de-brief on what worked and what didn't. Does that work?"

"Yeah, I mean, we'll probably waste our breath, but I'm game." Sunita didn't sound too certain. "What'll we do about Bobby? He's going to be pissed."

"Thanks Sunita. I'll reach out to Elke and get a slot on the next enablement community call. Leave Bobby to me."

Hilarious, Kate thought as she crafted her email to the leader of the team responsible for landing initiatives created by the headquarters team. These kinds of changes would allow her team to execute quickly through a bunch of products.

No wonder things had been stalled for years. The field did not require perfection. They just needed to understand the why behind making changes. She would teach this team how to do change management and results would come pouring in.

Well, results would come trickling in before they poured in, but every step closer to their transformational vision was a step in the right direction. When people trusted you, you had a lot more leeway.

She would prove it and create the next batch of change management-savvy leaders on the program strategy team.

---

"I'M HOME." Kate hung her keys on the hook by the door and went in search of James. She found him playing video games with some friends online. She waited at the door until he noticed her. After a few seconds, he looked up and pulled his headset off one ear.

"Hey Bug! Looks like I lost track of time, unless you're home really early."

"Nope. It's after seven. I got caught up writing a change management plan for a small business contracting policy and platform change."

"Sounds exciting." He put his headset back on. "Hey guys, the wifer is home. I gotta go. Same time tomorrow? Later!" He laid his headset on the table.

*At least he stopped the game*, she thought. "I'm hungry. What's for dinner?"

"Oh crap, I meant to defrost the chicken, but I forgot. Let's go out."

Kate didn't want to go out. They were eating out more and more which was putting a strain on her pocketbook. She didn't want to cash out even more stock to pay for their new lifestyle. But she was tired and didn't feel like cooking either, so out they went.

"What'd you do today?" Kate looked at James over her water glass.

"I found this great guide in Spain who leads motorcycle tours. Trevor, Ross, and I are talking about heading over there and doing a tour with him after our trip to California." Kate was happy he was having a good time, but looking for a job was curiously absent from his description of what he had done that day.

"That sounds like a lot of fun. How much are we talking for a trip like that?"

"We didn't get that far – we were just looking at dates.

According to Graham, he's the tour guide, the weather is good in southern Spain starting in May."

That was still within the six-month window of their agreement. She needed to let him explore. It would be okay.

## Chapter 32

"Thanks for joining everyone." Kate was ready to lead the session on changes to the small business approach. A good cross-section of stakeholders from the team was there, mostly from the enablement team responsible for landing changes. "Our goal today is to outline a roll-out plan for some policy and platform changes and get your feedback on how we can improve it. Changes won't go live for several months. We have plenty of time to incorporate your feedback."

Kate noticed some shocked looks on people's faces. She continued to explain her approach. "We'll have four meetings on this topic and will follow the same arc for future rollouts. Meeting one is this one where we'll outline the plan and get your initial thoughts. Meeting two is next week and we'll use the time to hear your more specific feedback after you've had a chance to digest today's conversation. The third meeting will be our recommendations for how we'll integrate your feedback into the plan. The fourth meeting is a placeholder to go over any final feedback. If we finish in three meetings, we'll cancel that one. Let's begin."

Kate walked through the plan and asked three pre-prepared questions to get the conversation rolling. Her team stayed pretty quiet. She hoped they were still engaged while she facilitated a sometimes-heated discussion of the goals and outcomes.

She and her team had a thirty-minute de-brief after the meeting. "Okay folks, what jumps out at you from that meeting?"

"They were so nice to you!" Sunita sounded shocked. "They let you finish your sentences and didn't attack. Their comments made sense."

Kate was pleased she noticed. "Is that different than how you usually engage with that team?"

"Totally," Tamar interjected. "It made such a difference that we have a couple months before roll-out so there was no panic."

"Exactly. When you explain why we're doing something and guide people through the logic, they partner. When you drop something on them, they push back."

"This is a totally different approach than we're used to. And the way you outlined the specific agendas for the next meetings was awesome. Everyone knows what to expect, and if they don't show, it's their problem." Sunita was doing pretty well until that last point, but Kate was reaching them. Little by little.

"Now how are we going to incorporate their feedback? What changes do you think we need to make?" Kate wanted to doublecheck her own understanding of the conversation. She was still new to the space, and it was easy to miss things when you were both facilitating and tracking a conversation.

They dug into the feedback and debated a few changes that were mostly in positioning. None of it changed the goals or desired outcomes. Perfect.

▭

"WHAT'S this I hear about you talking to the field?" Bobby stopped her in the hallway. She thought he was just saying hello, but that was not the case.

"Oh, hey Bobby. Yeah, we previewed our implementation plan for the small business contracting changes to the enablement team for feedback."

"That's not how we do things here." He looked angry.

"I'm trying a new approach. One that's worked on a lot of teams."

"All you're doing is creating headaches for me and my team by giving the field hope they can mold our strategy to their liking." Bobby clenched his fist to underscore his point. "We don't have time to make any more changes to the functionality."

"I'm not asking you to." Kate put up both hands in a show of surrender. "I'm working with the people who have to actually use the policies and tools. I won't be coming back with tool changes. If anything, I'll be changing policies to ease the transition based on your functionality release schedule. It'll be okay."

"Give 'em an inch and they'll take a mile." He shook his head at her. "That's why we don't talk to them until it's done."

*Shit, she should have listened more closely to Sunita and pre-briefed Bobby.* More bad feedback could go to Charlie. She steeled her face so as not to give anything away. "I hear you, Bobby. We're aligned on our outcomes."

"Fine, but I'm sending everyone to you when they call my team whining about changes."

"I would love that. I want to hear their feedback." *And that's why I'll make more progress faster than this team has in the past*, Kate thought.

He smirked at her before walking away.

*What the hell?* Why was he so anti-field? She hated seeing that the stereotype was true on this team – that engineering people didn't talk to their users as much as they should. *Right.*

Whatever you do, don't talk to the users. They might teach you something. Kate sighed before continuing to the coffee maker for a late morning pick-me-up.

⸻

"BOTH MOTORCYCLE TRIPS ARE SHAPING UP." James was excited to tell her about it. She liked seeing him happy. "Trevor and Ross are definitely in. We'll go to California at the end of April and Spain in the middle of May. Are you sure you're okay with me going?"

"Yep. It sounds like a lot of fun." Kate was fine with it. He hadn't asked for additional money. And May was still within the six-month exploration window. Everything was fine. She chose not to point out why she was okay with all of it. She didn't want to dampen his excitement about the trips.

She had missed out on her trip to Brussels. Maybe she should go with him to Spain.

No, that wouldn't work. She would still be new in role and that was the most critical time for performance management. The April/May timeframe was when performance review meetings started to happen and there was definitely a recency bias in the process. If she had done remarkable things for Charlie's team by the middle of May, she would be in a good place come fiscal year-end review time. She couldn't afford to take the time away from work for a boondoggle in southern Spain.

She would leave the fun to James.

## Chapter 33

"You're doing a fabulous job, Kate." Charlie beamed at her. "The team is thrilled. I'm thrilled. You've hit the ground running and haven't stopped. I can't believe you were able to retire those two gnarly programs in just two months without a negative peep from the field. And everyone's talking about the new change management approach you employed with the small business team. It's amazing. You dug into the details, created a great plan, and led the team through the execution."

Kate flushed at the praise. She was loving this team and this job. "Charlie, I couldn't have done it without you. You're such a great sounding board."

"That's why we're a great team."

Kate liked where this review was going. It's like her last one never happened. "What's next, boss?" She wanted to tackle the next big problem.

"Since this is your review, I want to take some time to talk about succession planning."

"But I just got here." A spurt of panic flashed through

Kate. Maybe things weren't as good as he made it sound. Had she disappointed him somehow?

"That guy really did a number on you," Charlie quipped. "I mean for me. One of the reasons I took so long to fill your position is because I was looking to hire my successor. I thought it would be Scott, but he decided to leave the team. My plan is to be outta here in eighteen months and I want to know whether your plan is to stick around or not."

This was what Kate craved. A real career discussion about a job she actually wanted. "Yes, Charlie, that sounds amazing. I can't imagine this team without Papi Chuck, but I'd be delighted to step in for you when you decide to go."

"Thanks. But don't get any ideas. I have two kids in college and need to get that paid off before I can ride off into the sunset. Eighteen months. And that's not public information."

"You got it, boss. Thanks for trusting me with the team."

"You earned it. This means I'm going to be putting you in front of Dan a lot more and asking you to lead all discussions. I'll provide color commentary and continue to be your sounding board, but you need to think of yourself as leading this team now."

Excitement filled her. Her team was coming along, and she felt like she had taken a lot of lessons from Julia's proverbial management book. She was developing the same kind of loyal following. She could do this.

"And lastly, I'm not supposed to tell you this, but I'm submitting your year-end review with the highest rating possible and a pitch for a promotion. You should be in line for a nice, fat bonus given the quantitative impact you've had. We can see the savings and new revenue from your programs. You're in great shape. I should have just promoted you on hire like we originally talked about. You've really proven yourself in this role."

Relief and excitement filled her. It was the final step in closing the door on the Randall situation. A good rating would erase the bad one and she would never have to talk about it or mention it again. And that promotion. Woo hoo! She was getting there!

KATE LOOKED at her phone as she walked down the hall to her next meeting. James had sent another picture of an unbelievably windy road serpentining its way up a steep hillside.

James relayed a story via text of Trevor making it to the top first and being crowned the King of Alto Velefique, which she surmised was the name of the road.

The tour guide used to be a software salesperson and knew a lot of the tools that James managed at work. They immediately hit it off and had a lot to talk about.

She was glad he was having fun.

Kate put her phone away because she had arrived at the conference room for her next meeting.

"THAT'LL NEVER WORK. We can't get partners to move to the new platform when half of the products they want to buy aren't available!" Kate was in the thick of it with another field team, this time the partner organization.

LampLight sold a lot of their technology through partners and from Kate's perspective, LampLight was getting a little arrogant about how they treated the ecosystem. Partners had choices and could sell LampLight's competitors' products as well.

"We hear you, Vic. We really do." Tereza leaned in. "What would make them more interested in moving?"

Vic tossed his head of long hair as he thought about it. "Cheaper prices and more incentives. There would have to be carrots and not just sticks."

"Yeah, it's a tough message." Kate loved the problem-solving energy she got from Tereza as they leaned into the situation. "We're basically asking them to sell some of our solutions through one platform and contract while selling other solutions on another. Even the contract itself is different. Our sellers are having the same challenges with it."

"Thanks for hearing me. That's what Bobby and team have been pushing for this whole time. We keep asking them to finish the tool and they keep yelling at us about why partner adoption is low."

"I'm going to talk through some options with my team. Perhaps we could offer promotional pricing or higher rebates for using the new sales platform. Thanks for the input."

## Chapter 34

"The anger is starting to pass." Kate was in Charlie's office for her one on one a few weeks later. "It used to take ten minutes of venting before we could get down to business in meetings with the field, but we've built enough trust now that we can just dive right in. It feels good."

"That's great, Kate. But I have to talk to you about something that I'm not happy about."

"Are you okay, Charlie?"

"Yeah, just really really pissed."

"At me?"

"Of course not. Would you please stop fearing the worst?" He rolled his eyes at her. "You're doing a great job, and your team loves you."

"Sorry. Knee jerk reaction after my last, um, situation."

"Speaking of that guy, I'm sorry to tell you that you won't get that promotion we talked about."

Her shoulders fell. She was bummed, but not surprised. You couldn't go from a bad rating to promoted in three months. "I get it. That's the system."

"Thanks for being understanding about it, but there's more."

Kate didn't like the sound of that.

"No bonus and no stock either." Charlie hung his head and wouldn't make eye contact.

"What do you mean I don't get any stock this year?"

"I'm so sorry Kate. I did what I could. When I left the performance review meeting, you were in the model at the highest rating like we discussed. The team supported your promotion. Even Bobby had given a thumbs up which is no easy feat."

"Then what happened?"

"I just got the final locked results, and it shows no bonus and no stock. When I asked HR what happened, they said Randall had used his influence to change it."

Kate felt the sting of tears but willed them away.

"How can he do that?"

"Apparently, he went to Dan and said your five months with him were half of the fiscal year. You've only been here three, so his rating trumps mine."

"And Dan agreed?"

"He folded like a cheap lawn chair."

"Why is he going after me?" Kate already knew the answer. She had reported him and then rejected him by leaving the job as his Chief of Staff.

He was worse than an angry ex-boyfriend.

"I can't answer that. But I know you're amazing and you have a safe home on this team. The high rating on your fourth quarter review still stands. You just didn't get the money and promo that goes along with it."

"Is there anything I can do to challenge it?"

"I wouldn't. I'd just let it go. I'll put you up for that promotion again at mid-year and it'll stick. But if you decide to pursue it with HR, I'll have your back."

Kate let that sink in and was quiet for a moment.

Charlie continued. "Sorry to dump bad news and run, but I have my own review with Dan now."

Kate left Charlie's office, head hanging down. Nothing was official until the model locked, she knew that from managing people. But she had wanted to believe that Charlie's rating would stick.

She knew she shouldn't take action when she was angry.

She would check with Julia.

▭

"HEY J-MONEY. Are you tired of me talking to you when I need something?"

"Absolutely not. I love that we have our monthly get-togethers now that you don't work for me. You know how I feel about fairness. We couldn't hang out as friends before." She clinked her glass against Kate's. "Is working for Charlie as magical as we hoped it would be?"

"Yes, definitely." Kate nodded for emphasis. "Charlie is great and told me I'm first on his succession plan. He gave me a stellar performance rating."

"Woo hoo! See? I told you! Randall who?"

"Yeah, about that. Apparently Randall intervened and gave me zero rewards. No bonus, no stock."

Julia flumped back on the vinyl booth. "Are you serious? What's his problem? You got out just like he asked."

"I know, right? But apparently, he chose to peek into another team's model, and influence Dan to change it."

"What're you going to do about it?"

"That's what I wanted to ask you."

"It's retaliation. You were an excellent Chief of Staff. Florence agrees." Julia looked incredulous.

"I would report him, but Lorna would just protect him again. I don't trust HR."

"You could try the investigations hotline. It's separate from HR. LampLight created it a few months ago because so many people were complaining that workplace violations were being swept under the rug. Email them."

"I think I will." Kate was determined. Charlie had her back, and this was bad.

━━━

KATE CAREFULLY CRAFTED the email the next morning. She kept it short and sweet.

*Hello Workplace Investigations Team, I believe that my rewards reflect retaliation from my former manager Randall Cunningham for reporting a bullying incident involving him and a person on my former team.*

*My Human Resources counterpart was involved in the situation. I do not feel comfortable working through HR at this time, so I am reaching out directly to the Workplace Investigations team. My current manager is aware of the circumstances. There are two sides to every story, and I could use some help from an objective group.*

*Thank you,*

*Kate*

She read and re-read the email, checking for tone. She thought the last part was a good addition, showing that she was open to feedback. She hit send and went back to work.

KATE and her team worked hard with the seller and partner incentives team. Of course, they were a completely separate team from her team, but alignment was critical to drive the right behavior with sellers and partners.

It required a lot of influence without authority to get them on board with a promotion to increase platform adoption. But with enough math, butt-kissing, and promises to roll the promotion back once the functionality of the two platforms was at parity, she and Tereza got what they wanted.

Her extended team couldn't believe it.

But she could. Kate believed in her skillset and knew that she was a good corporate citizen. Honesty and integrity clearly still mattered to some parts of this business.

A WEEK HAD GONE by since she sent the email to the investigations team and Kate finally had a response and a meeting request from the investigator.

"Why don't you tell me what happened." Dawn sounded crisp and matter of fact. Kate appreciated that.

"I'll try to tell the story with as little emotion as possible." Kate kept it professional. She described the situation. Embarrassingly, she almost cried twice as she relived the most horrible moments.

"I'm sorry those things happened to you."

"Thanks Dawn. Do you believe there's something here that should be investigated?"

"I can't comment on that until I've done some background work on my end. I'll be in touch. Thank you for bringing this matter to the Workplace Investigations Team. We take every complaint seriously and will get back to you in a timely manner."

It sounded like she had read that part from a written script. "Thanks, Dawn."

Kate let out a long breath when she was done. Talking about it brought everything back to the surface. The emotions were all right there again, creeping into her head and heart. After months of pushing them down, she didn't like them rearing their ugly heads.

Each time made it harder to push them back into their little box.

JAMES WAS OVERLY solicitous that evening, bringing her a glass of champagne and trying to take her mind off of work. She appreciated his efforts, but he was going overboard.

"I don't know if anything will come of this, but at least I tried."

"Yes. I'm proud of you. Too few people stick up for themselves. I mean, they had to create a whole team just to deal with stuff like this, so you know it's common. I'm glad to be out of there."

Kate just wanted to change the subject. "Is that a new shirt? It looks great on you."

"Thanks. Robert Graham was having a sale. I stocked up. My other shirts were looking a bit tired, and you know I like to look good for you."

"And you do." Kate leaned in for a kiss over her glass of bubbly. She didn't ask him how many he had bought. While unemployed.

He was still living within his allowance, so she couldn't comment. That was their agreement.

## Chapter 35

Kate got an alert on her credit card app that a large purchase had just been approved. After her meeting, she dug in to see what was going on. Her outstanding balance had been getting larger each month, but she thought it was regular living expenses.

James had just charged a motorcycle repair to their joint card. She took a moment to do a little more research and sorted charges by cardholder. James was using their joint credit card. A lot.

She tried not to get angry. Perhaps there was a perfectly good explanation. She scrolled through the expenses. Gas. Amazon. Grocery store. Those all checked out.

But there were a lot of meals at a restaurant in Seattle they never went to. He went there with the guys. Without her. Why was he charging the expenses to her? And then there was the motorcycle repair on top of that. That was clearly a James-only expense.

She would have to talk to him about this. She wasn't

going to pay him his salary and then also foot the bill for his fun while she worked.

Worked without getting paid fairly for it.

But rather than jump to conclusions, she would wait and talk to him. There might be a perfectly good explanation. Perhaps he was already planning to pay her back.

An email from Dawn, the investigator on her retaliation complaint, grabbed her attention. The James situation would have to wait.

She read the email.

*Hello Kate,*

*Thank you for speaking with me last week. I appreciate the information you shared with me. Based on our discussion, I have concluded that your concerns are not in scope for the Workplace Investigations Team.*

*I want to thank you for raising your concerns and sharing your experience with me. If you require additional follow-up regarding the concerns you raised, please contact Lorna Fernandez in Human Resources. She is copied on this email.*

*Dawn Houser*

They declined to investigate? Can they do that? What does "not in scope" even mean? That someone else should take care of it or that the investigations team was in cahoots with HR? They sent her back to Lorna, the very person involved in the cover up in the first place. She just couldn't win.

Shoulders slumped and feet dragging, Kate felt defeated. It was time to let it go. She'd been holding onto the anger for too long.

The money hit hurt, especially right now, but she would make it back next year. She'd be fine.

Next year at this time, Charlie would be a few months from retirement, and she would get his job along with a promo.

She just needed to play the long game.

"THAT KIND of thinking is super dangerous." Bobby pointed his finger at her. "You should know better than that."

Kate was taken aback by Bobby's words. His tone was vicious, and the content was nasty. She had just shared her opinion about a path forward on a new program. Charlie had asked her to proxy for him in Dan's leadership team meeting while he was at a doctor's appointment. Why did Bobby have to get so angry? She kept her tone light. "What do you suggest instead?"

"I don't know, but not that. Just leave it with me and I'll come back with the right answer."

"Hang on, Bobby." She kept her tone professional even though his was not. "I lead the program strategy team. It's my call. Your input is crucial, but I have decision rights on this."

"Not with that attitude you won't."

What did he mean? This was her job. This was her scope. Roles and responsibilities were clear. He didn't have jurisdiction. Why was he being such a jerk? And in front of Charlie's peers. "Why don't we take this offline so we can really dive into the details? I don't know how interesting this topic is to others."

Looking around the room, Kate could clearly see the discomfort on people's faces. Why couldn't Bobby read the room?

"Fine. But this isn't over."

As the conversation moved on, Kate scheduled time with Bobby to hear more of his feedback. She had been warned by Charlie that he was super insecure. They had gotten along well before. But something she had done triggered him. She would get to the bottom of it.

"I HEARD you got Bobbied in the leadership team meeting this morning." Charlie's eyes sparkled with laughter as he said it. "I heard from like five people he was a total dick to you but that you handled it well."

"He called me 'dangerous.' Riiiiight."

"His panties are in a twist because the platform is behind, and he's lost his way. When you come in with real vision and a plan that'll work based on what's actually been delivered, it forces him to admit he didn't meet his commitments. If he agrees with your plan, he looks really bad."

"Interesting perspective, Charlie. Here I was thinking I was saving his ass by putting lipstick on a pig." Kate appreciated that she could be herself with Charlie. Her tongue hurt from biting it in meetings with Bobby.

"There isn't enough lipstick in the world to pretty-up this pig. He'll calm down. Ten bucks says you get an apology call. That's his pattern. And why no one batted an eye at his behavior. They're all used to it. My guess? Mommy issues."

They had a good laugh together. "I already scheduled a one on one with him for tomorrow. I'm going to ignore his tantrum and focus on getting aligned on the plan. I don't want us going in different directions. That would be bad for the field."

"You're so fucking mature. I love having you on this team."

"Thanks Papi Chuck. And thanks for the support."

"You'll always have it. You're doing a great job."

---

KATE SAT IN HER CAR, checking her phone one last time before starting up. There was a text message from James saying he wouldn't be at home for dinner.

*Could he be cheating on me?* Kate was horrified that her mind went there.

It would explain the dinners out without her. The new clothes. Living beyond the payment she made him every month and hitting her credit card. Was she financing the oldest trick in the book? He was being secretive and not accounting for his time. It would certainly explain his overly-solicitous behavior over the last few weeks.

No, not her sweet James. They were tightly connected, and he wouldn't do that to her.

But the wife was always the last to know.

Maybe he got sucked into something and things got out of hand.

She had let her questions about James' spending go

unanswered for too long. She was going to drill until she got to the bottom of whatever was eating him.

It couldn't go on, or they wouldn't stay together.

KATE SETTLED onto the couch with a glass of wine waiting for James to come home after his dinner out. She finally heard the key in the lock.

"Hubs, can you grab a drink and meet me on the couch? I want to talk about something with you."

"Am I in trouble?" James hung his coat in the hallway closet. He looked amazing and too dressed up for dinner with the guys.

"Oh, don't start it like that, I just want to work something out." Kate saw the discomfort on James' face, a mix of a schoolboy-in-trouble and someone focused on making a drink.

He joined her on the sofa, the leather making a creaking sound as he turned to her. "Excuse me." James loved his fart jokes. Kate laughed to put him at ease.

"Are we in a safe emotional space right now?"

"We were until you asked me that." James' brow wrinkled with a look of concern.

"I just want to start with the fact that I love you. Period. New sentence." They both smiled at the joke. Kate used to have a boss who said that all the time because some corporate media trainer told her to stop using transition words like "but" and "although." Instead of listening, her boss just started saying "period - new sentence" as a break in thoughts. "When you left your job, we made an agreement that I'd pay you a salary so you didn't have to ask for money. But now you're using our joint credit card for a lot of expenses that are purely for you. That's not fair."

"We have plenty of money, Kate." James sounded confident and matter of fact. *Quite reasonable, actually.*

"You say that, but not getting a bonus this year is going to put some strain on our finances. And not getting more stock is a gift that will hit us negatively for four years. We're going to have to rethink this whole monthly salary approach."

"I don't think we need to do that. I like our approach."

"James. What's up? I'm giving you five thousand dollars a month. Why aren't you able to cover your lifestyle?"

"I have expenses."

"James, you're starting to scare me."

James set his drink on the nearby coaster, clasped his hands between his knees, and looked at them for several long moments.

Kate's mind went in fifteen different directions. She could tell that he was about to say something big, but she had no idea what it was. A second family? Cheating? His ex-wife stealing it? A bad investment? A drug problem? Giving it to his family?

"I've been struggling for the last few months, as you know, Katiebug. It's been hard for me to not make my own money." Kate tried to remain calm and focused on listening to James instead of screaming *get to the point* like she wanted to.

"I know it's been difficult. What else?" Kate dug deep for patience.

"I like having the latest motorcycle gear or tech gadget.

I like taking my friends out for dinner and drinks. I didn't cut back my spending when I left my job because, well… I don't know why."

Kate chose to stay quiet and not interrupt his train of thought. She waited for him to continue.

"Now it's kind of out of hand. I have credit card debt, and all the money you give me goes to paying the minimum payments."

Kate had exactly zero experience with credit card debt. She paid her bill in full every month and always had. How much did a bill have to be to have five thousand dollars of minimum payments and interest fees every month?

"How much are we talking here, like ten grand?" Kate couldn't imagine he could have spent that much money in just a few months.

Then she started thinking through the new adventure bike, the new mountain bike, the new trailer, the new riding gear, the new camping gear, the trip to California, the trip to Spain, the way he always seemed to be picking up a check for someone else while they were out.

Dread lodged in her stomach, a cold ball that drained the blood from her face.

"More."

"Thirty?" Kate knew she was over-shooting at this point but didn't want to make James feel even worse.

"More like fifty."

"Fifty thousand dollars? Of credit card debt? In five months?" Kate's head rolled back on her neck and a heavy sigh escaped her mouth as she stared at the ceiling.

She searched for calm before continuing. Piling on

when he already felt bad wouldn't help. "What're you going to do about it?"

"I've stopped buying anything that isn't absolutely critical. That's why I can't account for where the five thousand is going every month. I was already in debt when I left my job. I was too embarrassed to tell you. The debt isn't getting bigger, but it isn't getting smaller either."

Kate could see that James was shaking.

He kept talking. "I hate letting you down like this. I thought if I just kept paying the minimums and didn't spend more I could catch up. But it didn't work. I started opening new credit cards and transferring balances to get lower rates, but I still couldn't catch up. I'm such a statistic."

James looked absolutely miserable. His chin was trembling with the look of unshed tears, reminding Kate of Pa from Little House on the Prairie. Michael Landon's wobbling chin was always the portent of bad news – crop failures, drought, a dead horse.

Kate snapped back to the moment after the brief Laura Ingalls Wilder interlude. She wanted to fix it for James, as she always did.

She felt the importance of this moment in their relationship. If she screamed at him to get out, they might not recover from that.

If she leaned in and gave him a supportive hug, she would be denying her true feelings. She stayed quiet, thinking, while James' questioning eyes searched her face.

"Say something, please." James broke the silence.

"Fuck." Kate's word selection was meant to diffuse some tension, but she couldn't keep the tone and look on her face from broadcasting her disappointment in James. And he saw it.

"Do you want me to just leave?"

"I need some time to process this. I don't want to say anything I can't take back. You have to understand how angry and hurt I am right now. I think if you had admitted to cheating on me it would be easier for me to get over than hitting me in the pocketbook. It really hurts. That's all I should say right now."

"I know. It's really about the worst thing I could do. I appreciate you not screaming at me or making me feel even worse than I do. Actually, I don't think you could."

"I respect and love you, but if we keep talking about this, I'm going to lose it."

"What can I do?"

"I need to be alone for a bit. Why don't you go get all of the information from all of the cards on how much you owe, and we'll figure out a plan."

"Okay. I'll do that right now. Thanks for being reasonable."

"Reasonable. Yeah." A dismissive sigh escaped Kate's lips before she could stop it.

Luckily for her, James had already left the room before seeing her head shake in disbelief.

## Chapter 36

Kate sat for a moment, trying to get her anger under control. She had to get out of there.

"James? I'm going for a walk."

"Okay, thanks for letting me know."

At least he wouldn't think she was storming out in a rage. She needed to be out of the house.

She pounded her feet up the steep hill she lived on, the same thought swirling over and over in her head. *How could he?*

He knew how important money was to her. She was trying to be financially secure, working hard to build her nest egg so she could pursue her dream. And she couldn't trust her new husband with money after all?

Why did this happen? Why couldn't she find a guy who could hold a job and be responsible for his own financial health? This is why she didn't want to get married.

She was spiraling, her anger out of control. She had kept her shit mostly together through the entire Randall situation. But this was too much. This wasn't just her boss.

This was her life partner. The person she was supposed to be able to trust the most in the whole wide fucking world. And she couldn't. She couldn't trust him to not stab her in her soft underbelly of financial security.

She should slash his fucking tires.

But then she would just have to pay for new ones.

Where would he get the money to pay off the debt? He had no income to secure a loan with a decent interest rate to pay it off. She would have to co-sign for it and would wind up paying for it anyway.

How did normal people deal with this? It had to happen all the time. Did they just declare bankruptcy?

Kate had the money to cover the fifty-thousand-dollar debt. She could cash out some LampLight stock. The precious stock she had been slowly vesting. Her money. Her nest egg. Her blood, sweat, and tears at work.

The pain of not getting a bonus or stock in this year's review cycle hit her again. If she sold her stock and paid James' debt, she would get absolutely nothing out of it and again, James would get everything. All the toys, gear, trips, and meals with friends. And she would be left with a smaller portfolio, farther away from her goal. *What the absolute fuck?*

It would be just her luck to have the stock continue to go up – that was opportunity cost she would never get back.

She couldn't stay with him. He would have to leave. Move in with his brother. Get a new girlfriend. She didn't care. He just couldn't be with her. She was worried that *she* wouldn't be a good partner. That she wasn't marriage material. And now look at them.

How could she have been so dumb? Why did she marry him? If they hadn't gotten married, she could have just kicked him out. But not anymore. At least she had her pre-nup.

Would it stand up in court? Was he so far in debt he would challenge the legality of the document? She wouldn't put anything past him after this breach of trust.

A passing car forced Kate to halt her angry march up the hill.

She realized she was out of breath. In her anger, she had picked up speed and didn't even notice.

She couldn't stay this angry. That didn't serve anyone, especially her. A heavy sigh emptied her chest, and her shoulders lowered a couple of inches. *It's just money.* She would get through it.

*Right.* She felt the slap of lying to herself. She tried again. *Money doesn't equal happiness.* The words sounded hollow in her ears. The money grubber in her brain responded with Weird Al lyrics:

> You're dead for a real long time
> You just can't prevent it
> So if money can't buy happiness
> I guess I'll have to rent it

The rest of the theme song from *Johnny Dangerously* continued to play in her mind as she refocused on a slower walk up the hill.

She was spinning. She could process her anger later. Right now, she had to figure out a plan to stop the monetary hemorrhage. They were married and tied financially.

At least for now.

Every day with a credit card balance meant more money in interest and fees. She had to stop the bleeding and then triage the relationship.

Kate would stop paying James a replacement salary. She would make him close all his credit cards except one. It would have a low credit limit. He would have to give her access so she could see his expenses. She would take him off her credit card. She could control his spending through brute force.

But *fuck*, she didn't want to live that way, mistrusting and policing. That was no way to have a relationship of equals. *But they weren't equals.*

All he did was prove he couldn't be a trusted financial partner.

James had to get a job. Period. If they even had a chance of staying together, she needed a financial partner as well as a life partner.

She loved him. He provided a lot of non-monetary benefits. He was super fun to hang out with. He took care of her. He took care of the house. He was an animal in bed.

Were these enough reasons to keep him around?

Nope.

She had entangled her monetary health with his and he killed it. She had enough problems with the lack of a bonus and no stock. He was supposed to help make things better, not worse.

What was she going to do?

*Leave him.* She started to picture her life without him. Without the financial struggle. He was way more expensive than she was. She had been such a tight wad before she knew him. Always saving. Always squirreling everything away for a rainy day.

She could go back to that world.

He was more of a spend-it-now type. Whenever she didn't want to buy something or take a trip, he would yell "YOLO! You only live once" and she would usually acquiesce.

Her bank balance was smaller than she wanted it to be, but it was because she had lived a little in the last five years. Not too much, though.

She still kept a tight lid on the money because she wanted the security. She wanted the foundation so she could pursue her dream of being an author.

But now he took it way too far.

What did he expect? Did he think she'd just cave and cover his debt? While she supported his extravagant lifestyle?

That was asking too much. He couldn't have his cake and eat it too. He needed to step the fuck up or he was out of there. Maybe she needed to be out of there anyway.

She made it to the top of the hill. She had to take a break and catch her breath. In more ways than one.

How would she afford this extra expense?

She would pay it off for him and then kick him the fuck out.

She took a breath.

He didn't have a way to cover the debt. And he quit his job because she told him she'd support him. Well, the support stopped here. Five thousand a month for six months was one thing. Fifty grand on top of that was another.

One payment and done. He would be on his own. She would think of it like the cost of her freedom. She would pay off his debt and kick him out.

She didn't need him and his shitty financial management. She didn't need anyone. She had been right for the first forty-six years.

That fifty thousand dollars along with the missed bonus and stock meant another year of working. Another year of slaving away on other peoples' priorities instead of her own. Another year back from pursuing her own dreams. And all because she got married.

2016 was just a shit year she had to put behind her and move on. Shitty marriage, shitty boss, and a shitty career.

*Now what?*

## Chapter 37

Would she really kick him out or was that just her anger talking?

Would it be so bad to just work a few additional years? Maybe if she changed her goal of retiring and pushed it out to fifty-five. That wouldn't be so bad. She would still have plenty of time to be an author. Later. That would let some pressure off.

And there was a monetary benefit as well. LampLight had a benefit that if you stayed for at least ten years and hit the ripe old age of fifty-five, all your future stock grants vested immediately. She knew it was a way to push out older talent, but if she could just extend her retirement date out by three years, she could make it all work.

She could cover James' debt, still have some fun, and retire at fifty-five. That was plenty young enough to do what she wanted. Yeah, that was her new plan. Fifty-five. Her dreams would have to wait so she could cover James' debt.

Their relationship was worth protecting.

. . .

KATE'S BREATHING was back to normal as she crossed the street on her return home.

The warmth of the condo greeted her as she opened the front door. "Are you here?" Kate called out to James.

"Yeah, upstairs in the office." James was at his computer. "Feeling better?"

James' question annoyed her. It wasn't like she had a cold or something. She had a husband who royally fucked up. "I'm okay." Kate sighed and then charged ahead. "Have you closed your credit cards?"

"No, not yet. You can't have a balance when you close them. I need to pay them off before I can close out."

Duh. Kate hadn't thought of that in her rage. "That makes sense." She braced herself for the answer to her next question. "What's the final amount to get to a zero balance? I'll go write you a check." She had a glimmer of hope that James had been estimating earlier and it was actually lower than fifty thousand.

"I totaled it all up while you were gone. It's actually sixty-four, not the fifty I told you."

The rage returned. With a vengeance.


"SIXTY-FOUR. You just increased the amount by let's see…" Kate did the math in her head. "Twenty-eight percent. And you just casually throw that out without any preparation?" The calm that Kate worked so hard to create disappeared. "I can't even look at you right now." Kate turned on her heel and stormed out of the room.

Why was she with him? She had just told him how upset she was. And he glibly stated the additional expense now that he had *done the math*?

How could she be clearer with him? He should have sat her down and held her hand. Said things like he's sorry to make it even worse, but the number went up and here are the eight jobs he applied for while she was out.

*Then*, she could have handled it. Not when he just tossed it out there like it was no big deal. She could buy herself a lot of fun stuff or jet off to Spain with her friends like James or anything else she wanted with that money.

But she was supposed to just add it onto a check to the credit card company? What the fuck?

Of course, she thought all that while she pulled out her check book and wrote a check for sixty-four thousand dollars.

*Wait a minute.* She didn't even trust him to pay the credit card companies. She couldn't just hand him the check. What if he didn't do what she asked with it? Wow, her trust was really gone.

Could she get it back?


SHE KNEW IT WAS DANGEROUS, but she had to share this anger with him. It was new territory as the constant pleaser. But this went from annoying to abusive. It wasn't fair that she was carrying it all herself and he just expected her to write him a check.

"James, could you come in here." Kate called him into her office across the hall. She was very glad they each had their own spaces in the condo.

"Uh, hi." James stood sheepishly at the door, waiting for Kate to speak.

"I don't want to just give you a check."

"I understand." James looked panicked.

"No, I don't think you do, so I want to spell it out." Kate could feel the creases on her forehead and remembered her mother telling her not to frown so much because they would get stuck like that. This definitely felt like a frown-worthy moment. "I'll give you the money, but I literally don't trust you to take the check and use it to pay off the debt."

"Oh."

"Yeah, 'oh' is right." Kate couldn't keep the sarcasm from her voice. She had stayed cool for round one but couldn't for round two. "I don't know how to come back from this. Every minute we sit here, your debt grows from high interest rates, so I need to pay that off before we can have a productive conversation about going forward. How will you prove to me you paid off your cards, or do I need to do it myself?"

"I'll do it. Once I have the money, you can watch me send the payments in electronically from my bank account. You can stand over my shoulder. When the balance is zero, you can watch me close them. Meanwhile, I'll freeze the cards. I know I fucked up bigtime and the onus is on me to rebuild your trust. I'll do anything I need to do to get that back. Anything."

"Okay, here it is. To be clear, if you don't do what we just agreed, you're out. It's over. No more chances. I've told you I love you unconditionally. But if you fuck this up, I'll love you unconditionally from a distance."

It felt really bad to say that. Her nature was to be kind and smooth things over, not to threaten. She waited for the sense of accomplishment to overtake the guilt she felt at being mean, but it didn't come.

"Understood." James knelt at her feet while Kate sat at her desk. It made her uncomfortable for him to present himself that way. He took her hand. "Katiebug, there are no words to describe how much I hate myself right now or the horror I've felt at my behavior. I never thought I'd be this guy, but here I am. I'll do what you need. Counseling, getting a job, anything. Thank you for being so calm about this. I can only imagine how angry and hurt you are. Thank you for not making me feel even worse."

"You're welcome. Now go deposit that check and start the process."

"I will. Just one word change – this will *end* the process. It will not happen again. I promise." James held her gaze.

"Okay." Kate looked away, unable to look at him kneeling in front of her any longer.

She still wasn't sure they were going to survive this.

▭

KATE LAY in bed that night listening to James snore lightly beside her. It was going to be a rough few months. It wasn't enough that she had the fallout from Randall to deal with. Now she had to also work through rebuilding trust with James.

Could she? Or was the hurt too deep? How would she even know? How would she find out?

It would certainly be cheaper to just write the check,

kick him out, and tell him he had to pay her back over the next two years once he got a job.

He could stay with his brother for free for a while. She certainly wouldn't be the one to move out. She couldn't work from Chicago at Nina's apartment. She and her sister would be at each other's throats after a week anyway.

She loved the Steak and Bourbon ladies but wasn't close enough with any of them to just move in. Plus it was *her* condo.

She would make him start applying for jobs immediately. And no more replacement salary. She wasn't excited about that conversation with him either.

The hurt wasn't subsiding. She knew there was more to life than money, but at this moment, knowing it and believing it were two different things.

——————————

## Chapter 38

——————————

Kate was embarrassed to talk to her friends about this, but the best thing about having close friends was the no judgment zone they provided for each other.

She knew she could trust them. She couldn't trust her husband anymore, but she could trust her girls.

She invited Lesley and Melanie out for happy hour.

They met at the Rat's Nest because it was Melanie's favorite. Both Lesley and Melanie lived on the east side, so the trip to Renton was easy for them.

Melanie was parking her white SUV as Kate approached the door. They grabbed a seat after a quick hug and ordered their drinks.

Moments later, Lesley breezed into the restaurant sporting very short gray hair. She had made the bold move to cut off her long brown waves. The gray made her brown eyes look even bigger.

"Holy crap, what a difference! You look amazing!" Kate couldn't contain her exuberance at the change.

"You think so? I'm still getting used to it. Pretty

dramatic. I kept the hair and donated it to make wigs for cancer patients. A worthy cause."

"You're amazing, Les."

"And think of all the money I'll save on shampoo. But enough about me. What're we drinking?" Lesley asked with mock seriousness.

"Mel has her Jack and Coke and I have my bubbly."

"Bubbly sounds good." She pointed to Kate's glass and the server nodded.

"How's work going for you?" Kate asked.

"Work is work." Lesley shed her light jacket as she talked, still needing it in the late June rain. "This asshat I work with was talking through action items from our year-end review, and that jerk from the application platform team said, 'Okay, now let's get on those actions like a tall dog.' No one knew what he meant. Brad and I IMed a few interesting interpretations back and forth, but we really had no idea. He had to have meant something sexual, right?"

"Yeah," Melanie said. "That's just gross. How do these guys stay employed?"

"Seventeen years at LampLight and still going strong," Lesley replied. "How are the stores treating you?"

"Melanie was just talking about having to fire someone when you got here, Les."

Melanie picked up the story. "You wouldn't believe it. We just sent out a bunch of new products with labels all over them saying 'do not open until Thursday' and what do you think happened? Two store managers opened the boxes."

"Do you hire store managers who can't read?"

"No, they said they just wanted to be prepared for the launch. We had to fire both of them. It was really rough, because they had good intentions." Melanie looked like the decision hit her hard.

"Oh man, that's tough, but you had no choice. Product secrecy is so important. And that's the policy. It's too bad they couldn't get a warning first."

"Nope, it's a no tolerance policy coming straight from the President of the Product division. My hands were tied."

"What's the latest on that promo, Mel? I mean, if you're making these tough calls, they should be promoting you." Lesley was always the pragmatic one.

"Yeah, I keep thinking that if I just do a good job, they'll promote me."

That one lit Kate up. "There are so many people, especially women, who think that way. It's not going to happen without a strategy. Ask your boss what it would take to get promoted. Then, ask if it's okay to come back with a plan for how you'll demonstrate what she says you have to do and show her you're ready."

"Huh," Melanie said. "It's just that easy?"

"If she's a good manager, it is," Kate answered. "She probably already wants to promote you due to your awesomeness but doesn't know how to communicate that up the chain to her boss. Make it easy for her by giving her the answer."

"Wow. I never thought of it that way. I thought I had to convince her."

Lesley added to Kate's comments. "You do. Step one is to deliver. You've done that. But then there's step two, which can be kind of annoying, but is critical. If you and your boss are the only two people who think you should be promoted, it's not going to happen."

"I don't understand. My boss is the one who has to believe in me."

"Yes and no. She needs her boss to agree as well." Lesley pointed with a piece of free popcorn from the table. "How much visibility into your work does Kristen have?"

"My skip-level boss? None, really. I just get my work done and keep my head down. Isn't that enough?"

"It should be, but it's not. You have to get visibility up the chain. Come up with a reason to have a one on one with Kristen. You can't just ask her admin for a one-on-one meeting. He won't do it. You have to go directly to her, but you have to have a business reason. And you have to tell your boss you're going to do it before you actually contact the big boss."

"This is all so complicated," Melanie said.

"Not really, it's just business. You need to give Kristen a reason to talk to you. Aren't you almost finished with that vendor strategy overhaul project?" Kate remembered a story Melanie had shared at the last brunch.

"Yeah, we just hit the second major milestone. Once we get legal approval, we just have to roll it out and train people on the new approach," Melanie answered.

"That's it. Schedule a meeting to walk Kristen through the recommendation and pretend you need her guidance on something."

"Oh, okay, so then I do what she says." Melanie looked thoughtful.

"No," Kate said gently. "You tell her that you're stuck

and then offer her two paths that you could take. You explain the path you want to take and why and then you ask her opinion."

"But then I'm not really asking for her guidance," Melanie said, confused.

"Exactly." Lesley pointed at her with her glass. "You're showing her you own your decisions and want to be accountable for the outcome. Otherwise, you're just asking her to do the thinking. If she doesn't agree with your path, she'll tell you. But, I bet she'll agree."

"And then, you'll have an extra twenty minutes to talk about you," Kate finished with a flourish of her hands.

"Wow. That's kind of manipulative, isn't it?"

"I wouldn't call it that. I would call it knowing how to play the game. The management chain wants to reward the right talent. You just have to make sure they see you."

"Got it. I'll get on that Monday morning," Melanie said. "There's a reason your team loves you so much, Kate. You, too Lesley."

"I learned from the best." She clinked glasses with Kate.

"Whew, that was a long time talking about me." Melanie slapped her free hand on the table, careful to not spill her drink. "What's new in Kate-land?"

"Actually, I could use some advice."

"Ooooh, I love giving advice." Melanie leaned in while Lesley signaled for another round.

"This is really embarrassing, but my James re-employment plan has backfired. Big time."

"Oh no. He never wants to go back to work?"

"We haven't even gotten to that part yet. He racked up

a ton of credit card debt and has only been paying the minimums for months."

"Oh shit. That really builds up." Melanie made her famous "that's rude" face. "Didn't he learn that in his twenties?"

"Exactly. Now I need to write a huge check to get him out of debt."

"Wait." Lesley looked confused. "Why do *you* have to get him out of debt? Why can't he just get a job and pay it off."

"Because it'll just keep growing if we don't pay it off and then we'll be out even more money. It's a lot."

"Kate, I love you because you're kind and sweet and a problem solver. This is not your problem to solve. It's his." Lesley turned quite serious.

"I know, but –"

Melanie jumped in. "There's no but here, Kate."

"We're married, so this is our problem."

"Okay, I've registered my discomfort with this line of discussion, but I'm here to support you. What're you going to do?" Lesley asked.

"First, I wanted to kick him out. But then instead, I cashed out stock and wrote him a check. I don't know what happens next. He's totally blown my trust."

"Yeah, and then some." Melanie nodded.

"I don't know that I have the tools to rebuild it," Kate admitted. "With all my work stress, James was the one thing that was going well. He was working on figuring out what's next and being super helpful around the house."

"Do you want a really expensive housewife?" Melanie

asked. "I mean, it's worked for a ton of people over the decades."

"That part is actually nice." Kate smiled.

"Did he tell you why he did it?" Lesley asked.

"We haven't gotten to that part yet. After the big reveal, I was focused on solving the problem."

"I have a theory." Melanie raised her hand like she was in class. "While I was married to my first husband, we did some counseling, and it all came down to two truths according to the therapist. Men want to be admired, and women want to feel safe. My theory is that James wanted to be the big man on campus and treat himself and his friends well so they admired him. Of course, you want the safety net of money to feel safe, and the two worlds collided."

Kate sat back to absorb that. Money *was* safety to her. Was that why she was so hurt by this? Growing up, her mother used money as a weapon for affection and punishment. If you did what she wanted, she gave you money. If you did something she didn't like, she would take it away. Her aunts and uncles were always feuding over money. She couldn't count the times they had to do what her great-grandmother wanted because "she controlled the money."

She knew that underpinned her deep-seated desire to have enough money that she never had to rely on anyone else again. And James had violated that.

Lesley interrupted her thoughts. "In my own counseling, I had a few similar discussions. I like to help people, and I know you do, too. But my therapist helped me see that by helping people, especially when money was involved, it was really about control. I wanted them to do something. What're the chances that some of that is going on?"

"Whoa, that's deep. Let me process that." Kate started thinking out loud. "I know I have control issues about money. Having money means I'm empowered to make my own decisions. But I'm now wondering if encouraging James to take a break from work was actually me trying to control him. Wow." Kate looked down and scratched the back of her head. "I'm having a moment here." Her friends stayed quiet while she thought about it. "I wonder if I have some male characteristics."

Lesley and Melanie both laughed. "Of course you do. You have to in order to succeed in the workplace like you have."

"What I mean is, I want to be admired. I want to be respected. I give a lot of money to my family and a lot of gifts to my friends. Do I do that so they admire me, like I'm so cool because I can do that? Shit, am I just as bad as my mother?"

"Hold your horses there. I don't remember inviting Moaning Marilyn to this table. You're nothing like her because you don't manipulate or lord it over people. Your heart is in the right place."

Her friends knew her very well, but she could admit to herself she liked supporting James. She had thought it was about making him happy and giving him the freedom to explore, but was there a teeny tiny element that made him beholden to her? Was this situation her making?"

"I thought we were just having a drink, but the two of you are blowing my fucking mind." Kate admitted.

"That's what friends are for." Lesley sang it like the old Dionne Warwick song.

## Chapter 39

"Something's up that I want to talk to you about." Kate had an uneasy feeling based on the look Charlie gave her when he showed up at her door.

Kate was glad for the distraction. Her mind kept getting pulled back to her situation with James and the anger she felt. She didn't want to deal with that during working hours.

"Come on in and sit down."

He heaved a heavy sigh as he sat. Kate's Spidey Sense tingled – in a bad way. "Remember how I told you I was retiring in eighteen months? Well, that timeline just got accelerated."

"Are you okay, Charlie?"

"You're so sweet. I love that your first question is about me. I'll be fine. They're giving me a boatload of money to retire early. This is about you."

She was his successor. Why did a crackle of dread snake down her spine? It was probably just a flashback to the same conversation with Julia. This one would be different.

Charlie continued. "Dan and I had a detailed chat about you, and we agree you're the best candidate to be my replacement."

Relief filled her. "That's great to hear. What's the next step?"

"We're going to keep it quiet for a while, but everything is in motion and the new org should be locked in the next two weeks. Just a few loose ends to close up. Your super strong performance over the last few months made the decision easy and the transition will be even easier. My team loves you. You're by far the best people manager on the team."

"That would be you."

"Well, I'm leaving, so you can have the top spot. It's an incredibly under-valued skillset at LampLight and one Dan's team sorely needs. Maybe you can teach Dan and Bobby a few things."

"I'll try." Kate was filled with hope. It oozed out of her pores. "Will it come with that promotion?" She couldn't help but ask.

"Oh yes, definitely."

"That's amazing, Papi Chuck." In a flash, Kate's money worries were dramatically lessened. With a promo, there would be a raise.

"And I've put you in for a Special Stock Award. They can't expect you to get no stock at year-end and then stick around to do this really tough job. They aren't idiots, after all. Okay, got to run."

She sat for a moment, just absorbing the great news.

With the money issue off the table, she could focus on whether or not other parts of her relationship with James were strong enough and important enough to her to stay with him.

It was really happening. Her hard work was going to pay off. She just needed to work through the next couple of weeks and everything would work out.


"KATE, why don't you walk us through your strategy for that?" Charlie started taking more and more of a backseat in meetings, letting Kate be in the spotlight and lead the tough conversations. It was like he was slowly saying goodbye to the team while pushing Kate to the forefront. She appreciated him so much.

Kate walked through her plan and feedback from the field.

"Great work, Kate. Looks like we're going to wrap up the content early. Kate, would you mind staying behind for a couple of minutes? Class dismissed." The group laughed at Dan's joke as they filed out.

"What can I do for you, Dan?" Kate asked when the room was empty. She hoped it was about the re-org.

"I wanted to give you an update on the org changes that are coming down." She smiled in anticipation. "I know the original plan was to have you take over Charlie's team, but there's been a change."

Kate's heart sank. She stayed quiet. Maybe it was a good change? She tried to keep hope alive.

"We gave it some more thought and I've decided to

collapse Charlie's team and Bobby's team into one big team with Bobby in charge."

*Did that mean she would be following Charlie out the door?* she wondered to herself.

Dan continued. "You're so good at change management. I'd like you to focus on that full time and let Bobby handle strategy going forward."

No. No. No. Sure, that was part of her job, but she only did that to make sure her strategy was implemented. "Dan, just because I'm good at it doesn't mean I love doing it." He looked at her blankly, so she continued. "I was brought here to lead program strategy and have been doing a good job of that. Why the change?"

"I like you, so I'll give it to you straight. You aren't ready. In talking to Randall, I learned about some of your missteps and poor judgment calls in your last role. I haven't seen any evidence of that here, but it's only been a few months. You have a home here leading change management."

*He talked to Randall? Would that guy never quit?* "I'll think about it."

"Think about it? From what I've heard, you might want to adjust that attitude and be glad you aren't on the chopping block."

Kate's mouth almost dropped open in shock. She had the sensation of floating above herself looking down at the two of them sitting at the table, like this was happening to someone else. Someone's voice said, "thank you." It took Kate a moment to realize it was hers.

Somehow, she managed the grace to get up and leave the room without falling. She walked past her office and just kept walking. She needed air. She needed to get the fuck out of there.

Charlie called out to her as she passed his office. She didn't stop. Halfway down the stairs, he caught up with her.

"Did he give you the good news?"

"Good news? You think this is good news?"

"Yeah, you being my successor is great news."

He didn't know. And she had to be the one to tell him.

"Let's keep going outside. I'll tell you what he said."

Kate filled him in after they passed the smokers outside the door.

"No fucking way. That slimebag." Kate had never seen Charlie in a rage before. "That lying sack of shit. He played us. And I fell for it. Did he tell you why he had a change of heart?"

"He said he spoke to Randall who talked him out of giving me the opportunity."

"Randall? Dan doesn't give two shits about Randall. He's using that as an excuse so he doesn't have to take accountability for what he wanted to do all along. Did you notice how Bobby switched from lovey dovey to being a dick to you? It was all his move to discredit you to Dan. I'm so angry. I don't know what I'm going to do."

"You? You're going to ride off into the sunset on a big pile of cash. What the fuck am I going to do?" Kate couldn't hold it in any longer.

The stress of the James situation, the lack of a bonus, Bobby calling her names, the seesaw of thinking she would be fine only to have the opportunity yanked away from her, and Dan telling her to be grateful she had a job overwhelmed her. "I'm certainly not going to be the change management bitch. I mean, it's important work, but Bobby will make terrible business decisions, and I can't change manage my way out of shitty design. Fuck me."

They had made it to a bench on LampLight's campus. Kate's arms were folded across her chest and Charlie had his head in his hands. Kate was briefly concerned about what people would think was happening as they walked by.

"Fuck this place." Charlie said through his hands.

"PAPI CHUCK IS RIGHT. You have to get out of there." James was emphatic. "When are you going to admit that this systemic sexism has nothing to do with your actual capabilities and potential? This is unbelievable. You're telling yourself a story that you can get through it. Stop. Just stop."

Kate fell back on the sofa and groaned. "This is just so awful. Every time I get close, it's snatched away. The only common thread is me. I'm terrible. Yes, my teams love me, but my management chain rarely does. I'm always too outspoken, or too nice, or too something." Kate felt her tears trickle down her cheeks as she kept her head tipped back.

"No! You're just too female. LampLight keeps promoting insecure men who can't handle strong women. It's ruining what was once a great company! It's time to get out."

"Oh James. I thought we were getting to the light at the end of the tunnel, but it's just an oncoming train." The tears continued. She could taste their saltiness on her tongue.

"Kate, I get it. I love you. I respect you. I want to do everything I can to rebuild the trust I broke. But I have to say this even if you don't want to hear it. Just. Walk. Out. They don't deserve your tears. Or your big brain. Or the value you deliver. They don't deserve you."

"But it makes the fighting I've done for the last ten years absolutely meaningless. If I give up now, they win."

"Win what? The asshole Olympics? Other companies will fall all over you with offers. Go find out."

Kate sat up and wiped her tears. James calmed down enough to join her on the sofa and put his arm around her. "You don't understand, James. I would walk away from over a million dollars of unvested stock."

"Then walk away. You'll make more somewhere else."

Kate sat up, a defiant look on her face. "No. I'm not leaving the company without a fight."

Chapter 40

"Here's what you do. We write what's called a demand letter." Kate had asked Julia for Gertie's number so she could talk to the lawyer about options. "It states the legal basis for what you think he did wrong."

"Is that like suing LampLight?"

"No. That's what's great about a demand letter. It comes on legal letterhead, but it's just a statement of your *intention* to sue if you don't get what you want. We'll write it together. Then, you'll take the language from it and put it in an email you send to them first. If you don't like their response, then I follow up on my legal letterhead and they see you're serious."

"What could go wrong?" Kate asked.

"I'm glad you're thinking through the downside. Unlike actually suing, there's no case, so there's no public record of the complaint. That's the good news. Things could get really uncomfortable for you for the next few months while the process works itself through. You may wind up not wanting to work there anymore."

"That's big, but it's worth the risk."

"Okay, so the next step is to figure out what is actually illegal versus just annoying. It's not against the law to be an asshole."

That made Kate giggle. "It would certainly keep lawyers busy if it were."

"Oh, I'm plenty busy. Was there anything that created a hostile work environment or things Randall said that were discriminatory?"

"He called me a lot of names and told me to be quiet a lot, but nothing that I could prove. They would just say I was misinterpreting."

"This one might be harder to prove because you're a white woman, but was there anything racially motivated?"

Kate thought about it. "Well, this whole thing started because Randall bullied a Latino guy on my team and spoke Portuguese to him even through he's from Guatemala. When this kid pushed back, Randall accused him of being ashamed of his heritage."

"Bingo. I mean, that's terrible." Gertie corrected herself before continuing. "But we could use that. You reported him for racially-based harassment and then he retaliated. Now we're getting somewhere."

"But that's not even the bad stuff he does. And Lamp-Light already refused to investigate that."

"Doesn't matter. That's the *illegal* thing. And the rest of the behavior is likely to come out if they investigate the matter, which they'll do if the demand letter has merit. Let's get the details down in writing, and we'll be in business. Then we can walk through the timeline."

This was really happening. She was taking action.

Nothing might come of it, but she would only be out five hundred dollars in legal fees. It was worth a try.

"One of the important parts of the demand letter is a request for compensation for damages." Gertie was good at explaining the process. "This should be a big number because you'll never get more than what's in the demand letter. It should also be based on logic and math. The good news is that once the demand letter has been sent, the number and how you reached it are immaterial. It's just a requirement to state the value of the damages."

"That makes a lot of sense."

"So how much are we talking here?"

"Let me play with that for a minute." Kate started thinking.

"Get out those great math skills and get creative!"

"Two point two million." Kate walked Gertie through her math. If she had gotten a stock grant in line with previous stock grants, it would have been worth three-hundred and forty thousand dollars. If you follow the growth line of the stock for the last four years and forecast it out for the next four years, it would be worth one point six million. Kate added a hundred thousand for her typical bonus. She also added the missed money from not being promoted on hire in her current role. That would have been another fifty thousand in salary plus at least three hundred thousand more stock at year-end. Apply the same out year vesting calculation, and voila! Two point two million buckeroos.

"On it. I'll get you a draft of the letter. Keep fighting the good fight, Kate. We'll talk soon."

. . .

"WE COULD HAVE a lot of fun with two point two million." James smiled at Kate. "But we would spend it wisely and make all decisions jointly," he hurried to add.

"We would never get that much, if we get anything."

"Who's this 'we' you keep saying? This would be all *your* money. You've done all the hard work. You've suffered at the hands of idiots. You covered my debt."

"You know what I mean. I'd be happy with the two hundred and fifty thousand I missed out on from my stock. It was really painful doing all that math. One of the views I created for Gertie showed my compensation over the last five years and the nosedive it took because of Randall. History should count for something. It was hard to see that in black and white, but it certainly substantiates the story that Randall retaliated. I couldn't have just suddenly become an asshole."

"There's only one part of you that's an asshole, Katiebug."

Kate's face wrinkled in disbelief. "Uh, I'm looking for support here, not to be picked on."

"It's your asshole, of course. That's the only part of you that's an asshole." James laughed heartily at his joke.

Kate could only keep her bland face and raised eyebrow for so long before she laughed, too. *Punny James strikes again.*

"A NEW TEAM will be created by merging Bobby and Charlie's teams into one happy family that will be led by Bobby." Dan had called an all-hands meeting to announce the new organization. "There will be a few other changes. The program strategy team that currently sits in Charlie's org will move to report directly to Bobby. The part of Bobby's team that does field landing will move under Kate, and she will lead all our change management and field landing efforts."

Kate felt her team's eyes on her. Like Julia before him, Charlie hadn't made it a secret that she was his successor and now that wasn't happening.

Dan didn't even mention Charlie's departure. It was a huge omission.

Sunita raised her hand. Dan pointed at her. "Question in the front, go ahead."

"What's Charlie's new role?" Sunita asked.

*Good for her,* Kate thought.

"Oh, I should have mentioned that. Charlie will be leaving LampLight to pursue his personal passions." That was tantamount to saying he'd been kicked out. This team was not born yesterday.

Sunita looked right at Kate. Kate kept her gaze level and neutral. All eyes then shifted to Charlie who shrugged his shoulders and pursed his lips like it was no big deal.


THEY LEFT that meeting and went right into an All-Hands led by Bobby. "Don't think of it as me winning the role instead of Charlie. Think of it like a whole new job I just happened to get instead of him."

Change management was not Bobby's forte. Kate internally recoiled at his message. Putting it that way made it sound exactly like he had won. *Dickhead.* "Any questions?"

The room was silent. That's what happened when you hadn't created a culture of trust. She knew there'd be plenty of questions in her team meeting.

She braced herself for it.


"I'D BE SO mad if I were you." Tamar's hands were by her ears. Kate had created an environment where her team could speak their truth. Usually, she loved it, but it was hard to keep the façade up when she agreed with them.

All eyes were on her in her all-hands meeting and she had to keep going. The business and the team needed her to be cool.

"That's kind of you, Tamar, but I have a great job and an important spot on the team. I get to keep doing the important work of landing the strategy."

"Cut the crap, Kate." Jacob spoke up. "This is bullshit and you know it. You're ten times the strategist that Bobby is. I heard you didn't even get a shot, and that Dan and Bobby made the decision behind closed doors."

"I can't comment on rumors, Jacob. All I know is that we have work to do. Am I disappointed? Yes. Is it going to stop us from doing a great job? Hell no." *How had Jacob found that out?*

The grumbling subsided and the room was quiet. They seemed satisfied for now.

"The new org structure goes into effect immediately. Is

everyone clear on their new reporting structure, roles, and responsibilities?"

AFTER THE MEETING, Kate hit send on the non-legal version of the demand letter, explaining her situation and request. She and Gertie had added the additional retaliatory steps of Randall telling Dan not to give her Charlie's job. Even if Charlie was right and that wasn't true, it added more fuel to the fire.

It was the same content that would get turned into a demand letter if she didn't get the desired response, but it was just an email. No lawyer involved. She sent it to Ryan, her new HR business partner.

Game on.

## Chapter 41

"I'm so sorry you had to deal with all that." Kate was talking to Ryan from HR. "I was just heartbroken when I read your email. You were on such a strong trajectory on this team. I had no idea any of this was going on."

Kate's antennae were up. Ryan led HR for Dan's organization. He was instrumental in locking the performance review model. He was lying. Typical HR protect-the-company's-ass bullshit.

"Thanks for that, Ryan." Kate kept her answers short.

"I'm going to personally take this to Workplace Investigations to make sure this matter is dealt with by them. What was the name of the original investigator who declined to investigate?"

"It's all in the email, Ryan. Dawn Houser. I included her email as an attachment."

"Let's talk about happier things. Your new role sounds great. Very important work for you and your team. I hope you're jazzed about it."

*Yeah, really jazzed,* Kate thought. If jazzed meant ready to torch the place.

———

"THAT SOUNDS EXHAUSTING." James was on his best behavior and handed her a glass of bubbly. "I did a bunch of research and found this bubbly for nine dollars a bottle. I usually buy you the good stuff, but I know you don't like to waste the money by not finishing the bottle. This way, if you only have a glass, you'll feel okay."

Other women might be pissed he was economizing on something for her, but Kate felt seen.

"That's great, James. Thank you. I know you're trying hard to take care of me and make things better for us. I see and appreciate your efforts." Kate flashed back to Melanie saying that men like to be admired, so she was practicing saying that out loud to James. He beamed at her. Melanie was onto something. They still had a long way to go.

"I'm all packed and ready to go." Kate could feel James' excitement, even though the reason he was going was not a good one. She needed a few days on her own.

She was still very angry about the credit card debt and wanted some time to process it without him.

She offered to foot the bill for a long weekend motor-cycle ride. James, Trevor, and Ross were going to keep it on the inexpensive side by camping most nights. She was working hard to not use money as a weapon like her mother had when she was a kid.

Turning into her mother was her greatest fear. Even worse than being broke.

Understanding the motivations for Kate's actions helped her identify patterns that matched the shitty behavior of her mother and stop it.

Some might say she was being a pushover, a word that had been used to describe her a lot over the years. She preferred to think of it as rebuilding trust with her partner and rejecting destructive behavior.

It had allowed her to have very honest conversations with James about each of their motivations which had brought them closer together. They weren't all the way fixed, but trust was slowly rebuilding.

Four days apart might help them, too.

"I'll be very careful about money."

"I know you will. I'll foot the bill for one nice dinner out for the three of you. Other than that, please have them pay their own way."

"You bet. That was already my plan. I have some new skills to learn like not jumping on the bill when it arrives. I've talked to the guys about it, and they actually said they were surprised at how often I paid and that it made them uncomfortable. Good learning for me."

"Yeah, most people want to pay their own way." James gave her a really sad look. "That came out wrong. I just mean I know how they feel. I wouldn't like it if I had a friend who always paid. I'd feel like they were trying to buy my friendship."

"Noted. It just took me a second because that's clearly a sore spot. Please don't poke at it. I just got another 'thanks but no thanks' at a motorcycle gear company that advertised for a program manager. I want to do something that makes me happy. I don't want to just get a paycheck at a company that I don't believe in."

*Like she was doing*, she mentally added to the end of his sentence. She was barely able to keep that inside. She needed these four days apart.

She was different than James but she was taking action. She wasn't prepared to walk out before she had exhausted the possibility of getting paid to leave.

They owed her for the missed opportunities and the missing stock grant and bonus she should have gotten based on the high impact she delivered.

———

STEAK AND BOURBON was well-timed this month. *It was always a good time for Steak and Bourbon*, Kate mused. She had limped along in her new role for a few weeks and needed some girl power to help her get through the next.

This Sunday's menu started with a Bloody Mary bar. A pitcher of virgin mix sat on the counter next to a huge bottle of vodka and a platter of garnishes.

"You sure do spoil us, J-Money." Kate grabbed a long bamboo skewer and started loading it up with shrimp, pickled beans, olives, a lemon wedge, and a cocktail onion. She stuck a piece of candied bacon into the glass and called it done.

"Why do you call her J-Money?" Akiko asked around a mouthful of garnish.

"We were joking around one day giving each other rapper names." Kate explained.

Julia jumped in. "Kate was Girl Cares-a-Lot, like Sir

Mix-a-Lot. Oh, and Susan was Lil' Sue. Who else? Oh right, Jed was Jedinem."

"And because Julia's the pricing goddess, I wanted to come up with something that honored that without being gendered or religious." Kate stopped for a spicy sip of her drink. "I landed on J-Money. Which is, of course, spelled like the letter J and a dollar sign."

"Mine's the only one that stuck." Julia sounded proud.

"Yeah, because no one else liked theirs."

"And maybe because you kept it alive, Girl Cares-a-Lot," Julia shot back with a chuckle.

"Speaking of caring, what's the latest from our friends on LampLight's crack HR team?" Gertie sat down with a fresh Bloody Mary.

"It's only been a few weeks since my chat with HR. I haven't heard a peep from the investigations team." Kate was a little uncomfortable talking about this in front of the brunch ladies, but they all knew the story and would hold her confidence. It was the one place, other than with James, she could talk about it.

"Standard delay tactics. Or maybe they just have so many complaints it takes this long to get through them. All those potential clients." Kate laughed as Gertie rubbed her hands together with glee. "Are you ready to move to sending the demand letter on my letterhead?"

"It couldn't hurt."

"Actually, it can. Once you get a lawyer involved, things accelerate. And we could be talking about them making you an offer to leave. Are you ready for that?"

"You know, I really thought I would retire from this place, but at this point, I just don't see a home there."

"Okay then, give me Ryan's email address, and I'll hit send. Well, after I sober up. Great drinks, Julia… I mean J-Money." Gertie made rock and roll signs with her hands while pushing out her lips and shaking her head back and forth in a surprisingly good imitation of a rapper. She was full of surprises. "Time for a refill." Gertie headed back to the Bloody Mary Bar.

Kate met her there and lowered her voice. "How does that payment work? Will you get a third of the settlement if there is one or something like that?"

"We can do it one of two ways. You can keep paying my hourly rate. Or, if you don't want to pay me hourly, I can take a percentage of the settlement."

"I'd rather pay you an hourly rate in case I don't get anything. At least you'd get something. But, that feels unfair, you know, if I actually get a pile of money, you'll miss out."

"You're paying me the rate my company and I set. It's perfectly fair and the way most reputable lawyers work. And it goes both ways. If you don't get anything, I'm still compensated for my time."

"Okay, I feel better. Go for it." They headed back to the table with their full glasses.


"WHILE WE ALL HAVE DRINKS, I have some news to share." Melanie held up her glass. "I took the lovely advice of Kate and Lesley, had a meeting with my boss about my promotion, and now we have a plan! It played out just like they said it would. Next step is a meeting with my boss' boss. I'm on track!"

"Cheers!" Kate loved seeing the glowing smile on Melanie's face. It always warmed her when things worked out for people.

After the celebration died down, Julia piped up. "Okay, ladies, a question. I was reading a romance novel recently, and there was a section from the man's perspective. It was super dramatic and poorly written, but the point was that he could feel the woman's orgasm. There was something about 'feeling her walls clench him tightly' or some shit. Is that a thing?"

Nine pairs of eyes were on her. Brie was the first to speak. "Um, yeah. How did you not know that?"

"That's what Kegels are for," Gertie added.

"I thought those were to help women who had babies tighten up so they wouldn't pee when they laughed." Julia sounded confused.

"That too," Angela was the only mother in the group.

"Does it feel better during an orgasm?"

"Oh yeah. Really, Jules, how did you not know that?" Brie sounded incredulous.

"How did you learn it?" Julia shot back with a raised eyebrow.

"You know, media…" Brie trailed off. "And practice. Pelvic floor health should be taught in school. Totally underrated for men and women."

Everyone laughed.

It struck Kate as a special kind of magic to go from serious work topics to good news about progress toward promotions to pelvic exercises and sex in fifteen minutes of Steak and Bourbon.

She loved these women!

## Chapter 42

"I've got to have the story of that name." Gertie forwarded a copy of the demand letter and accompanying email to Kate. It had Gertie's full name and signature on it. "I thought it was short for Gertrude."

Kate heard a heavy sigh through the phone. "My creative parents, and I'm putting sarcastic air quotes around the word creative, made it up. My grandmother's name was Gertrude and my grandfather's was Bartholomew. Hence, I was named Gertholomew. For the love of shit, why couldn't they have just gone with Jessica?"

"At least you know no one else has the same name. And you needed something exotic to go with Smith." It wasn't the worst name Kate had ever heard. That went to Telmah Hamlet whose parents wanted to name their kid a palindrome.

"Yeah, you try it sometime, Kate. A name everyone can spell."

Kate tried to make it better. "Sometimes people spell it

with a C." This was not helping. "Why don't you use your middle name?"

"Because my other set of grandparents were Vladimir and Regina."

"Regimir?"

"Nope."

"Oh." Kate figured it out but had to wait a moment before she could say it without laughing. She put on a serious tone "So, Gertholomew Vladgina Smith, what's next?"

"Next is that you never call me that again. After that, we wait."

"Got it, Gertie."

---

"ARE YOU KIDDING ME?" Kate was on the phone with an angry Ryan from HR. "We have a chat and then you hit us with a letter from your lawyer?" The previous kindness from Ryan was replaced with anger. "What the heck, Kate?"

"Ryan, it's been three weeks since we talked, and I haven't heard anything. Given that my complaint was brushed aside last time, I don't want that to happen again. I've learned this isn't an isolated incident. I want to protect others from illegal behavior from Randall."

"You could have talked to me before getting a lawyer involved." Kate was astounded at his tone. He sounded positively affronted.

"I did speak with you before I got a lawyer involved." *Take that, you indignant prick.* "I look forward to hearing from the investigations team." Gertie had advised Kate to say as little as possible now that she was involved.

"The investigator was just about to reach out to you. I talked to her yesterday." *How convenient*, Kate thought. Here was the switch Gertie told her about. *Let the games begin.*

"LET'S MAKE A PLAN!" Kate liked to kick meetings off with a bit of fun and frivolity, so she put on her "Let's Make a Deal" voice. She was trying hard to be as normal as possible during this odd phase.

Charlie was gone and the team was still processing his departure. People were watching her reaction to the organizational changes, so it was time to model good leadership behavior. Continuing to act like she had before was important, even though it took more energy.

"The platform roll-out is delayed—"

"Again."

"Thank you, Tamar. Yes, again, but since this isn't our first rodeo, we have our Plan B. Let's dust it off and see if it needs any updating based on our last round of field feedback."

"How can you be so upbeat, Kate?" Jacob asked.

"Because it's just software and policies. No one is dying. No one is shooting at us. Let's keep a positive perspective here, team."

"You know, I used to think your super nice, accommodating, optimistic approach was annoying, no offense." Sunita looked sheepish... for a split second. "But you just keep plugging away. I'm starting to believe I can be more positive, too." That was high praise from the usually pessimistic Sunita.

"Thanks buddy. I won a perseverance award when I was eight for cleaning the most chalkboard erasers using a ShopVac. Someday, I'll win an award for being amazing instead of just persistent." She waited for the laugh, but it didn't come. Realization dawned on her. "Oh, you probably never used chalkboards or had to vacuum the dust out of them. Trust me, it's tedious."

"We'll give you an award for being brilliant." Tamar said. "For teaching us to not be afraid to gather feedback and to co-create with the teams using our stuff. Everything just seems easier now. I wish Papi Chuck was still here to see our successes."

"Thanks, Tamar. Collaboration is tough and taking the repeated kicks can wear you down, but you just keep going, showing progress, and incorporating the field's feedback and they become fans. Basic stakeholder management."

"That we didn't do before. We've learned so much from you." Jacob added.

"And there's more! Let's dig into our Plan B and make sure it shines. Once we're done, does one of you want to take a shot at leading the conversation with the field? I'll take the hits from the bad news of the delay and then hand it off to whoever volunteers to provide the updated plan. Bad news should always come from the manager and good news from the team."

"See? Another thing we've learned. But this time, I'd like to deliver the good and bad news knowing you have my back in case things go sideways."

"I love that, Tamar. Way to step up. You'll do a great job."

They got down into the nitty gritty details to make sure the plan was tight, and Tamar had what she needed to succeed.

This kind of conversation made the waiting game bearable. Kate was continuing to grow and mentor her team while making progress for the business. It refilled her energy coffers enough to sail through the rest of the week. And the continued waiting game.

<hr>

"I'VE GIVEN this a lot of thought, and I have a plan." James greeted her with a big hug when she got to the condo.

"For dinner?" Kate was hungry.

"No. Better. A plan for my next career."

"Oooh, I want to hear all about that. But full disclosure, I won't be able to give you my full attention if I don't eat something first."

The doorbell rang. "Way ahead of you. That's dinner." James collected the Thai delivery and got busy setting out plates and forks.

Kate enjoyed that she didn't have to put thought into dinner. She'd made enough decisions that day. "Okay, tell me about your plan."

"For years, I've been helping friends figure out where to ride their motorcycles all over the west coast. I know routes and bike rental companies, good restaurants, and decent hotels in multiple price ranges. Ever since I went to Spain, I've been thinking I could do what Graham does."

"Be a motorcycle tour guide?"

"More than that. Plan the whole trip for people. Chat with riders about what they want to do and how experienced they are and then set up a package for them. I can do an all-inclusive thing or just give them routes, all at different price points. I bet Julia would help me with what to charge, and you can give me pointers on the operations side."

"That sounds exciting. What would you need to get started?" Kate was concerned there would be a request for funding.

"That's the best part. Graham walked me through how he does it. He works with rental companies and people with rental properties. He doesn't own the bikes or the rental villas, he just arranges it for people. The capital outlay is super small. It's basically my time."

"With the flexibility you're looking for since you'd pick your hours."

"Exactly, and if the people wanted me to join their ride as a guide, I could charge them for that as well as the booking and arranging services. Over time, I could add additional services, and it would give me a way to write-off my own exploration tours as a business expense."

Kate could feel the excitement pumping off him. "I love it! How far have you gotten on the plan?"

"I have a lot more to do, but based on some of the numbers Graham shared with me, I should be able to start making money immediately with a run rate of ten to fifteen thousand within sixth months, and with an investment in marketing, could be looking at thirty to fifty in a year. I know that's less than I used to make, but I have so many ideas for how I could branch out."

"Oh yeah, like additional experiences a group would want, like hot-air ballooning, or a spa day. You could target women's riding groups or add-on events for people in the group who don't ride. Wedding parties, bachelor parties, birthday parties."

"Exactly. And if it failed, we wouldn't be out a whole lot of money."

"Let's not talk about that side of it. You'll be a success." Kate noted she could say things and mean them when they were about other people, yet she wasn't following her own dream. "I'm going to be super real for a moment. This plan also means more time without you contributing financially." They had promised each other honesty and full transparency.

"I thought of that and have a line on a few part-time jobs to tide me over."

Kate was happy to hear that. He was trying to get a job which helped rebuild some of the trust. "And let's see how this whole legal battle plays out. We might not have to worry so much about that." *Who said that?* It took a moment for Kate to realize that those words came out of her mouth.

Was she just trying to make James feel better or was his optimism rubbing off on her? She knew she had to keep going. It was the only way she could feel secure. One day, if his business took off, she would be able to take a break from the grind. But not yet.

"What do you think of this logo?" James slid a piece of

paper across the table at her. It was the acronym YOLO where the letter Os had been turned into the wheels of a motorcycle. The tagline said You Only Live Once. Ride More. YOLO Motorcycle Tours.

"Oh James, it's perfect. I love it! The little spokes on the tires are adorable."

"Adorable really isn't the vibe I'm looking for, but I'll take it."

"You're making progress. That's great."

"Yeah," James nodded. "Progress feels good."

Kate couldn't have agreed more.

# Chapter 43

"The whole thing is blowing up." Tamar looked more upset than Kate had ever seen her, her head shaking as she put her hands in the air. "How can the engineering team just not deliver? And they're acting like they never agreed in the first place. All of those meetings, for nothing."

"It's not that bad. They just aren't delivering *all* the functionality." Kate was annoyed, too, but didn't need to show it to her team.

"But we promised the field an improved experience. And now they'll have to manually enter the same information twice because engineering isn't going to deliver the migration tool."

"They'll deliver it, it'll just be a bit late." Kate realized she was being annoyingly optimistic, kind of like what James did to her while telling a story. She tried a more realistic question. "What if we delay the entire launch until the migration tool is done?"

"Engineering would kill us. You know the pressure

they're under. Amy will start firing people if the roll-out deadline slips again."

Tamar referred to the head of engineering for the entire sales platform. LampLight had a different team for everything. One for building technology, one for creating the plan for what to build, one to implement it, one to use it, and the list went on.

Amy was Bobby and Dan's key stakeholder. She ruled with an iron fist and a culture of fear. Everyone was afraid of her, especially Bobby and Dan.

The project was already about two years behind, so Amy's team kept cutting functionality to make it work. It wasn't that her team was bad, just that their priorities were different. Engineering preferred to turn off tools before new ones were ready.

Kate's team had to show the negative impact on revenue from doing that.

"I hear you, Tamar, but the bottom line is they aren't going to deliver and sent an email telling us instead of having a planning meeting to co-create a new strategy." Kate kept her tone light. "This is what we used to do to the field. Kinda sucks, doesn't it?"

"Yeah." Tamar looked thoughtful. "I see what you did there."

Kate would celebrate that later. "So, we'll hold engineering to the same standard that we hold ourselves. I'll reach out to Amy's Chief of Staff, and we'll get a meeting going."

"It'll take weeks to get that scheduled."

"No it won't. I bet it'll be tomorrow. I'll use the secret

Chief of Staff handshake that means we have to meet now."

IT WORKED. Kate was prepping her slide for the meeting with Amy. She and her team had done a ton of work on what functionality would unlock which growth areas. All she had to do was summarize the key bits into a table instead of the forty-two-page document the team used to capture their implementation plan.

The table was simple. It listed the expected functionality, the target audience, the time until results would appear, and the potential revenue. A simple quid pro quo. You give us this functionality, and we'll deliver this cohort of users.

She got together with her team to talk them through it. She knew that one way or another, she wouldn't be around much longer, and they needed to know how to do this themselves.

"How did you get these numbers?" Sunita was uncomfortable with the simplicity of the slide.

"It's the same cohort analysis we already did."

"Yeah, but you took out all the assumptions and how we got the targets. Without all of that, we're exposing ourselves. They'll make us deliver the growth without the functionality. That's how engineering works!"

"Sunita, they can say that all they want, but this clearly shows they need to deliver the key functionality before we can make the desired progress. No logical person would say 'do it anyway,' right?"

"You're still kind of new here. That's exactly what they'll say."

Kate laughed because she knew Sunita was right. "Then we'll bring friends from the field to back us up if things go sideways in the meeting. I'd rather try it on our own first. That way, we don't expose even more dirty laundry to the field leadership team."

"Okay, that makes sense." Jacob and Tamar nodded their agreement with Sunita's statement. "This is such a simple view, but it represents so much work, nuance, subtlety, and assumptions. I'm still nervous."

"That's good. That means you care." Kate nodded at them. "We need to hold our position and go in strong. Simple details are more effective than long documents. I'll add an assumptions slide into the appendix of the deck to cover our butts. Let's do this!"


KATE WAS ready for the meeting. Her simple slide was done, and quite beautiful if she didn't say so herself. She added the assumptions page that Sunita wanted. After all, Sunita, Tamar, Jacob, and others would have to carry on without Kate.

She wanted this to feel like their work too. She also added quotes from customers who threatened to switch to their competitor's technology platform if purchasing from LampLight got even harder.

Kate understood Amy's position and perspective. If she had the CEO breathing down her neck, she would feel pressured, too. Part of Kate was annoyed she would never know what that was like at this company even though she was confident she would have rocked in a role with that much visibility.

Kate, Sunita, and Tamar would be in the meeting, but Kate would lead it. She took the seat in the center of the table directly across from where she believed Amy would sit. She liked to sit across from her opponent.

Others were afraid of Amy and would try to stick to the corners. Not Kate. She needed to win this argument for customers and her team.

Amy hurried into the room and took the seat Kate hoped she would. It was go time.

"Okay Kate. Can we make this quick?"

"Absolutely, Amy. I just have one slide." Kate was secretly delighted Amy knew her name. She hadn't presented directly to her before. Usually Charlie or Dan had been the go-between.

Kate put the slide up on the projector and slid a hard copy across the table to Amy. "It's pretty simple really. We've mapped out the highest impact features we need and have calculated the usage and impact based on field adoption. For example, when you deliver the transition tool, we'll move four million of revenue onto the new platform within three months. Without these top features, we can't sign up for adoption and revenue numbers."

Kate didn't want to talk too much and overcomplicate the message. Amy was sharp and picked it up right away.

"Are you saying you'd block our launch if we don't deliver?" Sunita and Tamar looked absolutely stricken. Amy's tone made it clear she wanted the answer to be "of course not" so she could keep steamrolling the business.

Kate was going to do everything in her power to stop

this behavior. "Yes." Kate looked right at Amy, stand-off countdown starting in her head. Kate was tempted to sing the theme song from The Good, The Bad, and The Ugly. Dewy ewy oooo, wah wah wah.

The silence stretched on. Amy's eyes slanted closed a bit as she assessed Kate.

"Who do you think you are? You can't stop me." Amy leaned back and crossed her arms.

"You're right, I can't." Kate could meet blunt with blunt. "All I'm saying is that this is what we need to be successful. We're all aligned around the same goal there. I'm telling you what has to happen to drive adoption. I can't sign up for numbers without the capabilities. You can overrule me, but it won't change that reality." Kate heard Tamar's quick intake of breath. No one spoke to Amy like that. *Until now.*

Kate took a moment to inwardly laugh at how ludicrous this conversation was. They were all acting like this was life and death instead of technology. They weren't at war. And Amy couldn't actually hurt them. Why was everyone so afraid of her? And why had she been allowed to use a culture of fear to make her team perform unnatural acts?

Kate was glad her time at this company was coming to a close and she could bring a cool-headed perspective to the meeting.

"Lauren." Amy broke eye contact and addressed the lead developer. "What's the engineering estimate for how long it'll take to build and test the migration tool?"

"Three weeks." Lauren sounded confident in her estimate.

"We can handle a three-week delay. Prioritize it and push the launch three weeks."

Kate wanted to pipe in and ask for four weeks since she didn't want to sign up to release buggy code that hadn't been fully tested, but she could only take on so many battles at one time. "Thanks Amy."

"Kate, I'm glad you're here. Your team usually hits me with long documents and nested assumptions. You brought a clean, crisp, and clear plan. I appreciate that and look forward to our next meeting."

Kate nodded and the meeting broke up.

"HOLY CRAP, I WAS SO SCARED." Tamar waited until they were in the shuttle back to their building before exploding. "How did you just sit there, so calm, cool, and collected? Those meetings are usually screaming matches."

"Amy is human. Humans need clarity. Clarity sets you free." Kate thought that should become her new mantra. "And there was no downside, really. If she overruled us, we would have proof we couldn't deliver what she wanted. If she escalated, we could just share the slide with whoever she escalated to, even if it was the CEO."

"Nerves of steel. You were like a vision in that meeting. You're like, five levels below her in the organization, yet she totally treated you like an equal. She never talks to Bobby, Dan, or even Papi Chuck like that. I learned a lot from you today." Tamar's comments warmed Kate's heart. Teaching and helping was so important to her.

"Yeah, I wasn't actually sure she was human." Sunita laughed.

"I can't wait to tell the team and the field how amazing you were and how you got her to agree." Tamar bubbled with excitement.

"Hang on," Kate cautioned. "The field doesn't need to know we went toe to toe. We just present them a unified front that we jointly agreed to move the deadline to incorporate additional functionality that improves their experience, the customer experience, and meets our goals."

"Ever the political genius," Tamar said. "You could write a book about how to do this. How come you don't run this place?"

Kate had the same question.

## Chapter 44

"I did the right thing. I followed policy when racially-based discrimination happened. I spoke with HR and Randall." Kate was wrapping up her conversation with the new investigator assigned to her complaint. Leanne seemed more capable than the first person, but still sounded like she was reading from a script. "He continues to retaliate which violates LampLight policy and is illegal in the state of Washington."

Kate said all of the words Gertie advised her to use. Yes, the investigator would know she was being coached, but she thought that was a good thing.

"Do you have any written proof of the retaliation?" Leanne's tone was brusque. Kate felt like she was on trial.

"I have emails from before I reported him and after that show a marked difference in how he treated me. I have witnesses who are willing to share what happened in meetings that I was not in but heard about afterwards."

"But nothing in writing."

"Known bullies cover their tracks well. I know he's been reported before for similar actions." *Take that, Leanne!*

"Thanks for your time." It sounded like Leanne was finished asking questions. "If you do find anything in writing, please send it my way. Please follow up with the name, email, and contact number for the witnesses you would like me to speak with. We'll be back with our conclusion in the next several weeks."

*Several weeks?* This was taking forever. And Kate just kept cranking away at her current job. She didn't want anyone else to know about what she was going through, and she had to keep it confidential anyway.

Bernardo, Charlie, and Julia had all agreed to speak with Leanne. Bernardo would share what happened in the original bullying event. Charlie would talk about how Randall stopped her on-hire promotion, gave her an unprofessional transition review, influenced the review model, and told Dan not to hire Kate for the new position in the re-org. Julia would act as a character witness as her former manager.

Florence had declined to get involved. It hurt Kate's feelings, but she also understood that Florence was stuck in the political machine, still trying to make it work with Randall.

Kate prepared to keep up appearances for the next several weeks.

---

"I'VE GOT TO TAKE THIS." Kate walked out into the hallway when she saw Gertie's name flash on her phone screen. Talking to Gertie was way more important than sitting in a meeting with ten other people listening to Bobby drone on about his latest non-strategy.

It had been three weeks, and Kate was even more ready to walk out than before.

"I heard from LampLight's outside counsel," Gertie said.

Kate slipped into a conference room for privacy. "Outside counsel?"

"Yes. That's a good thing. They've referred the matter to outside counsel which means they found something in the investigation." Kate wondered what that could be. "It doesn't really matter if what they found matches our complaint. It just has to be something they don't want to have to expose through the discovery process. They know I can subpoena all the unofficial HR records for Randall and it would all get out there. Plus, they ignored you. And then there's the whole shitty treatment thing. They don't want that getting out."

"So what's next?" Kate was getting tired of the waiting game. She felt like she was lying to her team each time she made them feel better about what was going on. She really just wanted to tell them all to get out before they got screwed, too.

"Next, we wait. Typically, we'll hear the outcome of the investigation and things will move quickly after that."

"When do I tell Bobby this is going on? I mean, he's my manager, so do you think they've told him?"

"Don't say a word. This is a confidential matter among Workplace Investigations, outside counsel, you, and me. You shouldn't talk to anyone else about it."

"Okay, so just a few more weeks."

"Well, don't get too attached to that timeline. Things always take longer than expected. I'm going to help you by leaving the country."

"Um, what?" Kate was confused.

"Murphy's Law. Paul and I have an anniversary trip to Tuscany. We leave on Saturday and will be gone for a week. We'll be way out in the countryside where I hope, no offense, there's no cell reception. With any luck, me being out of the country will trigger the Divine Goddess of Settlements to make progress because I'll be unreachable."

"That sounds like a pretty good strategy. And I respect vacations. Even if I hear from anyone, I won't bug you. I can keep waiting."


GERTIE WAS RIGHT, as usual. Kate got the calendar request from Leanne for a meeting to discuss the outcome of the investigation. Someone from employee relations would be joining them as well.

They were all in different buildings on campus, so it was a virtual meeting. Kate donned her headset and dialed in. Leanne was there and introduced Ellen from the employee relations team.

"My role is to work with you in the aftermath of the investigation," Ellen explained. *Aftermath?* That made it sound like war.

"Nice to meet you."

"You too, but I'm not the star of the show. Leanne?"

"I'd like to start by thanking you for bringing this complaint to our attention." *Twice*, Kate thought. "We take every complaint seriously." Kate had heard it before. She wanted to hear the results. "Any questions before I share the outcome of the investigation?"

"No, thank you." Kate's heart pounded in her chest.

"Very well. We've completed our investigation and found your claims to be unsubstantiated." *Unsubstantiated? Nice.* "Your witnesses and documentation did not prove any wrongdoing on the part of Mr. Cunningham. There was no evidence he influenced your performance ratings unfairly. Your poor review was deserved. I'd like to remind you that the results of this investigation are confidential. Mr. Cunningham can report you for violation of policy and retaliation if you speak about this outcome with anyone. Again, we would like to thank you for bringing this to our attention and wish you a pleasant day. I'll leave you and Ellen to talk." And with that, Leanne dropped off the call.

Kate's first reaction was anger. Bitter, seething, anger. But that flash of emotion was quickly followed by resignation. *Of course it had gone this way.* All signs pointed to a cover-up and sweeping it under the rug. "Kate, do you have any questions?" Ellen clearly had training in using a soothing voice.

"It's very disappointing to know that people lie at this company. Why would they tell me one thing and the investigator another?"

"I can't answer that." Ellen shook her head.

"I did what I was trained to do in every corporate compliance training video." Kate dug deep for calm. Losing her shit wouldn't help. "I was trained to report policy violations. I was promised there would be no retaliation for reporting my boss, yet here we are."

"I can't comment on that." Ellen looked away from the camera.

"So what *can* you tell me?"

"Kate, I know this was difficult news to hear, but you should focus on getting back to work and putting this behind you. Our investigation process is fair and objective. I hope that in time you can accept the decision."

There was no sense in continuing the conversation with the very polite but useless Ellen. LampLight was closing ranks around Randall. It was over.

Kate couldn't help but let out a little of the rage. "Okay, thank you. I'll update my lawyer."

Ellen ended the call. Kate just looked at the blank screen for a few moments to collect herself.

She couldn't call Gertie because she was on vacation, and Kate didn't think this was important enough to bug her. She would just have to wait and see.

All of the waiting and seeing was killing her.

## Chapter 45

Kate pulled herself out of bed, bleary-eyed and achy. She was running late. Her quick shower did nothing to clear her mind.

She bypassed all of her fun, colorful clothes and grabbed gray from the hangers. Gray shirt, gray pants, gray shoes. Because it suited her mood.

The horror of the game of pretend-to-care-about-your-job-while-you-wait-for-an-offer was taking its toll on her mental health. How much longer could she keep it up? Gertie would be back soon and she would find out whether an unsubstantiated investigation meant it was over.

She had to snap out of this. No one was shooting at her. She had her health. She had a partner who loved her. Trust was slowly being rebuilt with James. Things weren't that bad. She could get through this.

The sun started to peek over the 520 bridge as she headed to the LampLight office. She appreciated the beauty, willing herself to be in a better mood by the time she got to her building.

. . .

"WE COULDN'T WAIT to tell you." Sunita, Tamar, and Jacob were waiting in her office. Tamar's smile lit up the room as she spoke, even brighter than the rising sun had been on the drive in.

"I'm all ears." Kate smiled to herself remembering her series of corn puns with James.

"The partner team approved the strategy, policy changes, and implementation plan!" They looked at her with great excitement evident on their faces.

"Another milestone reached! That's amazing."

"You're amazing, Kate. Your approach totally works."

"Okay, okay, let's take a step back here." Kate always liked to give credit away. "All I did was make a few suggestions and lead a couple of meetings. The three of you rallied your teams, wrote the documents, managed the design sessions, wrote the plan, and presented it at the last meeting. You three and your teams get all the credit."

Tamar and Sunita both blushed. Jacob looked away. Kate found it adorable. "That's kind of you, Kate, but it was a huge accomplishment, and we couldn't have done it without your leadership," Jacob said. "You guided us through the whole thing and let us run it so we really learned."

"But never felt exposed," Sunita added. "Because we knew you were right there with us."

"The three of you couldn't give me a nicer compliment. I get a lot of joy out of helping people see how far they can run."

"Oh, and we ran." Tamar laughed. "We got way

farther along the change curve than we thought we would."

"We want to share the news with the team, but we thought you might want to send the email. I mean, it was all your idea." Kate was going to complete their lesson right now.

"Absolutely not. This is your victory. You send it. And please copy the partner leadership team on it along with a thank you."

"I'll take the first crack, Tamar and Jacob, and then you can review and we'll send it out later this morning. Achievement unlocked!" They all laughed.

"Great job. Really. I'm proud of you!" Kate beamed at them. Sunita looked like she might cry. Jacob and Tamar murmured their thanks and left her office.

Kate congratulated herself on a job well done. She hadn't even set her laptop down in the excitement of seeing the three of them in her office. She pulled it out of her bag and snapped it into the docking station. She had a couple of minutes before her first meeting and would use it to catch up on any emails that arrived during her commute.

There was a message from Gertie who was clearly back from vacation. The subject said "offer." Kate opened it with excitement, her heart racing. *This is it*, she thought. *The moment of truth!*

Eighty-five thousand dollars? That's it? Kate felt the anger fill her, hot and red. After all the pain, agony, frustration, and legal issues, they were going to offer her a tiny settlement to be quiet? No, just... no. Kate took a couple of breaths and didn't hit send on her "that's bullshit" email to Gertie.

Could there be another explanation? Like, it was eighty-five thousand on top of a typical severance package? She looked at the angry words on her screen and decided she was over-reacting to the wrong person. She re-crafted the email to just have the professional message rather than the emotional vitriol. She thanked Gertie for the help and asked her if it was possible to counteroffer.

Was she at the end of her rope? She sat at her computer staring at the number. How much more of this deceit and lying could she take? Every time she scheduled a meeting more than two weeks out, she felt guilty because she hoped she wouldn't still be there when the date arrived.

No. She could handle anything. It's just that, well, she was fucking tired. She was sick of the poor treatment and the mixed messages and the lying. All while continuing to do work that contributed to LampLight's success. The company certainly wasn't investing in hers.

Gertie called her. "Sorry about just sending that over with no explanation. I thought I'd be able to talk to you before you read it since you seem to always answer my calls."

"That's because there's nothing more important to me than you right now."

"Oh, all the girls say that." Gertie laughed which seemed out of character. It must be the post-vacation glow.

Kate wasn't all the way numb. She could still laugh along and appreciate the distraction. "First of all, welcome back. How was the trip?"

"We can talk about that at brunch. Bottom line is it was

great. Ten out of ten. Would watch again. Now back to you. I got your email about the result of the investigation."

"Is that why the offer is so low?"

"Oh, honey, I should have explained this. Of course that was the result. If they said anything other than unsubstantiated, it would give us more of a case. Once this was referred to outside counsel, I knew you'd get an offer. And that the first would be a low ball."

It didn't make much sense to Kate. "But they didn't find him guilty."

"The fact that they involved outside counsel shows they found something bad. Getting an offer after an unsubstantiated investigation means that what they found was even worse than we thought. There's definitely something they don't want to have to deal with." Kate started to feel a little better. "It could be a pattern of poor behavior, it could be something that was covered up, it could be that someone knows you and knows you aren't a wanker. Who knows? The important thing is that we're going to counteroffer and worst case, they say no and you walk out with eighty-five thousand. That's better than a sharp stick in the eye."

"You're right, you're right. I just got stuck that there was a digit missing."

"We'll get it back up. What would you like your counteroffer to be?"

"It should be at least as much as they're offering people at my level as severance packages."

"And do you know those details?"

"Actually yes. I guess that's one good thing from being a Chief of Staff. It would be about three hundred thousand plus a year of future stock vests. So please counteroffer at six hundred thousand."

"Sounds reasonable. I've got about four hours into this thing, and I bet there's only an hour or two left, so it won't cost you much more to wrap this up."

"Worth every penny."

"All the girls say that, too."

⸻

"SHE'S RIGHT," James said. "Better than a sharp stick in the eye. I'd like to remind you that eighty-five thousand dollars is a lot of money." James was being his usual optimistic self. "More than I would have made if I took that full-time role at LampLight."

"Yes, I know, but less than my bonus was last year. And less than the bonus I deserved this year. It's really insulting."

"Don't be insulted. It's just a game. Gertholomew has got you. Hey, that rhymes." James started to sing it. "Gertholomew… Uh uh uh uh …. will help you… uh uh uh uh." He shook his hips back and forth and pumped his fists. "Gertholomew… went to law school. Uh uh uh uh. Gertholomew… has got to poo. Uh uh uh uh." He was laughing too hard at this point to keep going.

Kate was glad she didn't finish the first version that came to mind and instead sang, "Gertholomew… thinks you're real cool."

# Chapter 46

"I've got my first customer!" James' excitement was evident in his flashing eyes and bright smile. "It's a couple looking to do a ride from Seattle over Lolo Pass and back. They have five days of vacation."

"That's plenty of time to do that ride, even if they want to go back and forth over the pass a couple of times." Kate was happy to see James in good spirits. "How'd they find you?"

"They're Trevor's cousins. He doesn't like them a whole lot and doesn't want to ride with them. But I'm happy to work through the details with them, design a ride, give them options of stopping points. They might even want me to lead the ride. She's the more experienced rider, but she rides a cruiser and doesn't like to lean over too much because she'll scrape her pegs. But she's game for a long ride and he says he can keep up with her."

"That all sounds great. Anything I can do to help?"

"Just continue to be the delightful and supportive wife that you are." He kissed her on the nose. "I might not make a whole lot of money on this one, but they've agreed to put quotes on my website. They have the same last name, but since I would only use their first names anyway, I can use quotes from both of them."

"The power of marketing. Woo hoo!"

"How would you like to celebrate?" James asked.

"How about the Trattoria for dinner?"


THEY SAT in Eve's section because she was James' favorite server.

"Hey Eve, how goes the dating scene?" James hung his jacket on the hook under the table and put Kate's purse next to it.

"Ugh. I'll be back to tell you about that." She wiped down the table. "The usual?"

"Yep. We're celebrating," James said.

"Celebrating sounds like something that requires champagne." She headed back to the bar to place their order.

"How's Tia?" he asked another server as she passed by after dropping off an order at a nearby table. She immediately got out her phone and showed him her latest picture of her Pomeranian. Kate didn't even remember that she had a dog, let alone her name.

It was these moments that made her glad she hadn't just ended things with James when he made his stupid money mistakes. They had come through the drama stronger. Better communicators.

She had wanted to just walk out. But, like her Perseverance Award from 1978, she persisted. Sometimes, giving up or giving in was the best thing to do. But this felt right, and they were happy.

"Okay, love birds." Eve was back to take their orders. "Are you changing it up for your celebration?"

"Nope. We'll have the usual." James ordered for both of them. Eve knew the drill.

"Okay. What're you celebrating, anyway?"

"James' first customer in his new business venture."

"Oh wow! Champagne's on me!" Eve clapped her hands together and went to put their dinner order into the system.

Kate was excited about the future and that James was getting back into the game. "What's your vision for this company you've started?

She wanted something open and future-focused to talk about rather than her work situation and the seemingly never-ending waiting game.

"It could be anything, really. I'll start with motorcycle tours. But I could start selling merchandise with the logo on it and come up with fun sayings to add. I could even have a retail presence, like a pop-up store at motorcycle events throughout the summer to drum up business. Graham talked about having a cross-continental partnership. He already has a guy in the UK he works with and a woman in Thailand. I would be his US person. We wouldn't go into an official business together, just be partners who recommend each other."

Kate sat with her elbows on the table and her hands holding up her head as she listened to him talk about his vision. It seemed like there was no end to his excitement. If he had stayed at LampLight and taken the full-time gig, he would have been pressured to start working LampLight hours and he wouldn't have been able to follow this dream. She loved seeing him like this.

James changed the subject. "How're we going to get you to the same headspace as me, where you can think about what's next instead of the horror you're dealing with now?"

"I'm sorry. I know I've been a grumpotamus lately." Kate combined grumpy and hippopotamus to make James laugh. "It's so stressful keeping up the façade at work while playing this waiting game."

"I know. That's why I want to talk about what's next for you. You've given me this amazing freedom to try something. You stuck with me when I fucked everything up. It's your turn. What's your vision for your next move?"

"You know I want to be an author."

"Yep. What's stopping you?"

"Um, well." Kate was slightly annoyed by the question even though she knew James meant well. "That whole filling my brain with work so I can support us thing."

"But I'll get a job and you have savings. It's not true that you have to keep working at a job you hate."

"It's more true than ever right now." Kate could feel her anger rising but lowered her voice. "You can say that because I'm keeping us afloat financially. If I stop, we'll be screwed."

"Except that we won't, Kate. We have plenty of money.

*We have sixty-four thousand dollars less than we should*, Kate thought. Reflecting on some of her management training, she decided to get curious about James' thought process instead of being shitty. "We're so far apart on this issue. Where are you coming from?"

"I always think there's a way. You have to set this view that you don't have enough aside and really live. Live, dammit." James took her hand. "I'm watching it kill you. You've aged ten years in the last year. You're unhappy and exhausted, and you keep going through the motions because you think you're not in control." He paused to take a breath. Kate chose not to interrupt. "You are in control."

"But I'm not! I can't make them promote me. I can't make them repay the bonus and stock they took from me. I'm not in control of anything!" Kate was almost in tears. She thought they were talking about James tonight.

"Katiebug," James' tone softened. "Look at me." Kate pulled her eyes from the spot on the carpet that suddenly seemed very interesting and looked right into James' imploring hazel eyes. "You're in control of what matters. You choose what you do every day. You choose how to spend your time. You're in control of what matters."

Kate tried to pull away, but James held on.

"You don't understand the pressure I'm under." The tears threatened again.

"You're right. I don't." Kate appreciated the acknowledgement. "I see it differently. You hide behind this fake need to make money for both of us to protect yourself from the tough choice of leaving LampLight."

His words hit her like a slap in the face. Kate was silent for a moment. James just held her hand, watching the emotions flit across Kate's face.

Was it that simple? No, it couldn't be. She wanted her

hard work to pay off. She wanted the equation to be righted. She wanted bad behavior to be punished. "I don't have the freedom to make that choice." Kate's voice was small as she said it out loud for the first time.

"You do, Bug. That's the whole point. You don't make the rules for the game that Randall, Dan, HR, and Lamp-Light are playing. You can only play by your own rules. Let's say they handed you a huge check and Randall issued a public apology. Then what would you do?"

"I would feel vindicated. I would feel like it was all worth it."

"Kate, I love you so much." James looked directly into her eyes. "But you are fucking infuriating." He emphasized each word but still said them softly.

"I'm infuriating? You're the one who refuses to hear me."

"I hear every word. There's a difference between not listening and not understanding. Katiebug, I really want you to think about your next steps. Randall will never apologize. LampLight may or may not give you a big check. You don't need either of those to know you're a good person who does the best thing for her company and her team. You just suck at doing what's best for you."

Her eyes filled with tears. "It's not that easy."

"Of course it's not, but I know you're strong and capable and can do anything. If you don't believe me, ask any of your friends. Try to see yourself through my lens. Or your Steak and Bourbon friends. If you met you at one of Julia's brunches, you'd come home telling me about the coolest woman you'd just met and how she was going to be a great author because she was an amazing storyteller and had so much to say. Stop seeing yourself through Moaning Marilyn's shitty, shrinking lens and really see all your power."

Kate sighed and hung her head. "You make it all sound possible."

"I'm your biggest fan and will always cheer for you. Feel it. Know it. And get the fuck out." James looked at her for several seconds. Then he started to chant.

GGGG

TTTT

FFFF

OOOO

GTFO Get the Fuck Out GTFO

He lightly banged on the table with each syllable.

"Okay, okay, I get it." Kate interrupted his bizarre cheer.

"Thank you. You know me. I can't stand to see you this way, so I have to be silly."

# Chapter 47

James had given her a lot to think about. A lot. What was so bad about leaving? She had a whole career before LampLight. Why did she feel so stuck here? Two words. *Unfinished business.*

She wanted to go out on her own terms, not because someone else labeled her a bully and kept following her around to take chances away from her.

She remembered James' words. Would she actually feel better with a check? She knew money shouldn't solve everything, but she certainly believed it wouldn't hurt. She could walk out with eighty-five thousand dollars. She would give Gertie a couple of weeks to counteroffer and then just take it. She needed to move on and do what was next.

So what was next? Kate wanted to be an author. Deep down in her little heart of hearts, she wanted to write. She had an inkling she wanted to write when the dot com bubble burst in 2002. She had time on her hands in between jobs and had written a tongue-in-cheek exposé of the management consulting industry. After nine rejections from agents, she paid her six hundred dollars to self-publish the book. It was still available online, under a pen name, of course.

She had loved spending two or three hours a day telling stories of her life and her experiences. She didn't want to write about bitterness, though. She wanted to write women's fiction novels with happy endings – provide a little escapism for people dealing with the same issues she was tackling at work.

She had never found a book like that out there. Most women's novels seemed to end with marriage and babies. The protagonists' career was rarely the focus. She wanted to change that.

James' face flashed to her mind. *Try to see yourself through my lens.* It was so hard. Moaning Marilyn's voice was so much stronger than anyone in the brunch group or even James' voice. It was hard to admit she had fallen victim to a common pattern – being fucked up by your parent's shit. Dammit, she was smarter than that.

She would push that voice out and focus on her friends. She would hear Julia, Melanie, Lesley, Gertie and the rest of the Steak and Bourbon group pushing her forward and supporting her on her journey rather than the voice of "no."

She would start her first book. Well, technically it was her second book, but the first one only sold a few hundred copies, mostly to her friends, so that didn't count.

*Shit*, there it was again. Yes, it counted. It didn't matter that it wasn't a raging success. She had done it. She had put seventy-eight thousand words together in a coherent set of stories. That was a major accomplishment. She wasn't bragging or being egotistical in being proud of that. She was just owning the achievement.

It felt weird. Arrogant. Smug. She sat with those emotions for a while. They didn't get more positive.

Next came fear of complacency and worry that she would get blindsided by criticism if she wasn't careful. Holy shit, this negativity was strong. And she didn't realize how often it was there. She thought it was the voice that drove her. But she had listened to it long enough.

She would try the next forty-six years a different way. Telling herself positive stories. Believing she could do things. Choosing her own adventure.

She read somewhere that it takes up to a year to truly break a habit, especially a life-long one. Today was a good day to get started. By this time next year, with positive self-belief and a plan for how she'd become an author, she would be on her way. It would be a long, tough year, but she could do it.

The negative thoughts immediately tried to batter down the edges of her hope. She could almost see them, like little Vikings with battering rams running at her doors. She had to keep her defenses up. If even one of those little fuckers got through, others would follow them.

Kate remembered that she had an army of her own to combat them – her friends. She would go to brunch every month and provide an update on her progress. She would ask them to help her focus on the positive. That's what a personal board of directors does!

"GOT MY NEXT CUSTOMER!" James was brimming with excitement when Kate came into the kitchen after a long commute in heavy traffic.

He turned from the stove where he stirred a pot to smile at her. "And this is a large group. They want the whole shebang. Me as a guide, me planning the trip, commemorative t-shirts, everything. They agreed to my guiding rate plus the twenty percent upcharge I have on the bike rental and hotels to manage the bookings." He gestured at her with the spoon. "I also negotiated a five-hundred-dollar fee for trip insurance so I could lock in non-refundable lower rates but get the money back through trip insurance if they have to cancel."

"Wow Sweetie, that's great. When's the trip?"

"It's not for a few weeks so I have plenty of time to map out a course. This is really picking up speed. Pun intended."

"And it sounds like you've thought of everything. The details all come out when the rubber hits the road."

"Yeah, my background in software contract negotiation helped me sit down and work through all of the possible costs so I don't get stuck in a ditch."

"It's wonderful to see you excited about it. Your puns come out the strongest when you're happy."

"It feels really good. I've got a spreadsheet going to track the trips and a calendar so I don't double book myself. Trevor and Ross are both interested in helping me lead rides in the future, too. It's all coming together." James' positivity was starting to rub off on Kate. She sloughed off the pain from the day.

"What am I smelling? I'm getting butter and white wine."

"The nose strikes again! I'm trying a white coq au vin. It needs about ten minutes which is just the time I need to finish the couscous." Kate loved coming home to a nice meal. "I saved you a glass of the Verdejo I used in the sauce. Help yourself." He nodded toward the fridge. "I would get it for you, but I'm supposed to keep stirring during this part."

"MMMM," Kate said around her fork. "This is so good. Thank you."

"You're welcome. I'm trying to make sure I'm pulling my weight around here. I know I have some money coming in now, but I want to make your life as easy as possible. You've been so supportive."

"I appreciate that," Kate said with a smile.

"Any news to report from Gertie?"

"No, still in the waiting game."

"Okay, but that's only part of your life. How're your plans coming on the book front?"

"I don't really have plans. Just the idea."

"Katiebug. It was before my time, but you said you loved writing your first book. Why don't you try distracting yourself from the crap at work by writing in the evenings? Hell, you could do it during work hours, too."

"Good idea, except the part about doing it during work hours. That doesn't feel right."

"Like you've never worked on a weekend or an evening. It would be payback."

"It doesn't look good, and I wouldn't want my book to ever be on a LampLight computer anyway. Bad juju."

"I get it. What's your book going to be about?"

"I have about fifteen ideas," Kate admitted. "I want to do happy endings where it doesn't always end with a man showing up and saving the damsel in distress or the main character feeling fulfilled when she finally has the baby she always dreamed of." Kate snorted. "I'm so sick of those novels. They don't represent my reality, and I can't be the only one."

"People say to write what you know. Maybe you should write an autobiography."

"Nah, too personal."

"That's what makes it good. You can always fictionalize it."

"I'd have to in order to have that happy ending."

"I'm not so sure about that, Katiebug. Give it some time and start writing!"

THE NEXT EVENING while James was out on a motorcycle ride with the guys, Kate sat with her fingers poised over the keyboard. She was starting her novel.

She had captured various ideas over the past several years, but none had coalesced into a full concept for a novel yet. A writing course she had taken a few years before taught her to have an outline before starting writing, but she wasn't even sure what she wanted to write about. She went against the grain and started writing.

About herself. About her struggles with love and work.

About her relationship with money. About the interior of her favorite restaurant.

Scene after scene started flowing out of her fingertips. She didn't know if it was any good, but she had over five thousand words when she got too hungry to continue.

She felt a lightness she hadn't experienced in years. She mentally patted herself on the back. Even if it was crap, at least she had started.

Kate made herself a sandwich and sat back down at her laptop. She reread the scenes and laughed out loud a couple of times. Maybe she was onto something.

## Chapter 48

"Latest offer in." Kate saw the text from Gertie out of the corner of her eye while in a quarterly skip-level one on one with a member of her team. "When can you talk?"

Kate couldn't walk out on this person, but it was tempting. As much as she was trying to embody her new take-care-of-herself approach, she wasn't prepared to be rude.

She snatched her phone as soon as Natalie left the room.

"Call anytime you're available. I'll answer," she typed.

It was an excruciating twenty minutes before Gertie called. "Sorry to keep you waiting, it's been crazy over here."

"No worries. I've already been waiting months, so what's a few more minutes?" Kate was glad she had the capacity to joke when she really just wanted the number.

"They came up to two hundred thousand. That's a good offer, but I still think we can do better."

Holy shit, it was happening. "What're the terms?"

"Oh, there's a whole agreement you'd have to sign. The highlights are that you release LampLight from all further claims of harm. In other words, neither side admits wrongdoing. You could never work at LampLight again."

"I would never want to."

"Hang on there, Captain Moves Too Fast. You should read the language of the agreement before you get too excited. Plus, the tone of the negotiator suggested there was more wiggle room. Well, after I laughed at them and said 'nice try' before telling them to up the offer."

"You're worth every penny, Gertie."

"Tell me something I don't know." Gertie's semi-evil laugh floated through the phone. "I, of course, have to bring you the offer even though I don't think you should take it. You can. And we would be done, but if you can remotely stand it for one more week, I think I can get you more."

"As much as every fantasy has me walking right out the door, I've made it this long and can make it one more week."

"Good. I'll turn the screws on 'em and tell them we think you have a strong case and are insulted by the offer. That'll be good." Gertie sounded excited by the battle of wits.

"Bobby, my current manager, hasn't said a single word to me about this, and as per your guidance, I haven't said anything either. Is that weird?"

"A little. I bet he knows about it, but why poke the bear? You're leaving either way, so I would avoid an awkward conversation."

"Great point. There's only downside in talking to him

about it. I leave it in your very capable hands, Gertie. Thank you."

"Smart move. Smart move." Gertie sounded every bit the shrewd lawyer. "Will I see you at brunch on Sunday?" Gertie's tone shifted immediately to chirpy and happy. Kate bet that was super effective in the courtroom.

"You bet. Wouldn't miss it."

"Great, see you there, you big rich lady."

Kate laughed as she hung up.

"THEY'RE up to two hundred thousand." Kate shared the good news with James that evening.

"So you're done?" His voice was downright gleeful.

"No. Gertie said we should try one more round. Meanwhile, I have to read the offer when they send it over in writing. She says there's a lot of fine print."

"Well, it sounds like there's a LampLight at the end of the tunnel. If they go up again by the same amount, that's over three hundred thousand."

"Let's not get over-excited," Kate said as she got overly excited. She could do so much with three hundred thousand. She could take a break from work and focus on her book. She could save it all and build up her nest egg. She could invest it and make more. She could blow it on ten trips around the world.

James took her hand. "I want you to feel like you have options and can pursue your dreams. You've certainly helped me pursue mine, like not kicking me out when I royally fucked up, and still helping me create a new career for myself. You're one in a million and I'm lucky to be with you."

"I can't take all the credit. Yes, I'm a wonderful fucking person, but you worked hard to rebuild my trust and take finding a new career seriously." Kate squeezed his hand. "You're not totally done with the work of rebuilding my trust. You're making a lot of progress, but knowing you can keep something like that from me still hurts. Anything you want to share?"

"No. No more secrets." He squeezed back. "Oh, I thought of something."

Kate froze. "What now?"

"I farted a little when you squeezed my hand."

"That wasn't a secret."

They both laughed.

"But seriously, Bug, you know you'll get at least two hundred big ones. What're you going to do with it?"

"I have this little dream."

"No dreams are little. And if they are, you should make them bigger. You can do anything." His look was filled with support and love.

"I'm going to use it to fund a year off work to focus on writing my book." Kate paused, waiting for the embarrassment she usually felt when she talked about her dream to strike. But it didn't come.

"That's amazing. I'm with you one hundred percent."

Kate was uncomfortable but continued. "I've thought through the details."

"Of course you have," James said.

"With COBRA benefits for eighteen months helping with healthcare costs and you starting to bring in some cash, the money could technically carry us for more than two years, but I've set the goal for myself to write and publish within the year."

"That sounds really fast. Doesn't it take months to find an agent, let alone get published?"

"Yes, and there's also writing the damn book, but self-publishing tools have come a long way, and I can always do it that way so at least I have something to show for my year."

"I love everything about this plan, Kate. And I love that you're letting me come along for the ride. You're going to be a famous author."

"It's nice to have you in my corner." Kate meant it. She had almost kicked him out and was glad she could see all of him and love him for his goods and his bads.

<hr>

"I HAVE SOMETHING TO SHARE." Kate's heart was beating fast at Steak and Bourbon that Sunday. James was the only person she had shared her dream with so far. That was really hard, but she knew deep down he would support her no matter what. While this group of fabulous women had become her friends over the last several months, it still felt risky to say her plan out loud.

"First, I want to thank Gertie for helping me get a decent offer from LampLight to leave quietly." Kate led the whoop whoop for Gertie and raised her glass in Gertie's direction.

"Just doin' my job, little lady," Gertie said pretending to raise her imaginary cowboy hat with her index finger.

"It was more than that, and you know it." Kate gave her a stern look.

"Ooooh, Gertie is rubbing off on you, sweet Kate. I love it!" Melanie was all in on the celebration.

"This group has inspired me to dream big."

"And drink big," Angela interjected.

"Yes, that too. And learn about Kegel exercises to improve sex – thank you very much…" Kate had to take a break to make room for the cheering. "And with your support, I'm able to say something out loud for the first time outside of my condo."

"Drum roll please," Melanie called out as everyone started rolling their fingers on the brunch table.

"I've decided to take a year off from the corporate grind and focus on writing and publishing a book."

The table erupted in hoots and hollers.

"That's amazing, Kate." Julia exclaimed.

"How great." Lesley added.

"What will your books be about?" Akiko asked. "And please note that I made it plural, by the way."

"They'll be about strong women balancing career and love. Surviving corporate life and striving to meet their goals."

"I'd read that. I'd read the whole series." Alex said.

"Love it!" Melanie yelled.

"Can we be in it?" Margaret asked. "Can my name be something super dramatic and old-fashioned like Tuesenelda or Maleficent?"

"You can all pick your names because these brunches have been my lifeline during the last few months. I couldn't have done it without you all. To Steak and Bourbon!"

"Well that explains the four bottles of champagne you brought with you, Kate. We're drinking to your happiness and new career!" Kate beamed at Alex.

Kate felt the love and support from the room.

"I can't wait to read the first one! Let's start a book club where we only read your books!" Lesley suggested.

"I have to write it first."

"We'll be your beta readers." Akiko offered.

"Put a lot of sex in it." Margaret demanded. "You know we'd all like that."

"Give your main character a secret life." Brie suggested. It made Kate wonder what she might be hiding.

"Or amazing musical talents," Alex added.

"Just do your thing, Kate." Julia's advice stood on its own as everyone smiled and nodded at Kate.

— — — — — — — — —

## Chapter 49

— — — — — — — — —

By the end of the following week, Kate had over twenty-five thousand words. She was cooking with gas. Each writing session brought her closer to her dream and she loved the feeling of doing something entirely for herself.

In the book, she could be anyone. She could create rich, relatable, realistic characters as she mixed and matched elements from multiple people she had met and worked with into fictitious people. There was no end to the anecdotes she wanted to write.

She had switched tactics and had an entire outline. She had cut some of her first scenes as she landed on a writing style that was serious with light-hearted moments. She cut out adverbs and read her dialogue out loud to make sure it didn't sound stifled or weird. She was on her way.


IN HER OFFICE on Friday morning, Kate got a text from Charlie. He had landed a new job at a major competitor.

She sent back a congratulations message and asked to meet him for a drink to celebrate.

What great news. This meant that Bernardo was happily settled in his new role and Charlie was going to be okay. She felt a wave of relief that things were working out.

She had one more meeting that day – a one on one with Bobby. She hated these. She felt like she was lying every time she met with him. She hadn't mentioned the situation with the lawyers and neither did he. Did he really not know, or was he just acting like she was?

She tried to keep the meetings short, but he always gave her some stupid-ass assignment, analysis to do, a paper to write, or some bullshit. She was annoyed before she even stepped foot into his office. It seemed to be a permanent state lately. She walked slowly down the hall to the meeting.

"Hey Bobby."

"Kate. What did you say to Amy?"

Kate thought back to her last meeting with Amy as she took a seat. It had been a triumph that led to a brilliant solution and set of adopted policy changes by the partner team and the sales team. "Uhh, I believe it was a thank you for working through the change management options for the small business team." Kate searched her mind for what she could have done wrong.

"Well she fucking loves you. Whatever you did, keep doing it."

Kate was floored. "Oh, okay." She was so ready to be yelled at that she found it hard to believe when she was getting a compliment.

"You're really making a difference here and I'm glad you're on the team."

"Thanks Bobby." *Was he fucking with her?* Did he really not know what was going on? She was one email away from walking out and he was playing nicey nicey?

"What's the next trick you have up your sleeve? The strategic accounts team was all over me in our last review, angry about the delays. I mean, you know, and I know we aren't going to build that ridiculous solution they want. Can you do some of your magic and make the complaints go away?" He waved his hands to indicate magic. She found it dismissive. It wasn't magic. It was strategy. But he wouldn't recognize that.

"I can certainly try." Kate tried to keep the incredulity she felt off of her face.

"Okay great, anything else you want to discuss?"

"Nope, I'm good." She kept it short.

"Great. We'll talk soon."

*What the fuck?* This was pure insanity.

<br>

"THAT'LL SHOW 'EM," Kate said, clinking glasses with Charlie. She had brought James with her to meet Charlie and help them celebrate.

"You're heading to Serenity? The LampLight security and hardware teams have been watching them for a while and are appropriately scared of that company's steep increase in market share." James sounded intrigued.

"Yep. We're coming for blood." Charlie tried to fake an

evil face, but he couldn't hold it and giggled in the middle. "Or something like that. I'm just glad I can still afford college for my kids."

"You've been out of LampLight for, like, three months. Were you really worried?"

"Oh, that's the best part. My separation agreement has me on the books until my next stock vest, you know, so I don't sue them. Now I get double paychecks and my next stock grant. Drinks are on me!"

"I'm glad it's worked out for you. Sounds like an amazing gig with tons of potential for them to understand and leverage your big brain while exacting a little revenge on LampLight."

"Damn straight. Of course, I would never admit to agreeing with that in a court of law."

"I didn't hear a thing." James looked at Charlie with great innocence on his face.

"I like this guy. You can keep him." Charlie clinked glasses with James.

"Now what about you? I talked to the investigator as you know. They got all weird on me and kept asking me for written proof. I laid it on thick and explained they were splitting hairs and that a jury wasn't going to care if I heard it or read it. Either way, it had happened."

"Thanks again. I'm not supposed to talk about it."

"I know, but since I was part of the investigation, I got a letter about the outcome. That's a real bummer because that guy's a dick and was out to get you."

"My lawyer says it's not over. I'll get a good offer – not as good as yours, but then, I'm not as good as you."

"Are you fucking kidding me? You're smarter, nicer, more diligent, and you care a lot more than I do. Losing me was just an acceleration of an existing plan. They have no idea what they're letting slip through their fingers by letting you walk out."

"Thanks, Papi Chuck." Kate blushed. In her heart of hearts, she wanted that to be true, but the last year had shown her that they really didn't care about her or believe she could have a positive impact. She shook it off so she could continue to celebrate Charlie.

"What's next for you?" he asked.

"I'm going to take the money and run."

"To where?"

"To my home office for starters. I'm writing a book and will take a year off to finish it and try to get it published."

"What if I had a home for you on my team right now? Technically, I have a non-solicitation clause in my separation agreement that says I can't recruit LampLight employees, but you won't be one of those for much longer."

A zing of excitement went through Kate at his words. Part of it was because she had been at LampLight for so long it sounded weird for her to be separated from her employer. Part was the knowledge and validation that Charlie would want her to work for him again.

"Would you consider that, Kate?" An emotion she couldn't figure out flashed across James' face. And his tone was unreadable. Did he want her to say yes or no, she couldn't tell.

"It's lovely of you to offer that, Charlie. It makes me feel really good. But it's just too easy to take the comfortable path. I want to make a go of it as an author." James' smile burst onto his face.

"Right on!" James said, lifting his glass.

"I get it, Kate." Charlie smiled. "I don't have a Plan B. I'm not sure if it's a lack of skills, confidence, or vision, but I'm all about the comfortable path at this stage of my career."

"Yeah. That's what kept me at LampLight for so long even after I started being routinely treated poorly. I figured it would be the same everywhere and at least I was making good money. It's scary to venture out on my own and try to accomplish my dream. A few hundred-thousand-dollar cushion will make it easier. It's still scary. And I might fail, but nothing ventured, nothing gained." James was still beaming at her. "All I have to do is finish the game of chicken I have going with LampLight's lawyers, and I'll be on my way."

"You're already on your way, Kate." Charlie looked straight at her. "You have the skills and the vision. You'll rock this."

"To mentors and friends!" James added.

"I WAS worried you were going to take the job Charlie offered you," James revealed on the drive home. "When there's a safe path with assured money, it's easy for you to take it. I'm glad you stayed firm."

"I meant it. If I don't go for it, I'll never get it." Kate felt her conviction down to her toes. "And if it doesn't work out, I can always ask him for a job later."

"I can't take my eyes off the road, but I hope you felt my extreme eye roll."

"Okay, okay. *When* I'm successful, I won't need to ask Charlie for a job. But I can if I want to," she added quickly.

"Better, but still not great. Believe in yourself, Katiebug. All the people who matter already do."

# Chapter 50

Friday morning, the final offer was in. Four hundred and thirty-one thousand dollars.

The fine print said she could never work at LampLight again in any capacity. Not as a vendor, not as an employee, not even as a contractor fulfilling a contract she had nothing to do with selling.

LampLight was in the top ten employers in the area, and she was blocking herself from ever coming back. It made her feel like if the author thing didn't work out, she would have to move out of Seattle. It gave her pause.

The other stipulation was that the moment she signed the separation agreement, she was no longer an employee. Her team was completely unprepared for the announcement. She didn't even really know if Bobby knew the agreement had been sent. Kate was spinning on the ramifications.

"It's the best deal we're going to get without a trial." Gertie always gave it to her straight. "And it could take years in court."

"I don't want to deal with any of that."

"Then take the money and run." Kate had used those words with Charlie. "You know, Kate, only about ten percent of demand letters result in a response, much less a settlement. You must have been through a lot."

"Yeah, when you step back, the pattern is pretty strong." Kate reflected for a moment. "I was too close to it to really see it. Crazy that what we got Randall on wasn't even the worst thing he did."

"But it was the illegal thing. It's not illegal to be a dick-head. In fact, people make whole careers out of it."

Kate chuckled. "I'm going to sign."

"Excellent. And we can celebrate at brunch."

"Thanks for everything, Gertie."

"You're welcome. It feels good when it works out."


"WOO HOO! When will you be home?" James sounded like he couldn't contain his excitement.

"I can't just walk out. I have to do some transition work and alert my team and…"

"What do you care?" James interrupted. "You're done. Sign it and come home."

Kate thought a moment. "You're right. Once I sign, it's over. I'll drop my laptop off and hit the road. I already wiped most stuff off my laptop anyway. Everything the team needs is posted on the team's internal share. I'm good to go."

"Then you're done. I'll be waiting with champagne."

"It's only ten thirty."

"And your point is?"

KATE TOOK a deep breath and hit the electronic signature button to sign the separation agreement. She had thought about writing a goodbye email to everyone she would miss at LampLight, but then thought better of it.

She didn't want to be in this building any longer than necessary. She was in touch via LinkedIn with everyone she wanted to be and could find people through that tool if she needed them.

She wrote a quick email to her team saying she was no longer with LampLight, thanking them for everything, and providing her personal email address. She snuck down the stairs before anyone could read it. If they wanted to get in touch with her, they could follow up later. She wasn't allowed to talk about the separation agreement anyway.

She stopped at the front desk and set her laptop on the corner. "Hey Marcy. I need to borrow the corner of your desk for a moment."

"Take your time, Kate."

Kate typed a quick email to Bobby explaining she had signed the separation agreement and alerted her team that she was no longer with the company. As she re-read it, she realized she had typed Booby. She toyed with not correcting it. For just a moment. She was in a hurry to get out of there, so she corrected the spelling of his name and hit send.

"And Marcy, one more thing."

"What's that, Kate? Need me to order food for a team meeting?"

"Nope. I need to give you my laptop, badge, and

corporate credit card. I'm leaving the company, effective immediately."

Marcy's jaw dropped open. "But you're the nicest person in the building. You're the only one who always says good morning and offers to bring me coffee. You're not like everyone else."

That pretty much summed it up.

Kate walked out the door for the last time, head held high.


SHE CHECKED her phone before pulling out of the parking garage. They hadn't shut off her access yet, so she could see the incoming emails. Lots of surprise from her team. The email that caught her eye was from Booby, as he would forever be known from now on.

It was only one line.


What did you tell the team?


An asshole to the very last. Not, "Hey Kate, thanks for everything" or "thanks for being cool about it." Just a message that showed he only cared about himself.

She replied by attaching the email she sent to the team. Then she logged off and deleted the account.

Done. Done. Done.


KATE DROVE across the bridge to Seattle. It was over. She had wanted to retire from LampLight as a vice president or higher. Instead, she was being paid to leave quietly, a tacit acceptance of the bad behavior by execs that would continue unchecked.

She tried to convert her reaction to a positive one. She couldn't help feeling bad for all the people, especially women, she left behind to deal with the unrelenting negativity, sexism, retaliation, and inequitable treatment.

It made her feel slightly better that Bernardo and Charlie were in better places now. Melanie had gotten her promotion.

Snapping out of it as she hit the accelerator on the 520 bridge, she thought about pursuing her new dream. Her real dream. Being an author and helping other women see they weren't alone or making up their work drama.

She could help more women have the courage to pursue their real dreams. She could do it. She would do it.

JAMES ENVELOPED her in a big hug when she got home. True to his word, the bubbly was poured, and he had added some strawberries since it was still before lunch.

"What's next?" he said, releasing her.

"Come on, I just got home. I want to take a few deep breaths before I jump in."

"You already have jumped in, Kate. You're a quarter of the way through your first book already. Now you have more time to focus on the journey you've already started."

That was a great way to look at it.

"Let's celebrate with lunch at Pike Place Market and walk through the stalls," James suggested. "We could pick up food for me to make you a fabulous congratulations dinner tonight. And then tomorrow, I'll be guiding a day-long ride, so I'll be out of your hair, and you can write write write."

KATE WOKE up that Monday at five-thirty in the morning, like she had most mornings for the last twenty-four years. Except this time, it was for herself.

She didn't have to run through the shower and get to a meeting.

She didn't have to worry about a meeting with someone who was angry at her.

She didn't have to put on a fake smile and grit her teeth through an interaction with someone intent on belittling her.

She could have breakfast with James, linger over a second cup of coffee while reading a book, and spend the rest of the day immersed in the world she was creating for her future readers.

She was on her journey and had over half a book to show for it. Was it any good? That didn't matter…yet. She had a monetary cushion to get through the next year. She would finish her book, hire an editor, find an agent and get published. If no one wanted it, she would self-publish like she had her first book.

Either way, she would be an author. After that, she could see if she would stay on that path or return to the workforce.

It was liberating to not dread anything. To just be filled with hope and creativity to pour into her dream.

<br><br>

## Epilogue
### 1 YEAR LATER

"To being a published author!" Nine powerful women and friends raised their glasses around Julia's dining room table in celebration of Kate's first book.

Kate's cheeks hurt from smiling so widely. Each of the Steak and Bourbon ladies held their own copy of her book. They had all read early versions and provided feedback. It was almost as much their book as hers.

"Awwww, you dedicated it to us!" Melanie read the dedication on the first page. "To my board of directors in Steak and Bourbon. This book would never have happened without you."

"Well it's true! Each of you played a huge part in getting me to this place." Kate's voice shook a bit with unshed tears of thankfulness.

"Is James pissed you didn't dedicate it to him?" Gertie's question made everyone laugh.

"I love that man, but you are my girls. He can have the next one."

The celebration continued while Kate sat back and let the feeling of accomplishment fill her.

She had turned her corporate pain into a book that just might inspire others to make a change.

She took a moment to look at each brunch friend and send them a silent thank you. When she got to Gertie, they locked eyes.

Kate lifted her glass in thanks to the wonderful lawyer who got her through.

"You did it," Gertie said. "You are now worthy of your new name."

At Kate's puzzled look, Gertie continued and lifted her glass in return. "Congratulations, Kate-alomew."

<br>

The End

# About the Author

Laura Preslan worked in the technology industry for thirty years leading teams, delivering successful projects, and coaching colleagues through tough situations.

She found many of the same political and people-based issues at every company she worked at as a consultant, advisor, or employee from start-ups to Fortune 100 companies.

This experience influenced her goal to create a new genre of women's fiction written by and about powerful female executives and the unique challenges women overcome at work and at home.

When asked why this vision is important to her, Laura said, "So many of us have compelling stories to tell about terrible toxicity we have conquered at work and how we found balance at home. None of us are going through this alone. With courage, creativity, and self-awareness, we will succeed in work, life, and love. I encourage all of us to write our stories (fictionalized, of course). The more we talk about it, the better things will be for those who come after us."

Find out more about Laura at www.laurapreslan.com.